MARVEL

AVENGERS ASSEMBLE

P9-AOX-074

MARVEL UNIVERSE ALL-NEW AVENGERS ASSEMBLE VOL. 2. Contains material originally published in magazine form as MARVEL UNIVERSE AVENGERS ASSEMBLE SEASON TWO #5-8. First printing 2015. ISBN# 978-0-7851-9359-3. Published by MARVEL WORLDWIDE, INC., a subsidiary of MARVEL ENTERTAINMENT, LLC. OFFICE OF PUBLICATION: 135 West 50th Street, New York, NY 10020. Copyright © 2015 MARVEL No similarity between any of the names, characters, persons, and/or institutions in this magazine with those of any living or dead person or institution is intended, and any such similarity which may exist is purely coincidental. **Printed in the U.S.A.** ALAN FINE, President, Marvel Entertainment; DAN BUCKLEY, President, TV, Publishing and Brand Management; JOE QUESADA, Chief Creative Officer; TOM BREVOORT, SVP of Publishing; DAVID BOGART, SVP of Operations & Procurement, Publishing; C.B. CEBULSKI, VP of International Development & Brand Management; DAVID GABRIEL, SVP Print, Sales & Marketing; JIM O'KEEFE, VP of Operations & Logistics; DAN CARR, Executive Director of Publishing Technology; SUSAN CRESPI, Editorial Operations Manager; ALEX MORALES, Publishing Operations Manager; STAN LEE, Chairman Emeritus. For information regarding advertising in Marvel Comics or on Marvel.com, please contact Jonathan Rheingold, VP of Custom Solutions & Ad Sales, at jrheingold@marvel.com. For Marvel subscription inquiries, please call 800-217-9158. **Manufactured between 7/3/2015 and 8/10/2015 by SHERIDAN BOOKS, INC., CHELSEA, MI, USA.**

10 9 8 7 6 5 4 3 2 1

YA GRAPHIC
Avengers

MARVEL

AVENGERS ASSEMBLE

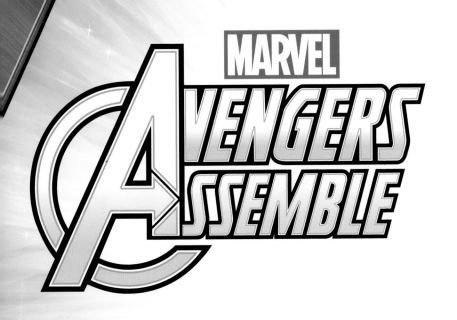

Based on the TV series written by
**MAN OF ACTION, JACOB SEMAHN, KEVIN BURKE,
CHRIS "DOC" WYATT & MICHAEL RYAN**

Directed by
TIM ELDRED & **PAUL PIGNOTTI**

Art by
MARVEL ANIMATION

Adapted by
JOE CARAMAGNA

Special Thanks to Jenny Whitlock, Henry Ong & Product Factory
Avengers Created by Stan Lee & Jack Kirby

Editor
SEBASTIAN GIRNER

Consulting Editor
JON MOISAN

Senior Editor
MARK PANICCIA

Collection Editor
ALEX STARBUCK

Assistant Editor
SARAH BRUNSTAD

Editors, Special Projects
JENNIFER GRÜNWALD & **MARK D. BEAZLEY**

Senior Editor, Special Projects
JEFF YOUNGQUIST

SVP Print, Sales & Marketing
DAVID GABRIEL

Head of Marvel Television
JEPH LOEB

Book Designer
JAY BOWEN

Editor In Chief
AXEL ALONSO

Chief Creative Officer
JOE QUESADA

Publisher
DAN BUCKLEY

Executive Producer
ALAN FINE

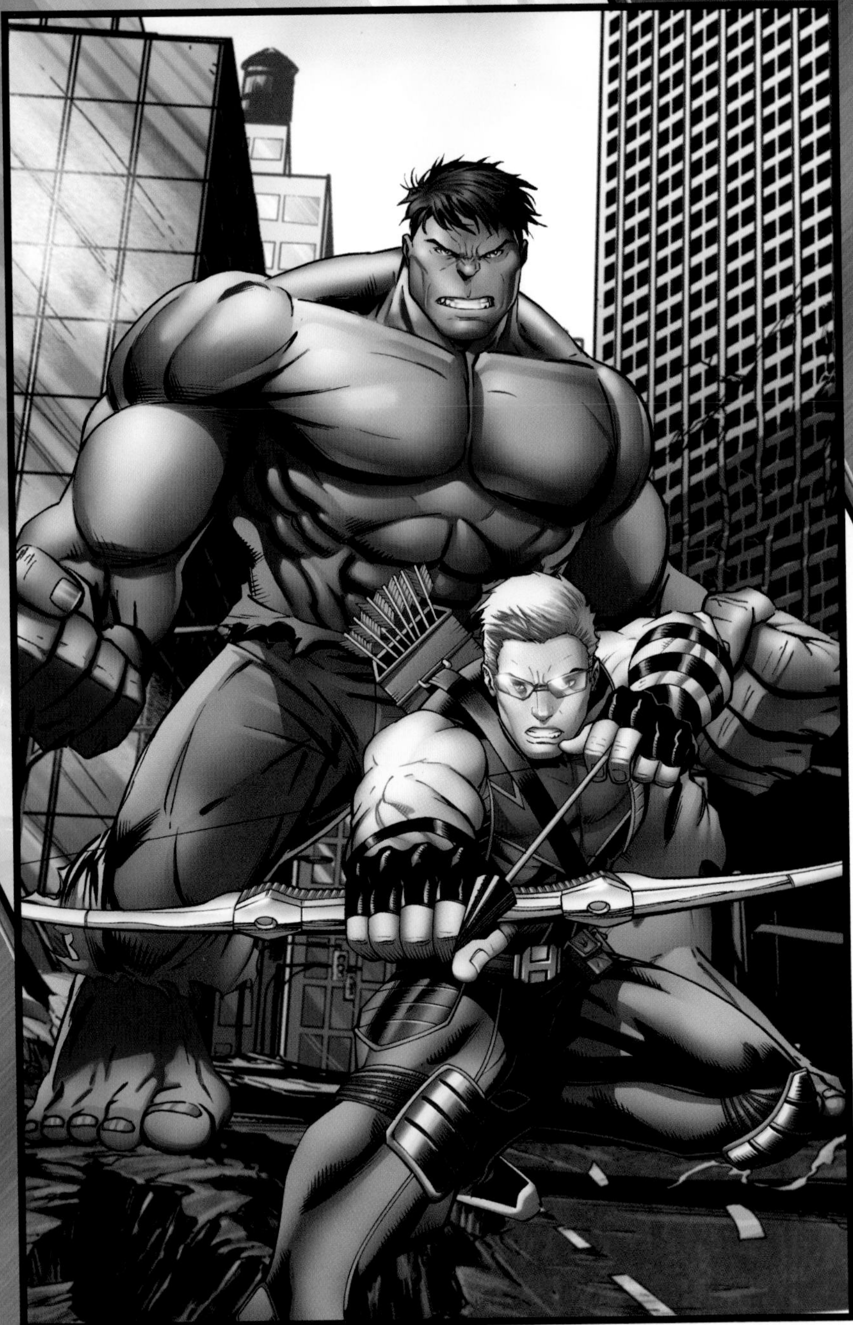

#5 BASED ON "MOJOWORLD"

MARVEL

AVENGERS ASSEMBLE

SEASON 2

And there came a day unlike any other, when Earth's mightiest heroes found themselves united against a common threat, to fight the foes no single super hero could withstand.

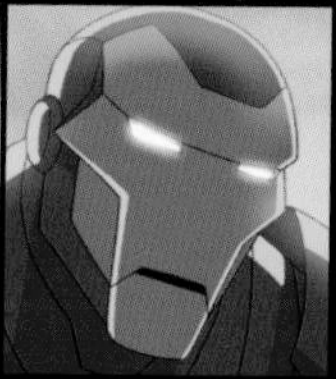

IRON MAN

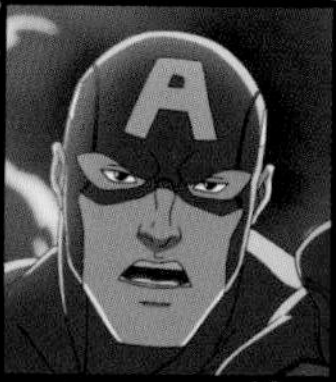

CAPTAIN AMERICA

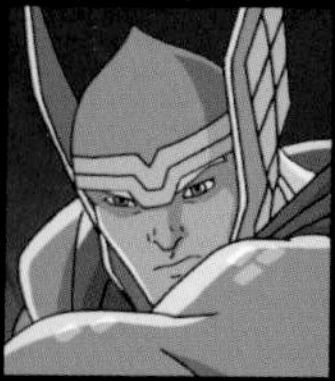

THOR

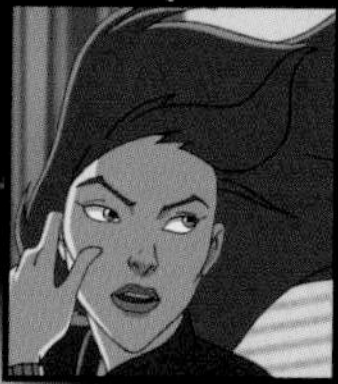

BLACK WIDOW

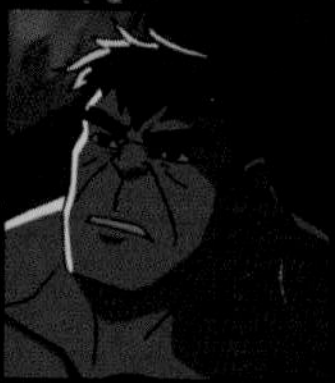

HULK

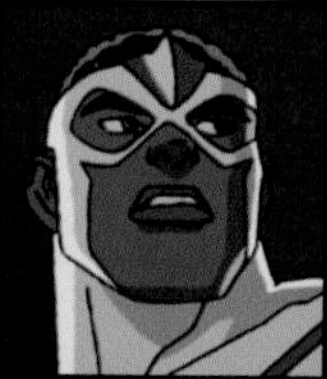

FALCON

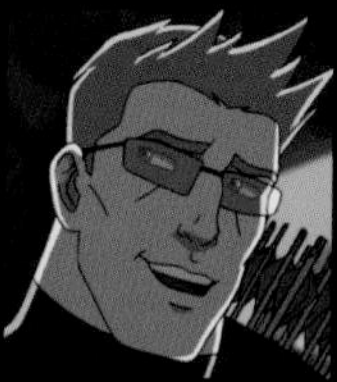

HAWKEYE

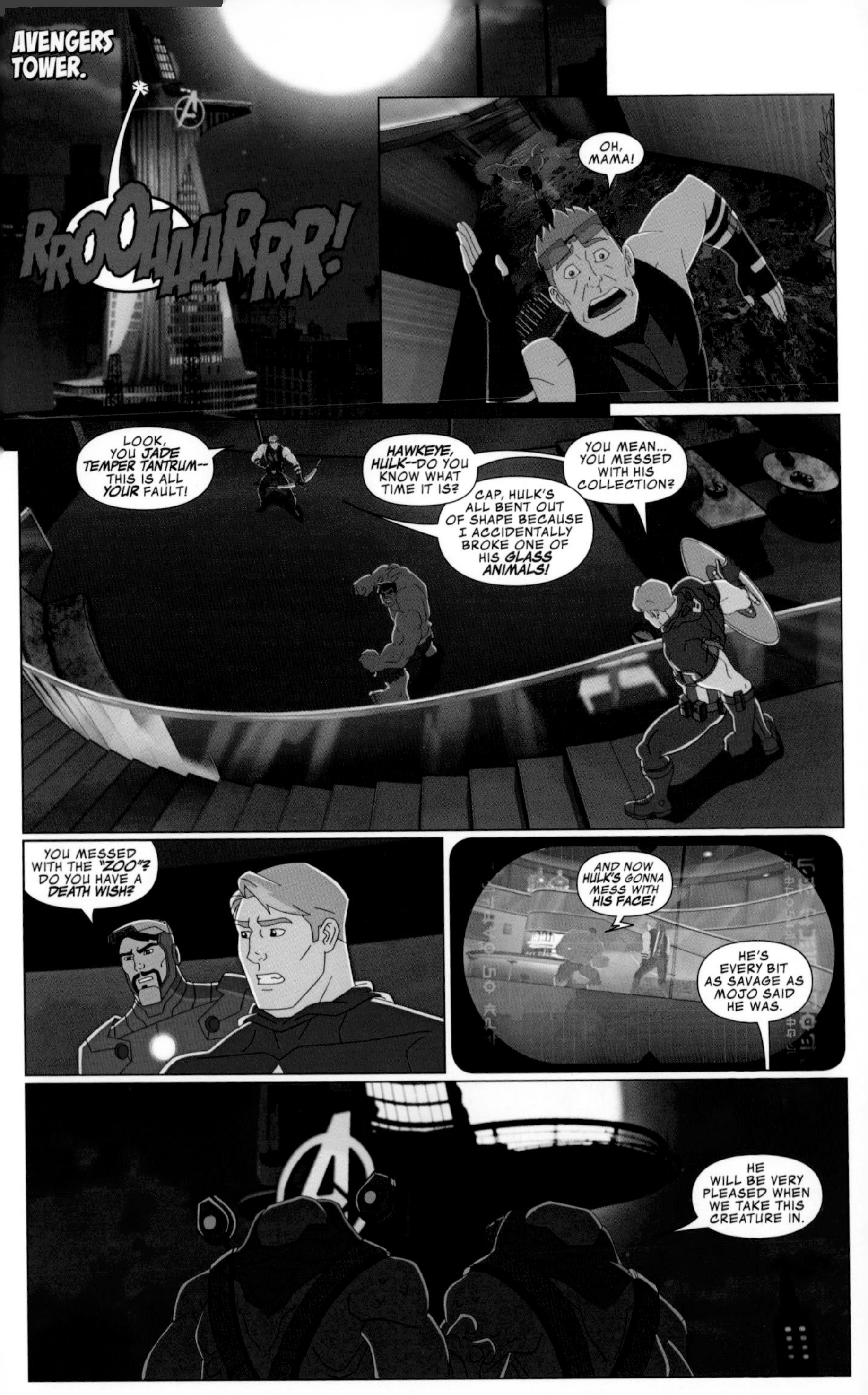
AVENGERS TOWER.
RROOAAARRRR!
OH, MAMA!
LOOK, YOU JADE TEMPER TANTRUM-- THIS IS ALL YOUR FAULT!
HAWKEYE, HULK--DO YOU KNOW WHAT TIME IT IS?
CAP, HULK'S ALL BENT OUT OF SHAPE BECAUSE I ACCIDENTALLY BROKE ONE OF HIS GLASS ANIMALS!
YOU MEAN... YOU MESSED WITH HIS COLLECTION?
YOU MESSED WITH THE "ZOO"? DO YOU HAVE A DEATH WISH?
AND NOW HULK'S GONNA MESS WITH HIS FACE!
HE'S EVERY BIT AS SAVAGE AS MOJO SAID HE WAS.
HE WILL BE VERY PLEASED WHEN WE TAKE THIS CREATURE IN.

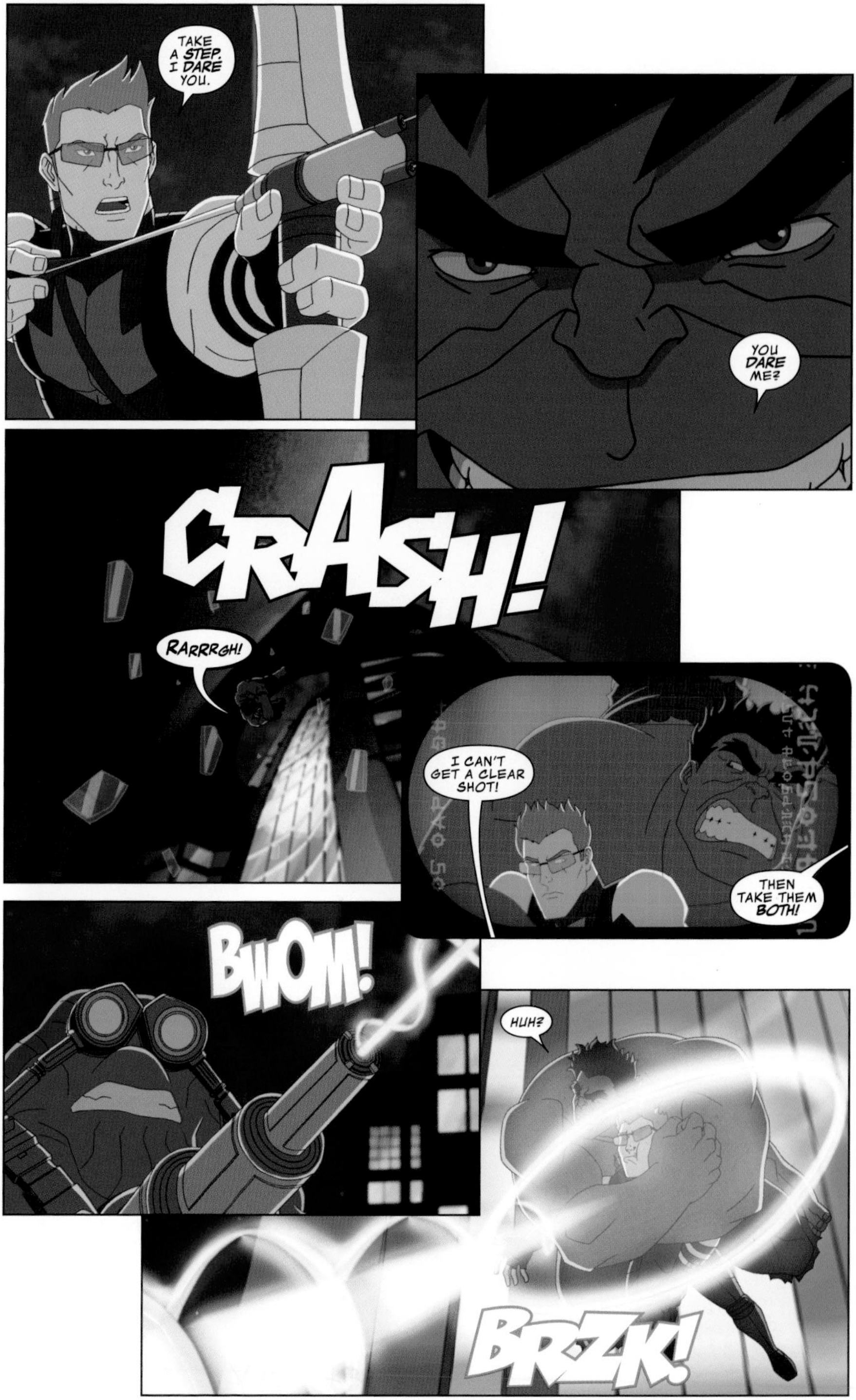
TAKE A STEP. I DARE YOU.
YOU DARE ME?
CRASH!
RARRRGH!
I CAN'T GET A CLEAR SHOT!
THEN TAKE THEM BOTH!
BWOM!
HUH?
BRZK!

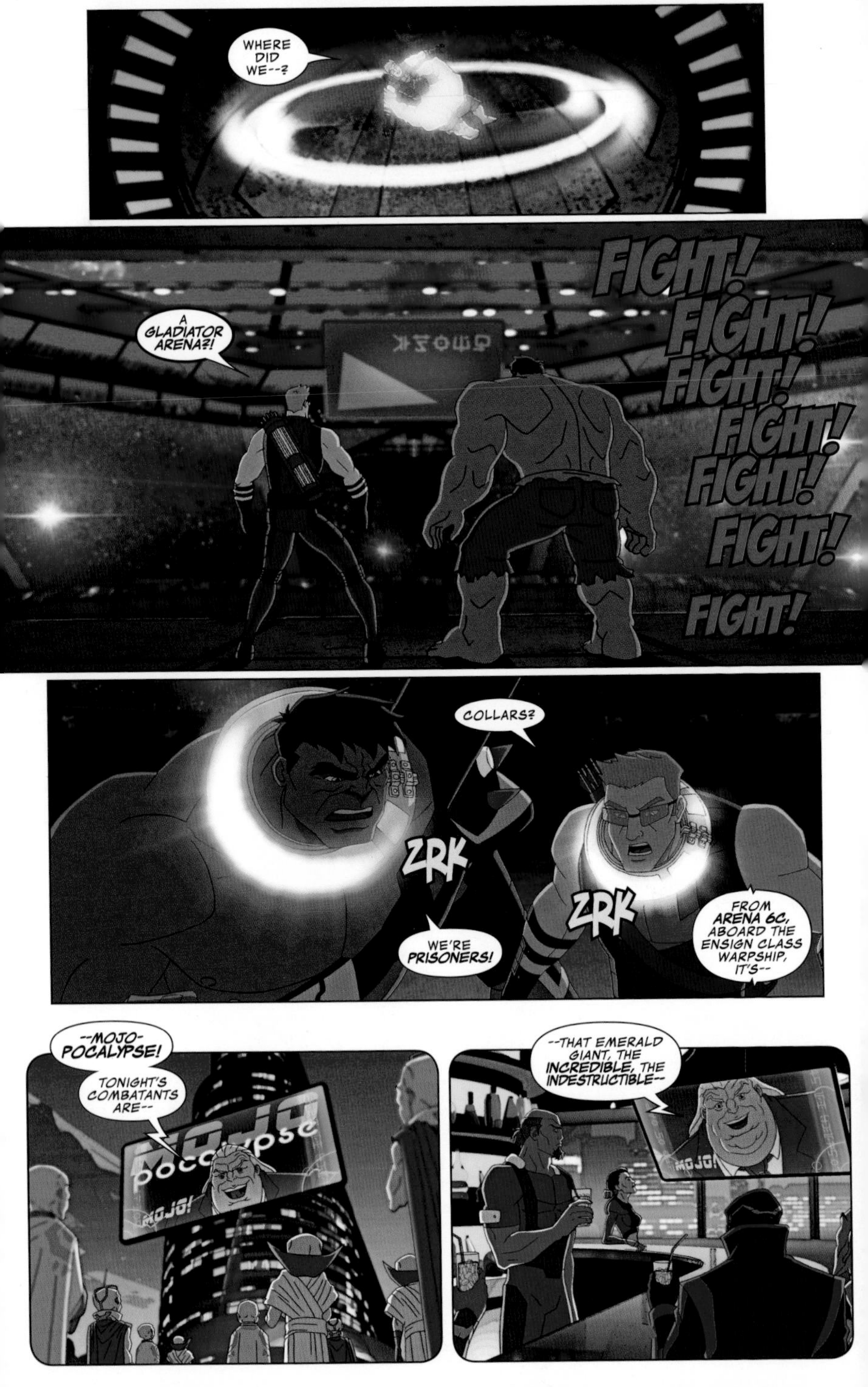
WHERE DID WE--?
A GLADIATOR ARENA?!
FIGHT!
FIGHT!
FIGHT!
FIGHT!
FIGHT!
FIGHT!
FIGHT!
COLLARS?
ZRK
ZRK
WE'RE PRISONERS!
FROM ARENA 6C, ABOARD THE ENSIGN CLASS WARPSHIP, IT'S--
--MOJO-POCALYPSE!
TONIGHT'S COMBATANTS ARE--
MOJO pocalypse
MOJO!
--THAT EMERALD GIANT, THE INCREDIBLE, THE INDESTRUCTIBLE--
MOJO!

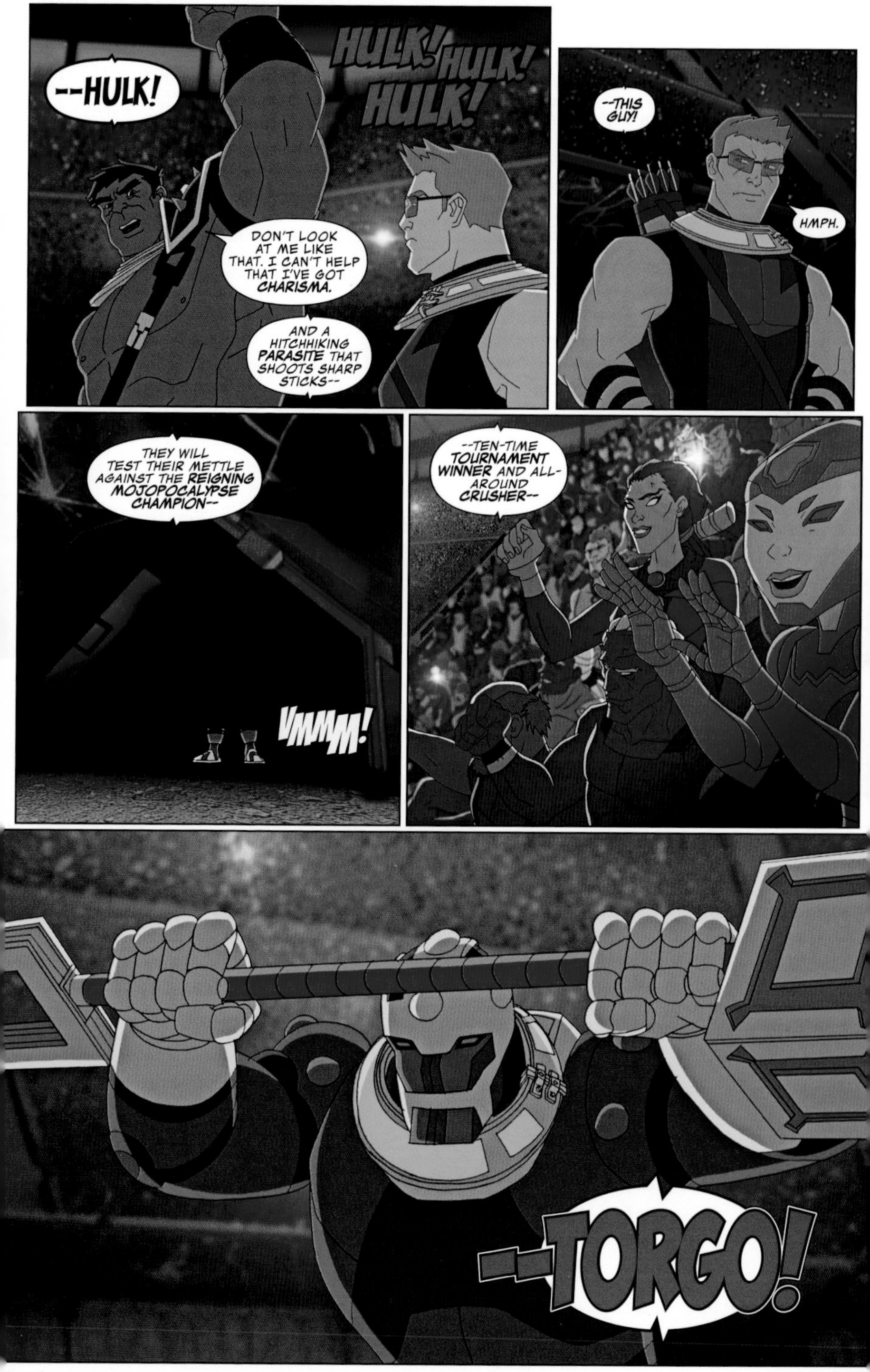
--HULK!
HULK! HULK! HULK!
DON'T LOOK AT ME LIKE THAT. I CAN'T HELP THAT I'VE GOT CHARISMA.
AND A HITCHHIKING PARASITE THAT SHOOTS SHARP STICKS--
--THIS GUY!
HMPH.
THEY WILL TEST THEIR METTLE AGAINST THE REIGNING MOJOPOCALYPSE CHAMPION--
VMMMM!
--TEN-TIME TOURNAMENT WINNER AND ALL-AROUND CRUSHER--
--TORGO!

ALONG WITH A FEW CHALLENGERS FROM THE PAST!

THOSE STILL *SURVIVING*, THAT IS!

THAT'S RIGHT, SPORTS FANS, WE'VE GOT OURSELVES A *DERBY OF DEMISE!*

THE RULES ARE SIMPLE-- THERE ARE NONE!

THAT TORGO GUY IS *MINE!*

EASE UP, HULK! WE'RE NOT EVEN SURE WHAT THIS IS ALL ABOUT!

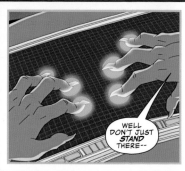

WELL DON'T JUST *STAND* THERE--

HEY! WHAT'S THE IDEA?

--*FIGHT!*

HE'S FORCING US TOGETHER AGAINST OUR WILL!

IT'S THE *COLLARS!*

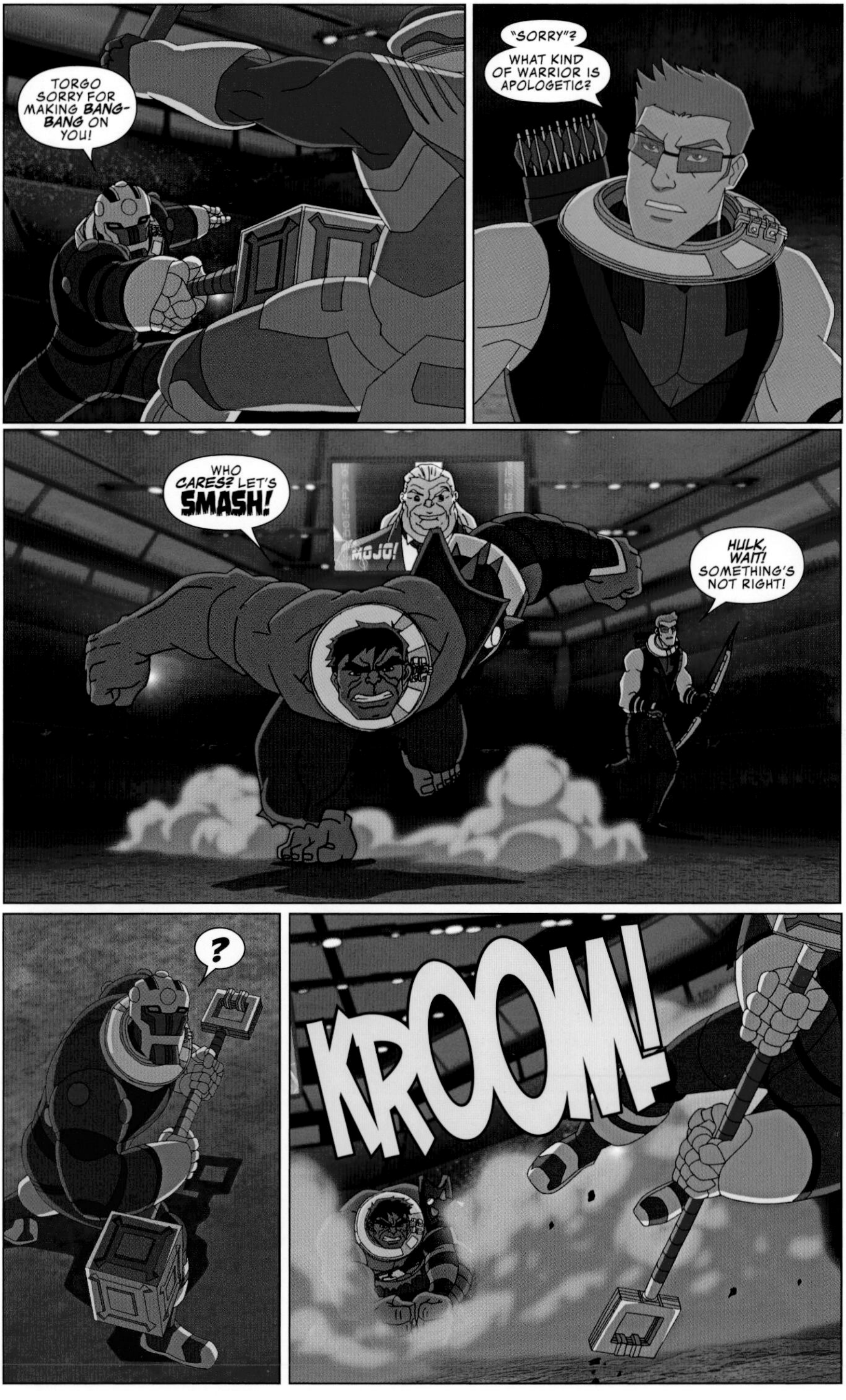
TORGO SORRY FOR MAKING BANG-BANG ON YOU!
"SORRY"? WHAT KIND OF WARRIOR IS APOLOGETIC?
WHO CARES? LET'S SMASH!
MOJO!
HULK, WAIT! SOMETHING'S NOT RIGHT!
?
KROOM!

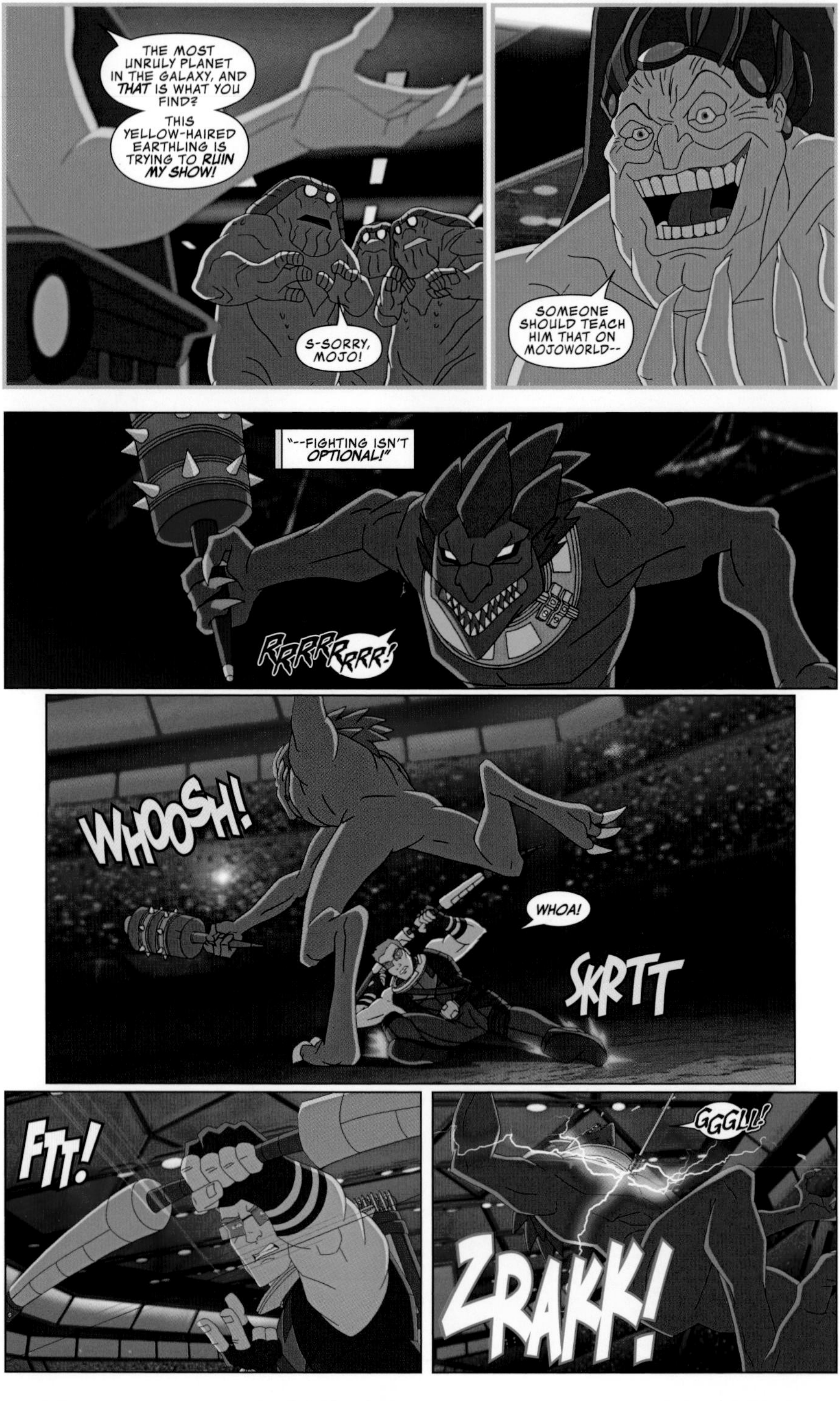
THE MOST UNRULY PLANET IN THE GALAXY, AND *THAT* IS WHAT YOU FIND?
THIS YELLOW-HAIRED EARTHLING IS TRYING TO *RUIN MY SHOW!*
S-SORRY, MOJO!
SOMEONE SHOULD TEACH HIM THAT ON MOJOWORLD--
"--FIGHTING ISN'T *OPTIONAL!*"
RRRRRRRR!
WHOOSH!
WHOA!
SKRTT
FTT!
GGGLL!
ZRAKK!

SORRY, HULK NOT SORRY!

MOJO BIGGEST FIGHT PROMOTER IN *UNIVERSE*, FINDS GREATEST *WARRIORS* FROM *EVERY PLANET*.

KRMMB!

TORGO *PRISONER*, LIKE *YOU*.

TORGO ALWAYS WIN SO MOJO NO CANCEL TORGO HOME.

"CANCEL HOME"? MOJO DESTROYS THE PLANET OF EVERY *LOSER?!*

WHAM!

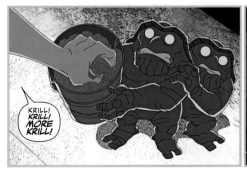

KRILL! KRILL! *MORE* KRILL!

THIS IS JUST STARTING TO GET *GOOD* AND I NEED MORE *FOOD!*

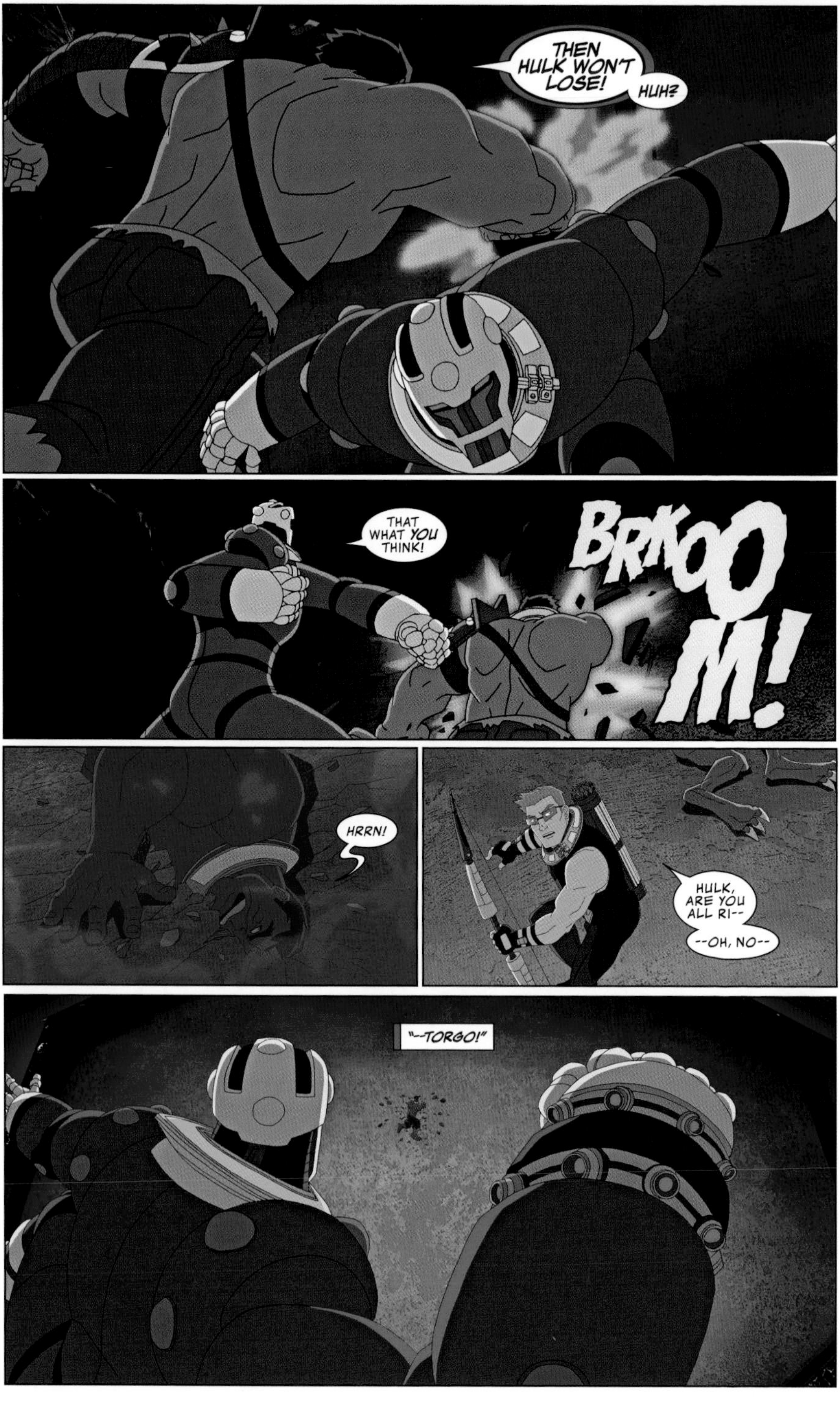
THEN HULK WON'T LOSE!
HUH?
THAT WHAT YOU THINK!
BRKOOM!
HRRN!
HULK, ARE YOU ALL RI--
--OH, NO--
"--TORGO!"

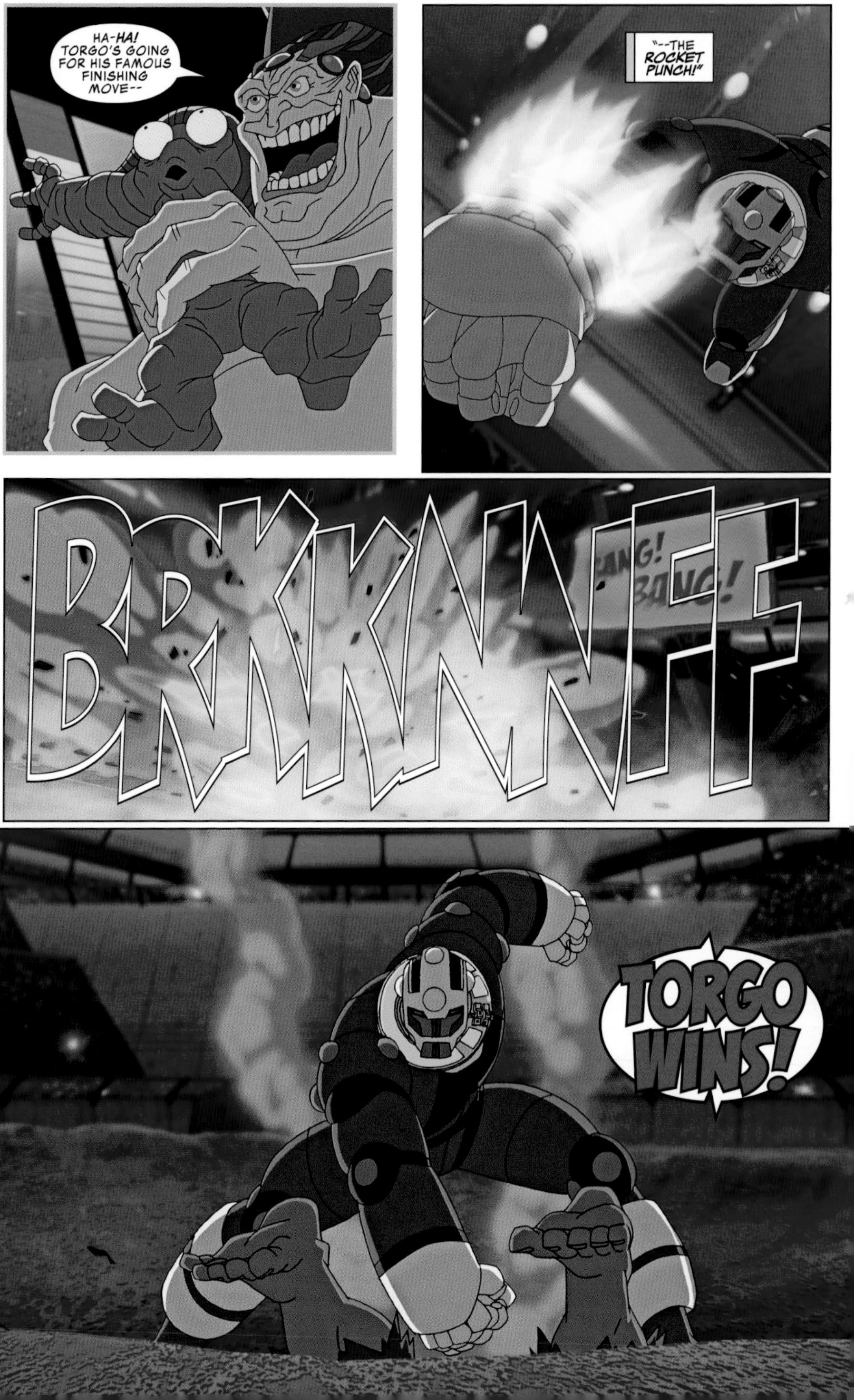
HA-HA! TORGO'S GOING FOR HIS FAMOUS FINISHING MOVE--
"--THE ROCKET PUNCH!"
BRKKNNFF
BANG! BANG!
TORGO WINS!

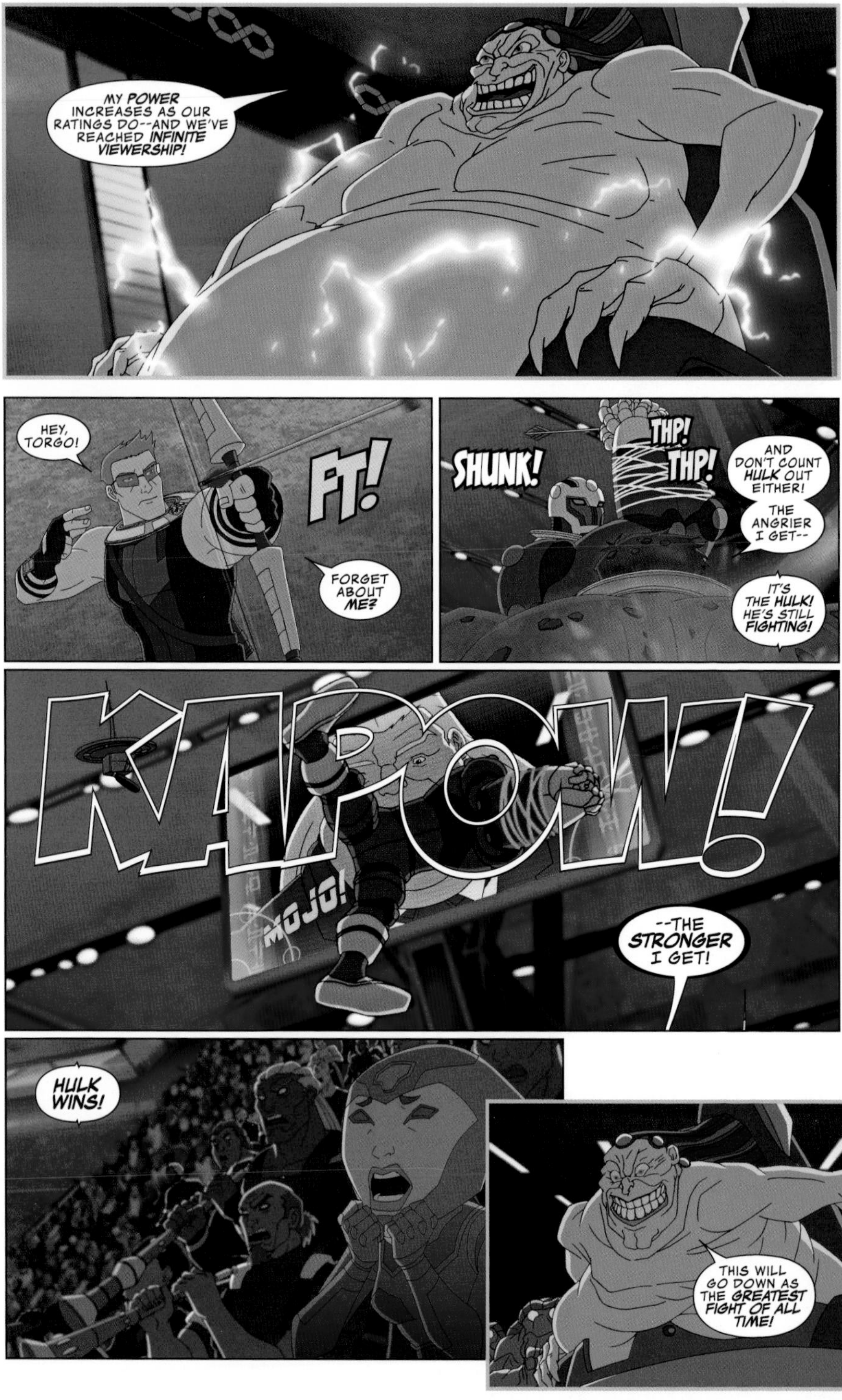
MY POWER INCREASES AS OUR RATINGS DO--AND WE'VE REACHED INFINITE VIEWERSHIP!
HEY, TORGO!
FT!
FORGET ABOUT ME?
SHUNK!
THP!
THP!
AND DON'T COUNT HULK OUT EITHER!
THE ANGRIER I GET--
IT'S THE HULK! HE'S STILL FIGHTING!
KAPOW!
MOJO!
--THE STRONGER I GET!
HULK WINS!
THIS WILL GO DOWN AS THE GREATEST FIGHT OF ALL TIME!

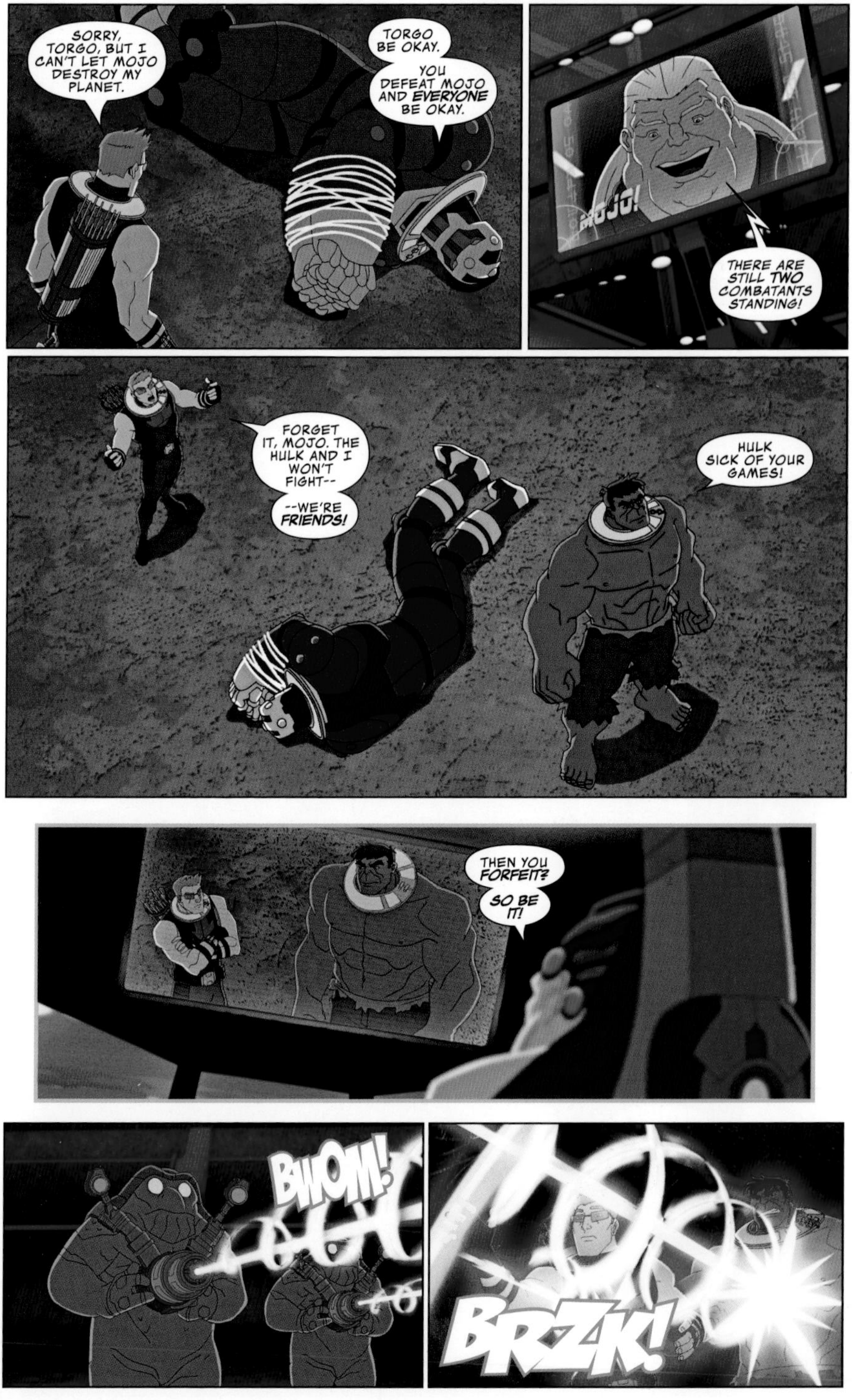
SORRY, TORGO, BUT I CAN'T LET MOJO DESTROY MY PLANET.
TORGO BE OKAY.
YOU DEFEAT MOJO AND EVERYONE BE OKAY.
MOJO!
THERE ARE STILL TWO COMBATANTS STANDING!
FORGET IT, MOJO. THE HULK AND I WON'T FIGHT--
--WE'RE FRIENDS!
HULK SICK OF YOUR GAMES!
THEN YOU FORFEIT?
SO BE IT!
BWOM!
BRZK!

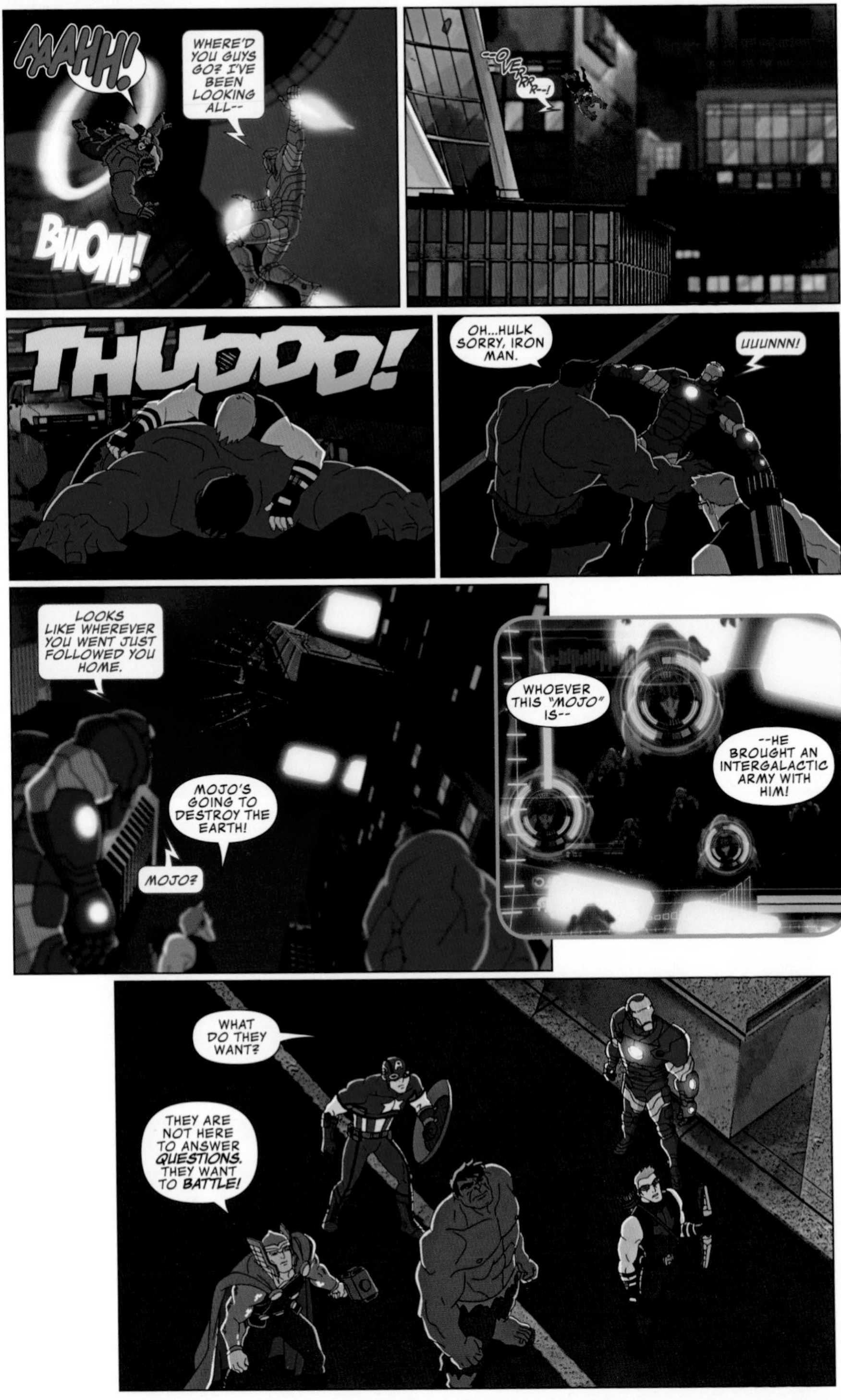

AAAHH!
WHERE'D YOU GUYS GO? I'VE BEEN LOOKING ALL--
BWOM!
--OVERRR--!
THUDDD!
OH...HULK SORRY, IRON MAN.
UUUNNN!
LOOKS LIKE WHEREVER YOU WENT JUST FOLLOWED YOU HOME.
MOJO'S GOING TO DESTROY THE EARTH!
MOJO?
WHOEVER THIS "MOJO" IS--
--HE BROUGHT AN INTERGALACTIC ARMY WITH HIM!
WHAT DO THEY WANT?
THEY ARE NOT HERE TO ANSWER QUESTIONS. THEY WANT TO BATTLE!

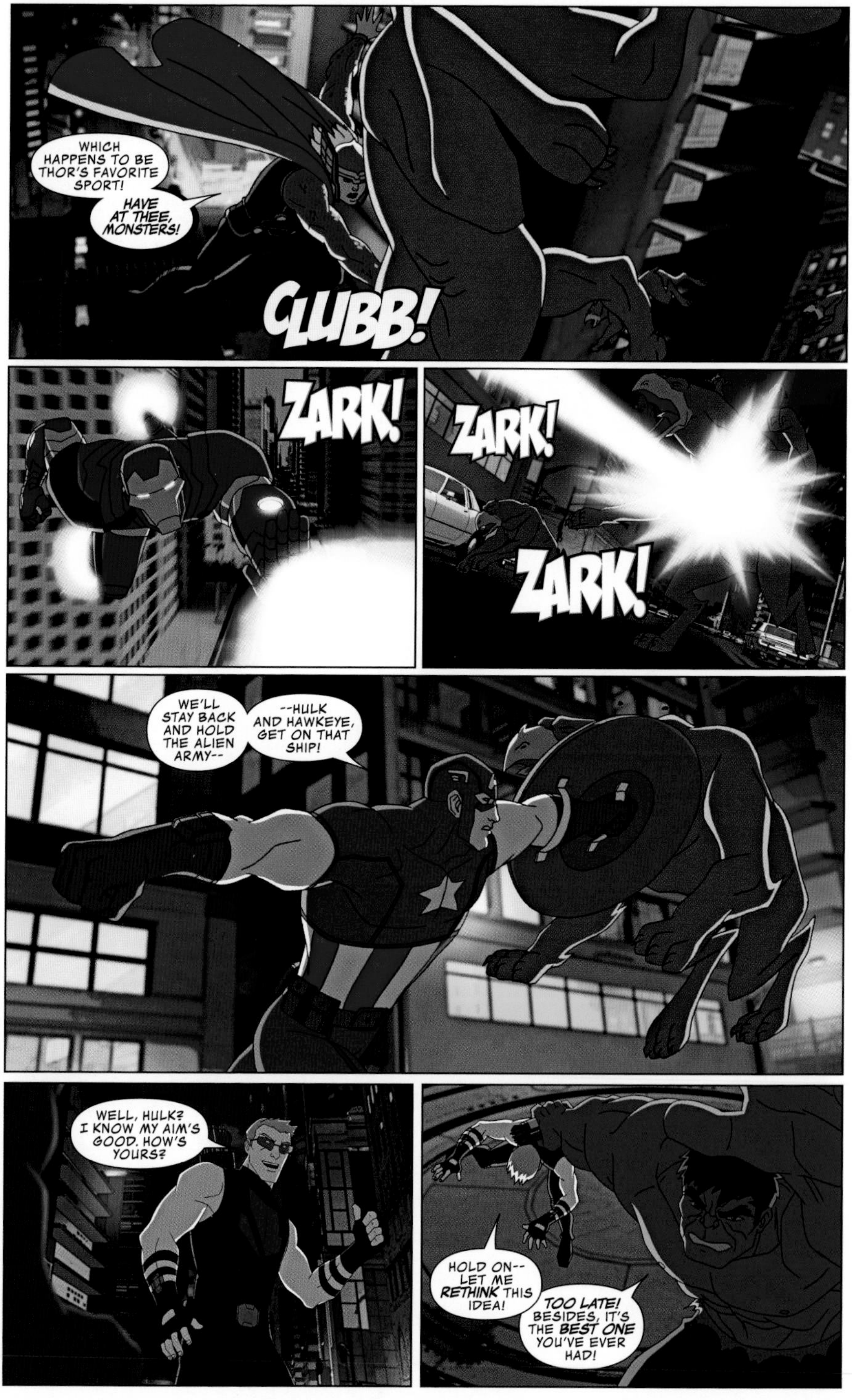
WHICH HAPPENS TO BE THOR'S FAVORITE SPORT!
HAVE AT THEE, MONSTERS!
CLUBB!
ZARK!
ZARK!
ZARK!
WE'LL STAY BACK AND HOLD THE ALIEN ARMY--
--HULK AND HAWKEYE, GET ON THAT SHIP!
WELL, HULK? I KNOW MY AIM'S GOOD. HOW'S YOURS?
HOLD ON-- LET ME RETHINK THIS IDEA!
TOO LATE! BESIDES, IT'S THE BEST ONE YOU'VE EVER HAD!

HULLLLKKKK--!

I AM AWESOME!

NOT *ONE*, NOT *TWO*, BUT WE'VE FOUND *FIVE* OF THE GREATEST WARRIORS ON THIS PLANET!

BUT BEFORE WE *BROADCAST*, CAN YOU DO SOMETHING ABOUT MY THIRD CHIN?

SORRY, MOJO--

--SHOW'S *OVER*!

WHY WASTE YOUR TIME BEATING ON ME WHEN MY *FRIEND* HERE WILL BRING IN *BIGGER* RATINGS?

VRRRT!

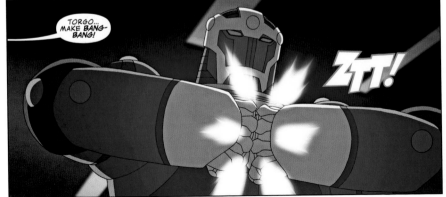

TORGO... MAKE *BANG-BANG*!

ZTT!

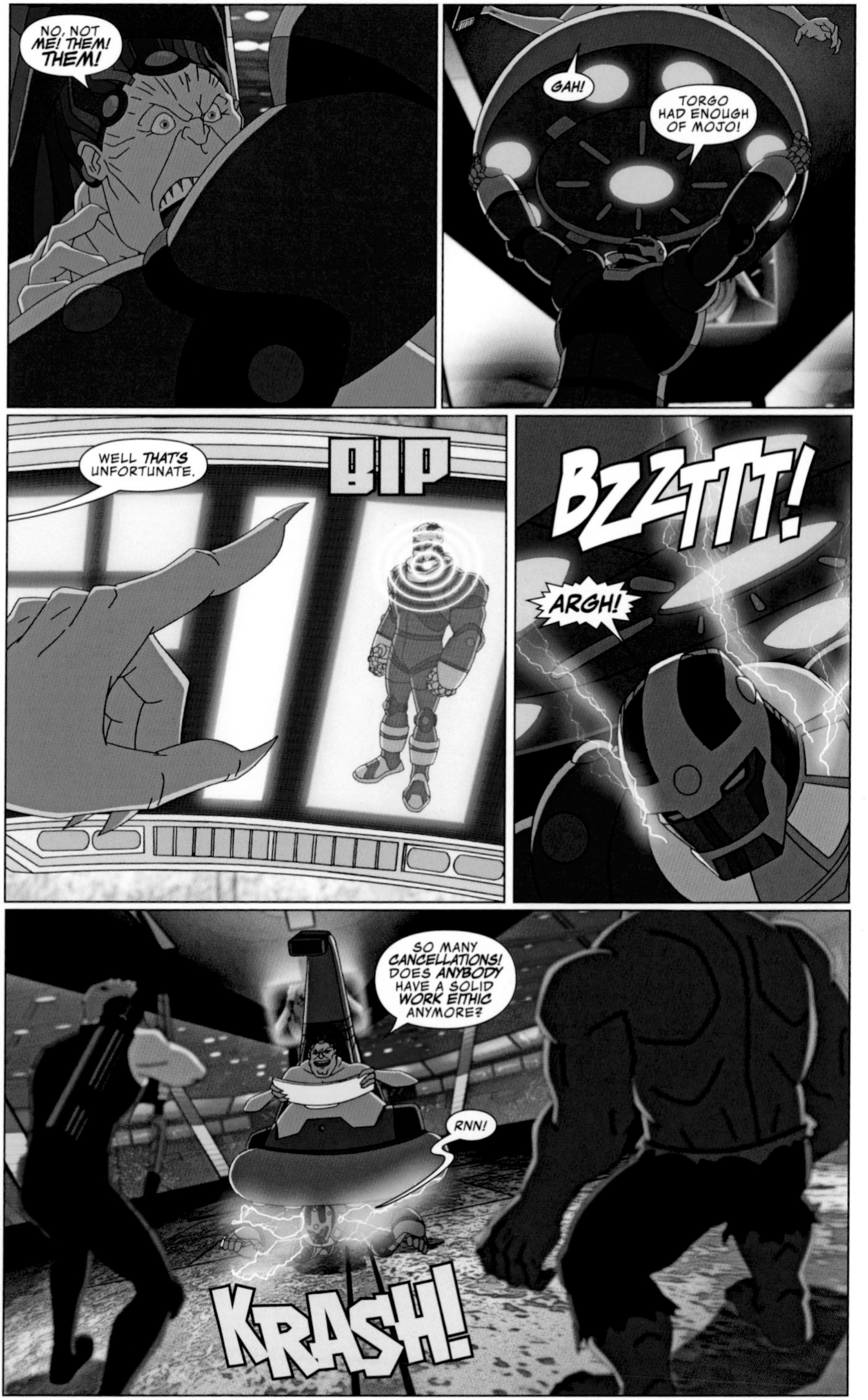
NO, NOT ME! THEM! THEM!
GAH!
TORGO HAD ENOUGH OF MOJO!
WELL THAT'S UNFORTUNATE.
BIP
BZZTTT!
ARGH!
SO MANY CANCELLATIONS! DOES ANYBODY HAVE A SOLID WORK EITHIC ANYMORE?
RNN!
KRASH!

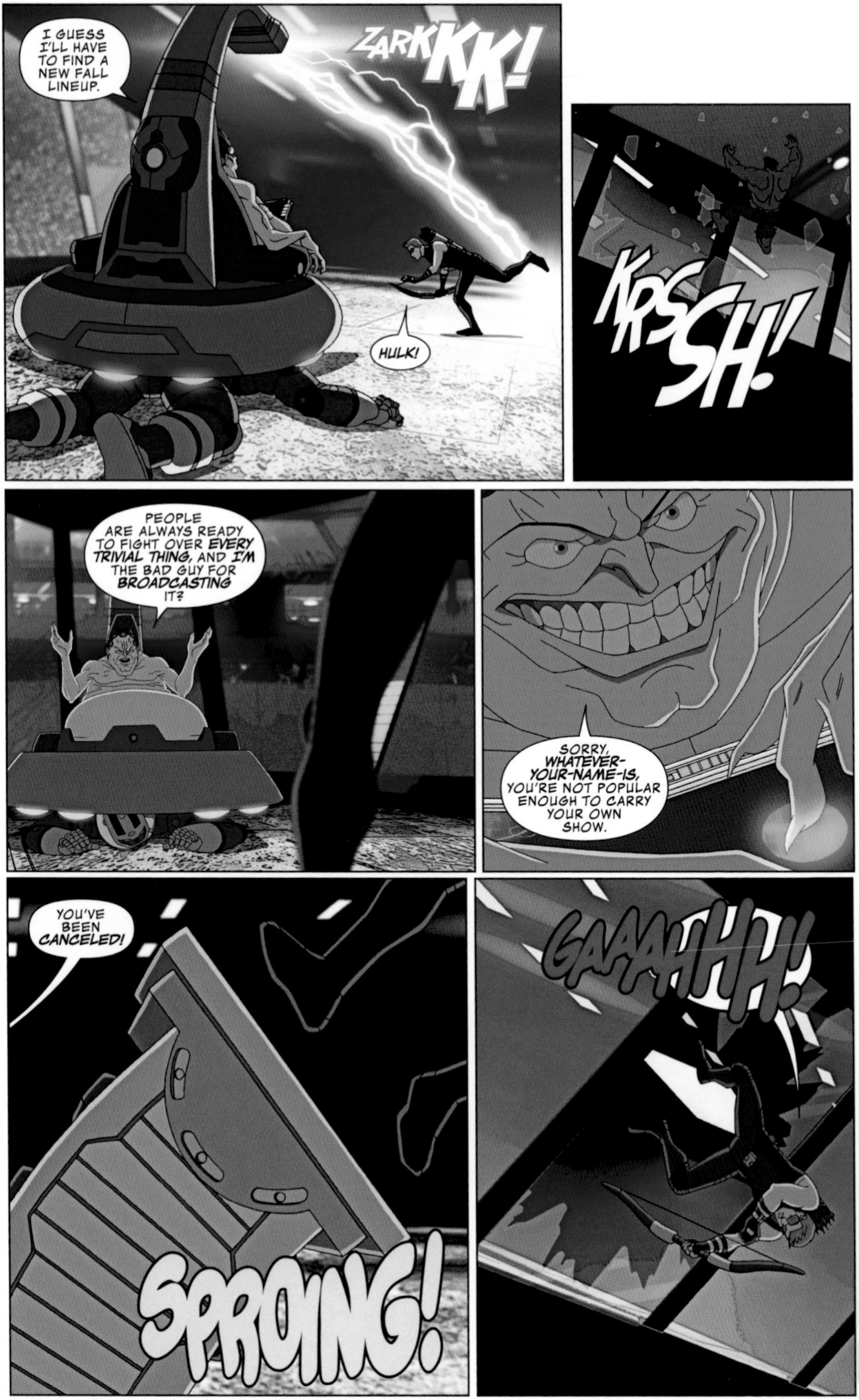
I GUESS I'LL HAVE TO FIND A NEW FALL LINEUP.
ZARKKK!
HULK!
KRSSH!
PEOPLE ARE ALWAYS READY TO FIGHT OVER EVERY TRIVIAL THING, AND I'M THE BAD GUY FOR BROADCASTING IT?
SORRY, WHATEVER-YOUR-NAME-IS, YOU'RE NOT POPULAR ENOUGH TO CARRY YOUR OWN SHOW.
YOU'VE BEEN CANCELED!
SPROING!
GAAAHHH!

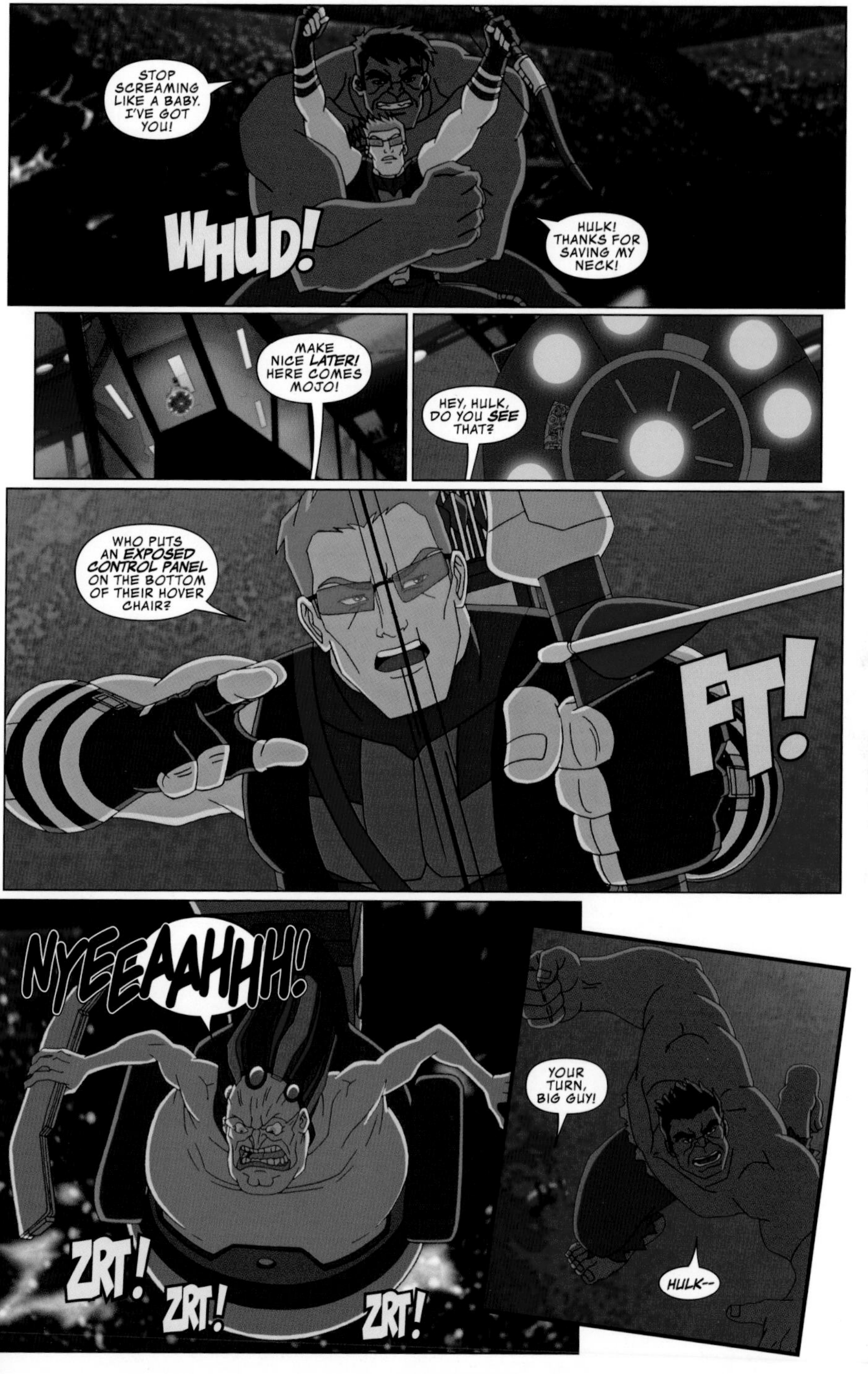
STOP SCREAMING LIKE A BABY. I'VE GOT YOU!
WHUD!
HULK! THANKS FOR SAVING MY NECK!
MAKE NICE LATER! HERE COMES MOJO!
HEY, HULK, DO YOU SEE THAT?
WHO PUTS AN EXPOSED CONTROL PANEL ON THE BOTTOM OF THEIR HOVER CHAIR?
FT!
NYEEAAHHH!
ZRT!
ZRT!
ZRT!
YOUR TURN, BIG GUY!
HULK--

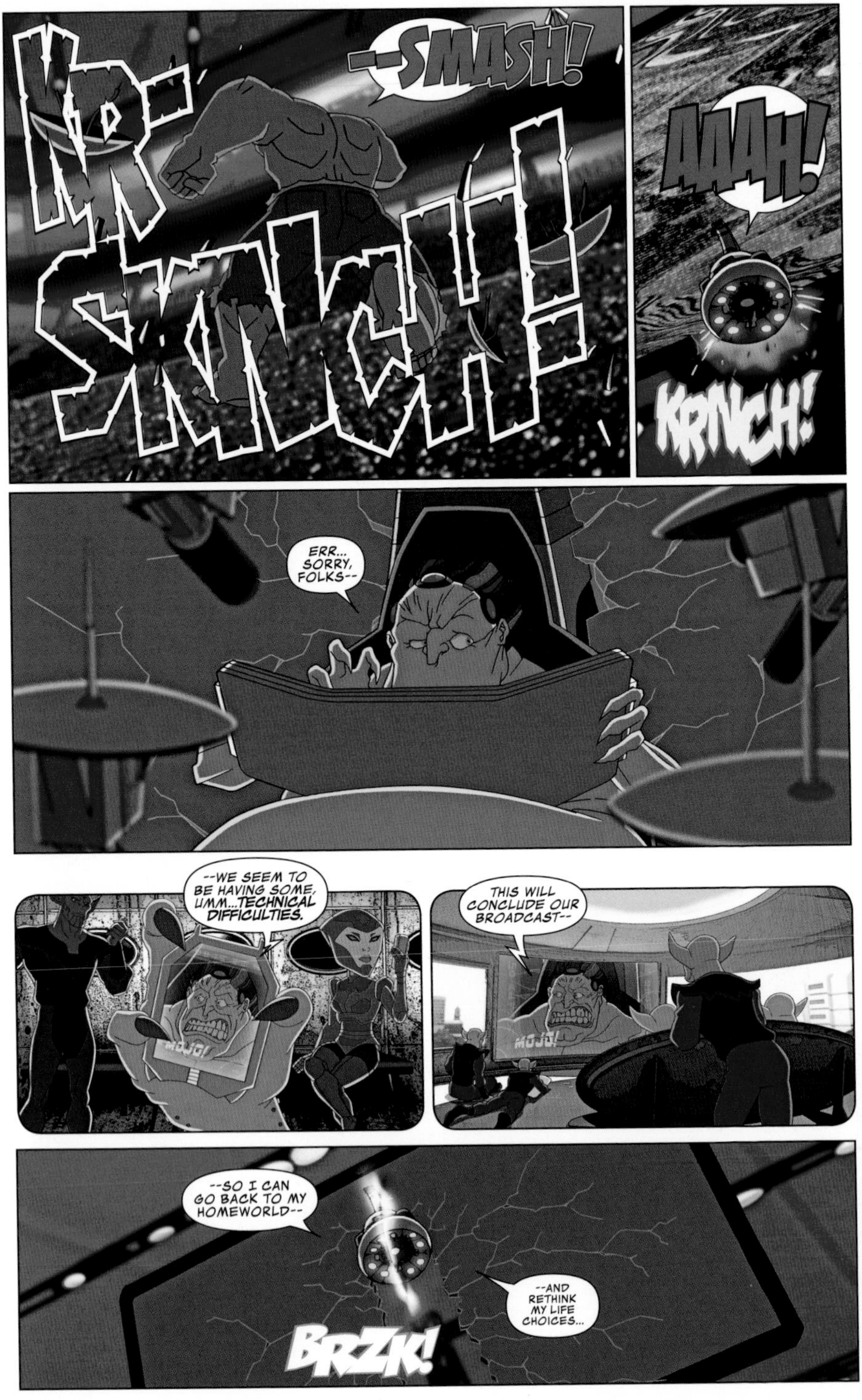
KR-
--SMASH!
SKRNCH!
AAAH!
KRNCH!
ERR... SORRY, FOLKS--
--WE SEEM TO BE HAVING SOME, UMM...TECHNICAL DIFFICULTIES.
MOJO!
THIS WILL CONCLUDE OUR BROADCAST--
MOJO!
--SO I CAN GO BACK TO MY HOMEWORLD--
--AND RETHINK MY LIFE CHOICES...
BRZK!

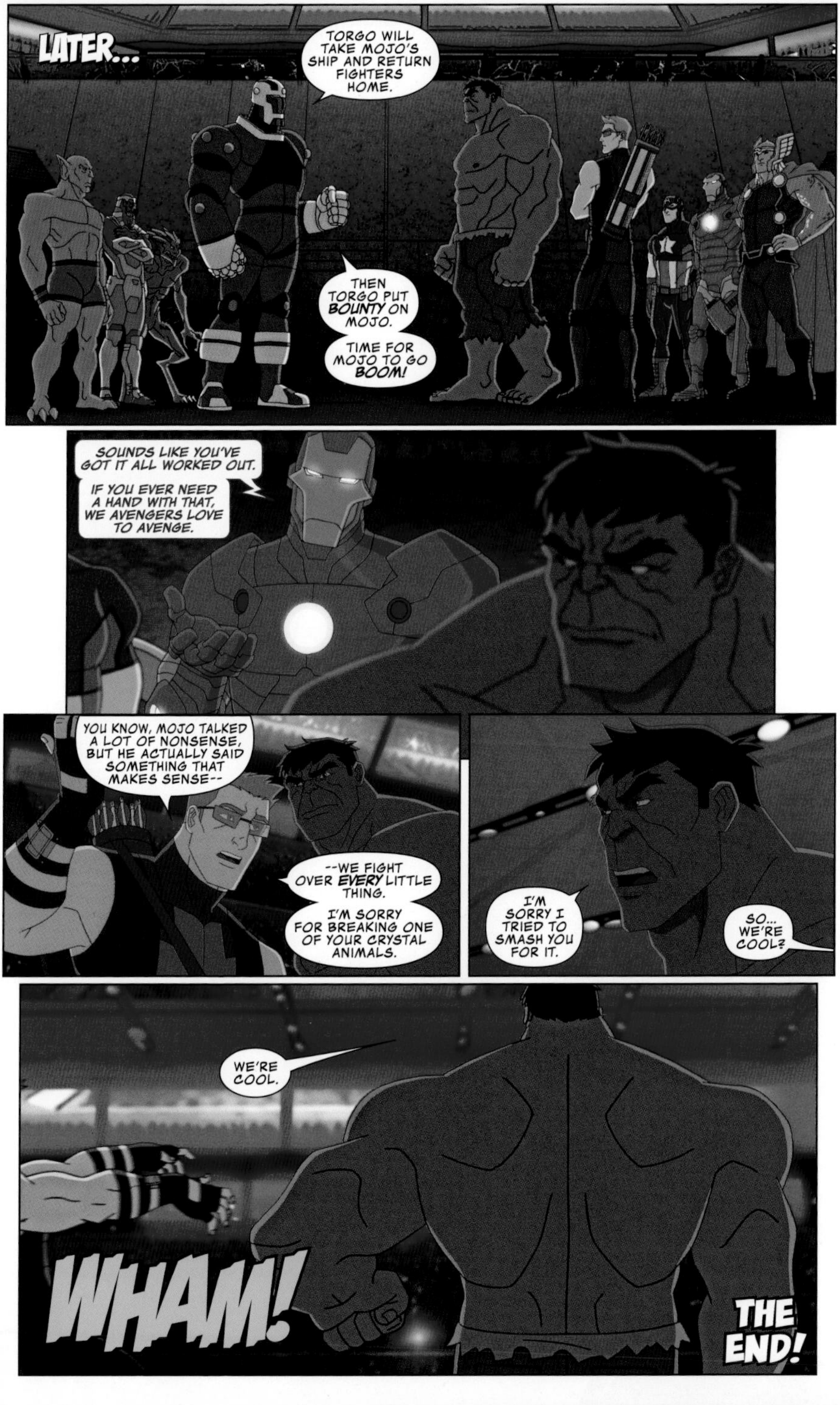
LATER...
TORGO WILL TAKE MOJO'S SHIP AND RETURN FIGHTERS HOME.
THEN TORGO PUT **BOUNTY** ON MOJO.
TIME FOR MOJO TO GO **BOOM!**
SOUNDS LIKE YOU'VE GOT IT ALL WORKED OUT.
IF YOU EVER NEED A HAND WITH THAT, WE AVENGERS LOVE TO AVENGE.
YOU KNOW, MOJO TALKED A LOT OF NONSENSE, BUT HE ACTUALLY SAID SOMETHING THAT MAKES SENSE--
--WE FIGHT OVER **EVERY** LITTLE THING.
I'M SORRY FOR BREAKING ONE OF YOUR CRYSTAL ANIMALS.
I'M SORRY I TRIED TO SMASH YOU FOR IT.
SO... WE'RE COOL?
WE'RE COOL.
WHAM!
THE END!

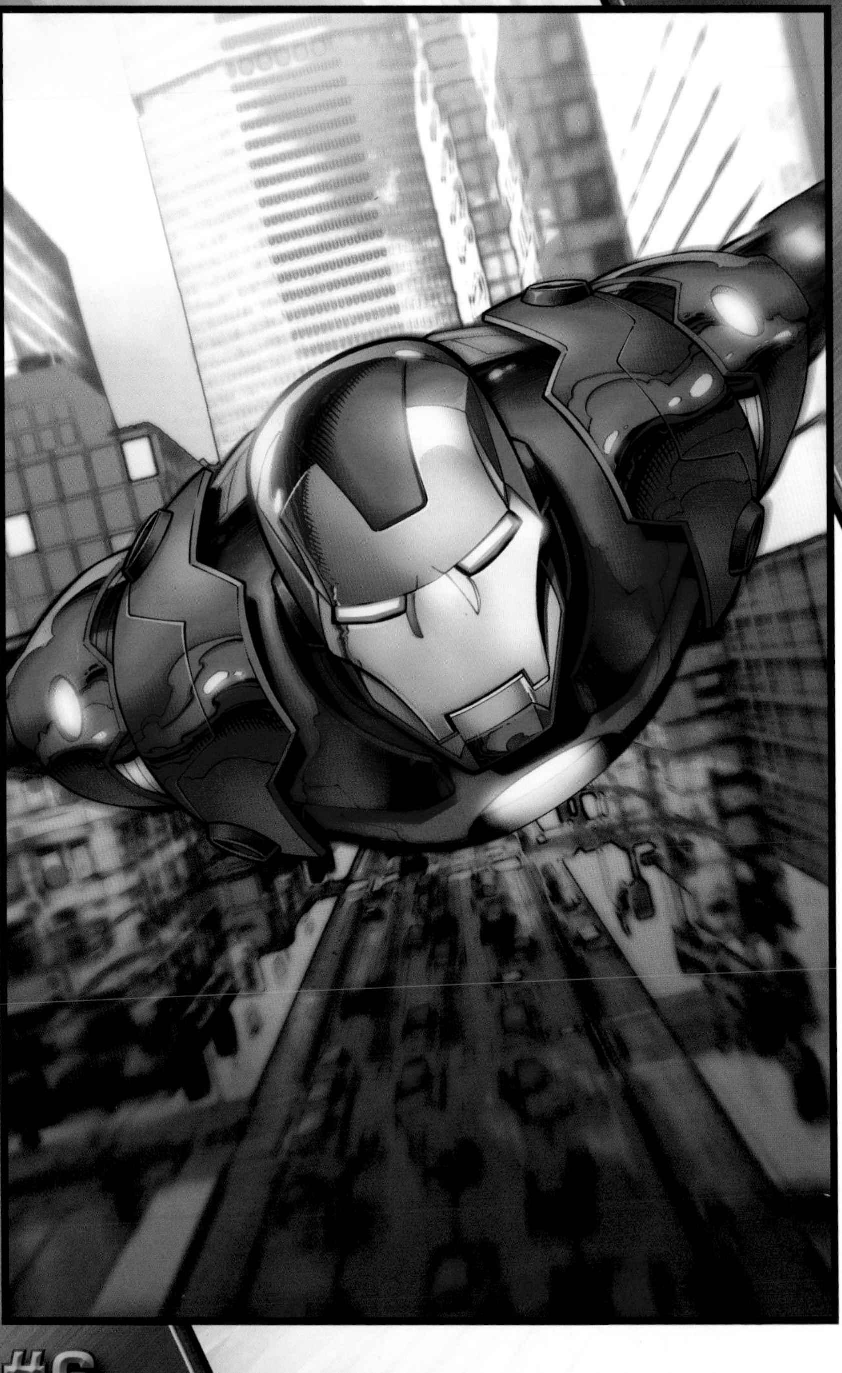

#6 BASED ON "THE AGE OF TONY STARK"

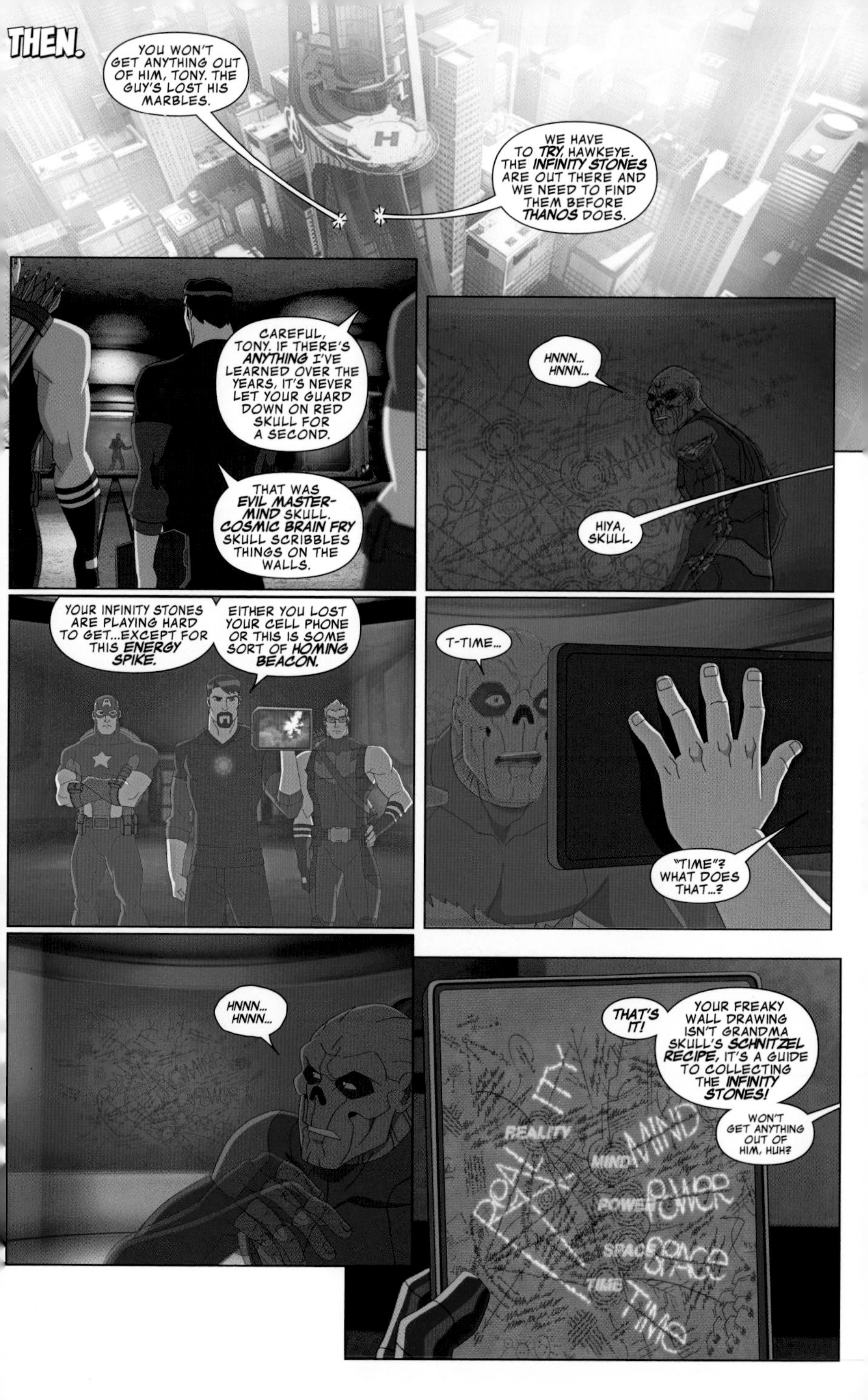
THEN.
YOU WON'T GET ANYTHING OUT OF HIM, TONY. THE GUY'S LOST HIS MARBLES.
WE HAVE TO TRY, HAWKEYE. THE INFINITY STONES ARE OUT THERE AND WE NEED TO FIND THEM BEFORE THANOS DOES.
CAREFUL, TONY. IF THERE'S ANYTHING I'VE LEARNED OVER THE YEARS, IT'S NEVER LET YOUR GUARD DOWN ON RED SKULL FOR A SECOND.
THAT WAS EVIL MASTER-MIND SKULL. COSMIC BRAIN FRY SKULL SCRIBBLES THINGS ON THE WALLS.
HNNN... HNNN...
HIYA, SKULL.
YOUR INFINITY STONES ARE PLAYING HARD TO GET...EXCEPT FOR THIS ENERGY SPIKE.
EITHER YOU LOST YOUR CELL PHONE OR THIS IS SOME SORT OF HOMING BEACON.
T-TIME...
"TIME"? WHAT DOES THAT...?
HNNN... HNNN...
THAT'S IT!
YOUR FREAKY WALL DRAWING ISN'T GRANDMA SKULL'S SCHNITZEL RECIPE, IT'S A GUIDE TO COLLECTING THE INFINITY STONES!
WON'T GET ANYTHING OUT OF HIM, HUH?
REALITY
MIND
POWER
SPACE
TIME

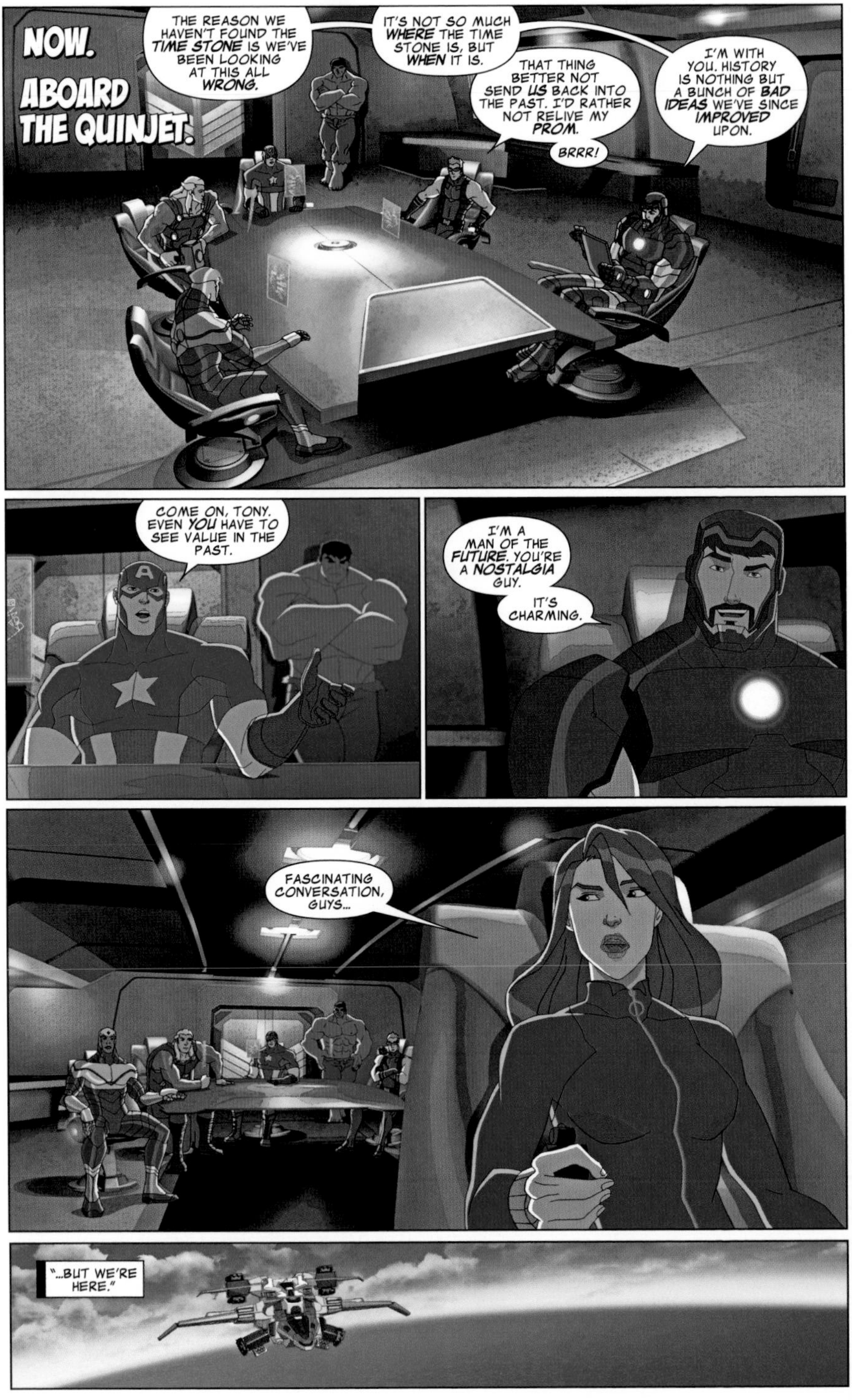
NOW.
ABOARD THE QUINJET.
THE REASON WE HAVEN'T FOUND THE TIME STONE IS WE'VE BEEN LOOKING AT THIS ALL WRONG.
IT'S NOT SO MUCH WHERE THE TIME STONE IS, BUT WHEN IT IS.
THAT THING BETTER NOT SEND US BACK INTO THE PAST. I'D RATHER NOT RELIVE MY PROM.
BRRR!
I'M WITH YOU. HISTORY IS NOTHING BUT A BUNCH OF BAD IDEAS WE'VE SINCE IMPROVED UPON.
COME ON, TONY. EVEN YOU HAVE TO SEE VALUE IN THE PAST.
I'M A MAN OF THE FUTURE. YOU'RE A NOSTALGIA GUY.
IT'S CHARMING.
FASCINATING CONVERSATION, GUYS...
"...BUT WE'RE HERE."

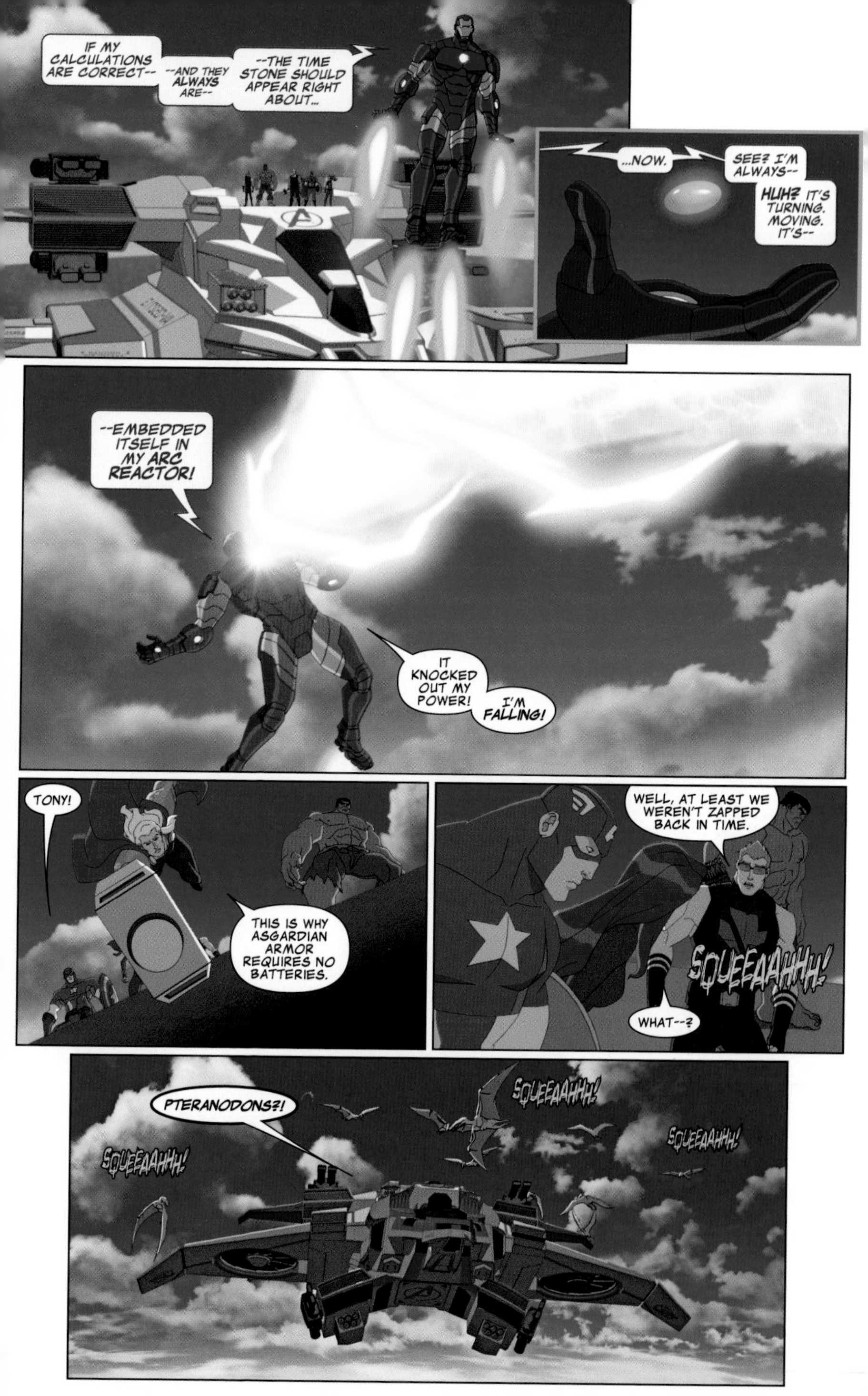
IF MY CALCULATIONS ARE CORRECT--
--AND THEY ALWAYS ARE--
--THE TIME STONE SHOULD APPEAR RIGHT ABOUT...
...NOW.
SEE? I'M ALWAYS--
HUH? IT'S TURNING. MOVING. IT'S--
--EMBEDDED ITSELF IN MY ARC REACTOR!
IT KNOCKED OUT MY POWER!
I'M FALLING!
TONY!
THIS IS WHY ASGARDIAN ARMOR REQUIRES NO BATTERIES.
WELL, AT LEAST WE WEREN'T ZAPPED BACK IN TIME.
SQUEEAAHHH!
WHAT--?
PTERANODONS?!
SQUEEAAHHH!
SQUEEAAHHH!
SQUEEAAHHH!

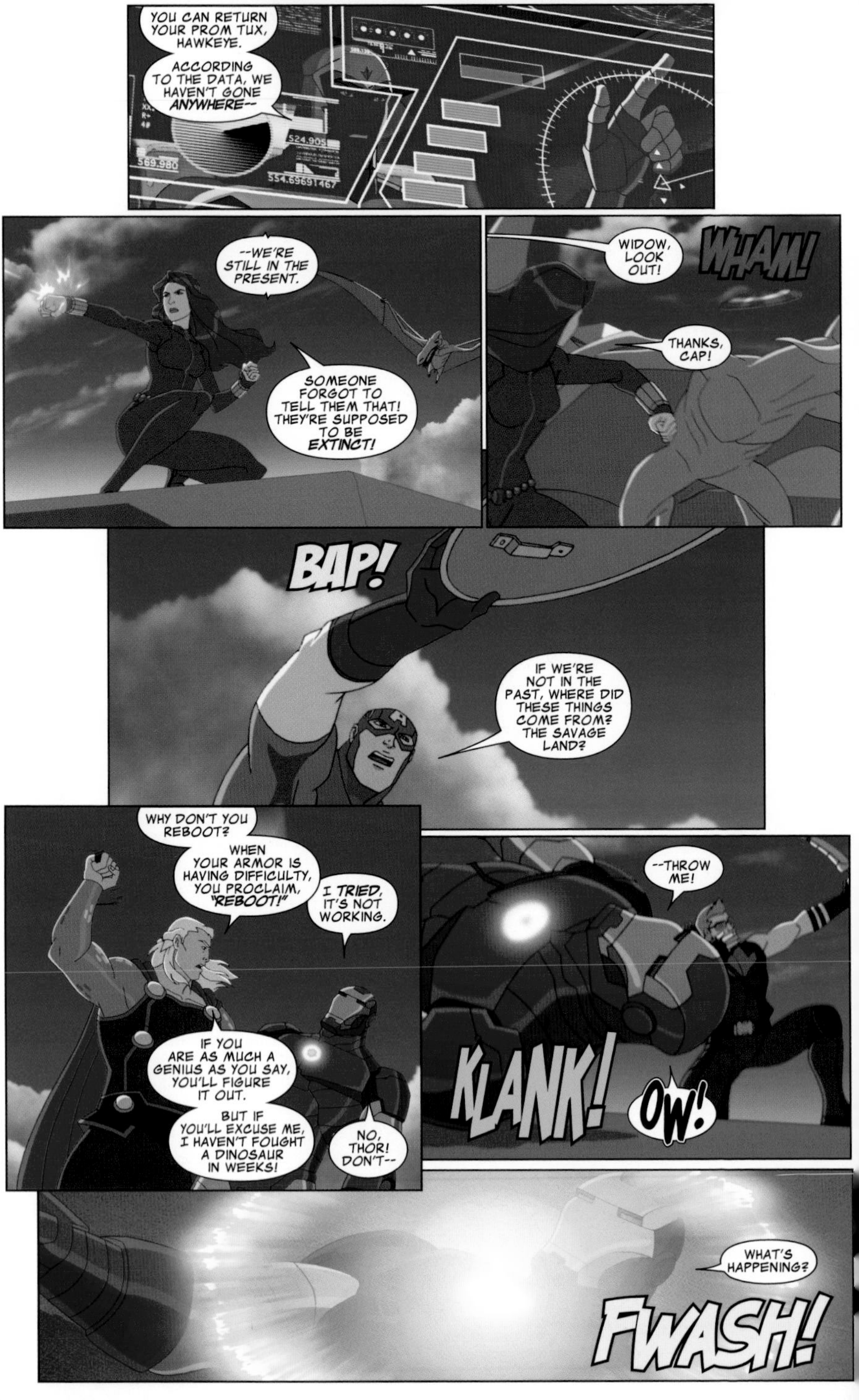
YOU CAN RETURN YOUR PROM TUX, HAWKEYE.
ACCORDING TO THE DATA, WE HAVEN'T GONE *ANYWHERE*--
--WE'RE STILL IN THE PRESENT.
SOMEONE FORGOT TO TELL THEM THAT! THEY'RE SUPPOSED TO BE *EXTINCT!*
WIDOW, LOOK OUT!
WHAM!
THANKS, CAP!
BAP!
IF WE'RE NOT IN THE PAST, WHERE DID THESE THINGS COME FROM? THE SAVAGE LAND?
WHY DON'T YOU REBOOT?
WHEN YOUR ARMOR IS HAVING DIFFICULTY, YOU PROCLAIM, *"REBOOT!"*
I *TRIED*, IT'S NOT WORKING.
IF YOU ARE AS MUCH A GENIUS AS YOU SAY, YOU'LL FIGURE IT OUT.
BUT IF YOU'LL EXCUSE ME, I HAVEN'T FOUGHT A DINOSAUR IN WEEKS!
NO, THOR! DON'T--
--THROW ME!
KLANK!
OW!
WHAT'S HAPPENING?
FWASH!

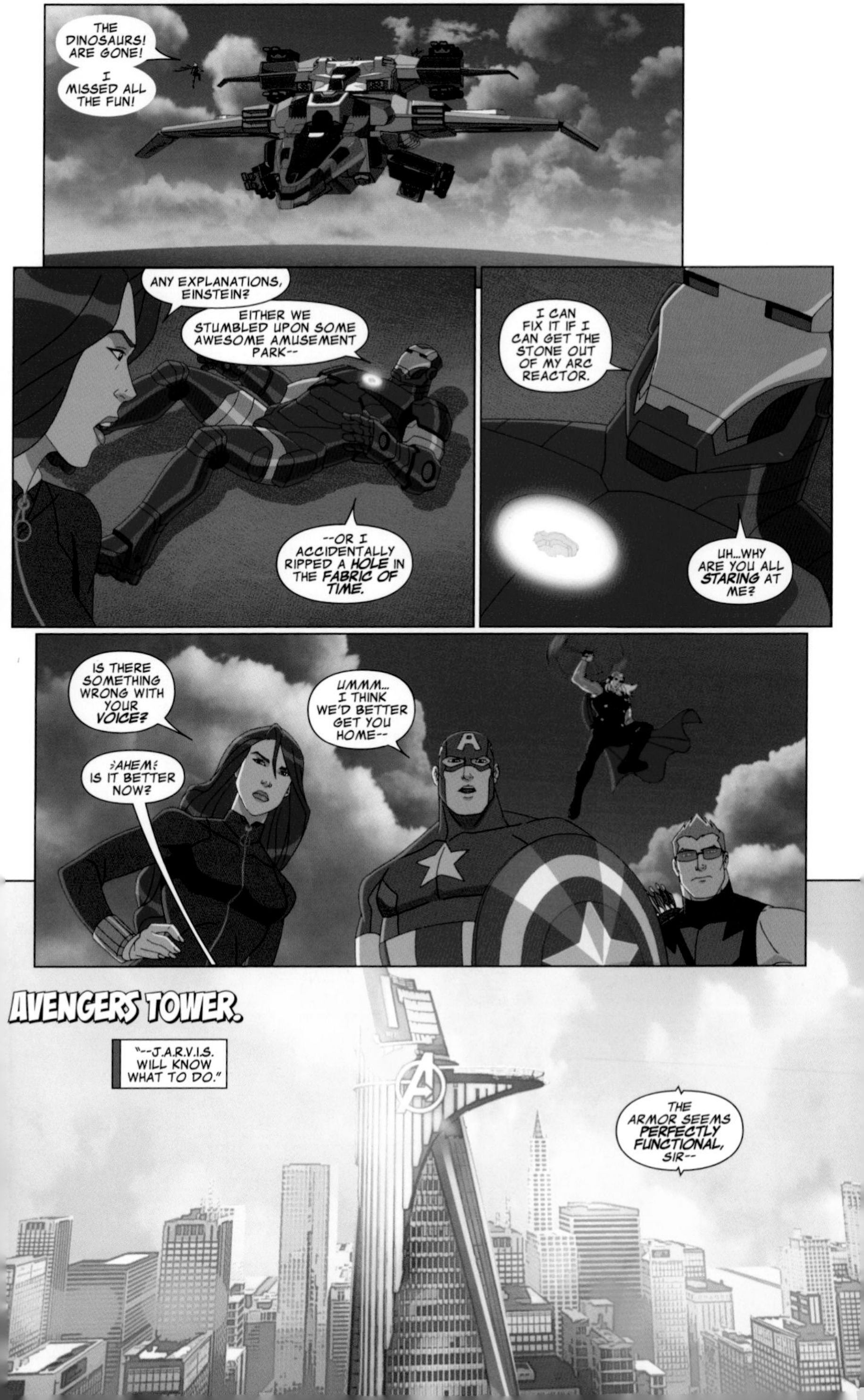

THE DINOSAURS! ARE GONE!
I MISSED ALL THE FUN!
ANY EXPLANATIONS, EINSTEIN?
EITHER WE STUMBLED UPON SOME AWESOME AMUSEMENT PARK--
--OR I ACCIDENTALLY RIPPED A HOLE IN THE FABRIC OF TIME.
I CAN FIX IT IF I CAN GET THE STONE OUT OF MY ARC REACTOR.
UH...WHY ARE YOU ALL STARING AT ME?
IS THERE SOMETHING WRONG WITH YOUR VOICE?
AHEM IS IT BETTER NOW?
UMMM... I THINK WE'D BETTER GET YOU HOME--
AVENGERS TOWER.
"--J.A.R.V.I.S. WILL KNOW WHAT TO DO."
THE ARMOR SEEMS PERFECTLY FUNCTIONAL, SIR--

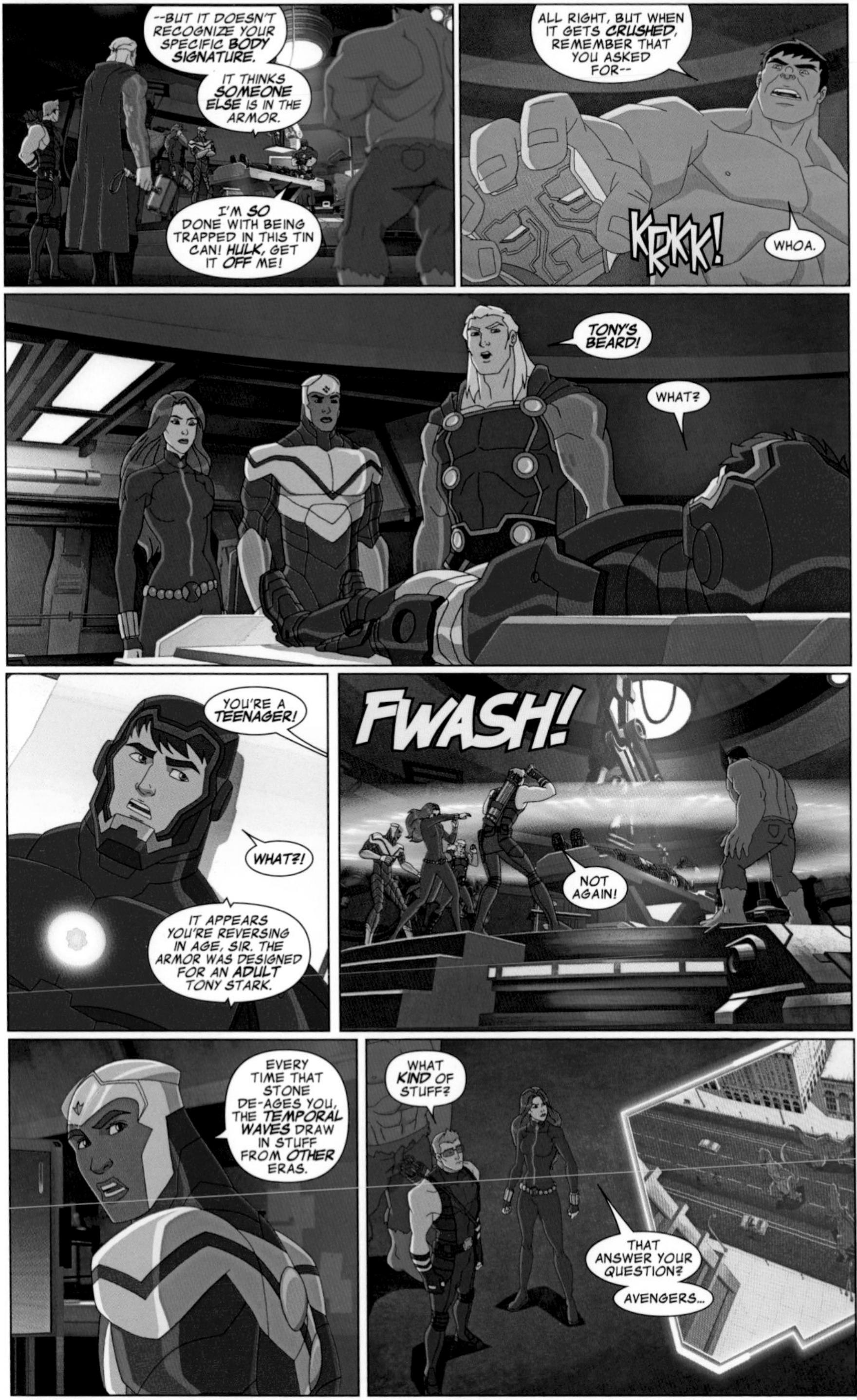
--BUT IT DOESN'T RECOGNIZE YOUR SPECIFIC BODY SIGNATURE.
IT THINKS SOMEONE ELSE IS IN THE ARMOR.
I'M SO DONE WITH BEING TRAPPED IN THIS TIN CAN! HULK, GET IT OFF ME!
ALL RIGHT, BUT WHEN IT GETS CRUSHED, REMEMBER THAT YOU ASKED FOR--
KRKK!
WHOA.
TONY'S BEARD!
WHAT?
YOU'RE A TEENAGER!
WHAT?!
IT APPEARS YOU'RE REVERSING IN AGE, SIR. THE ARMOR WAS DESIGNED FOR AN ADULT TONY STARK.
FWASH!
NOT AGAIN!
EVERY TIME THAT STONE DE-AGES YOU, THE TEMPORAL WAVES DRAW IN STUFF FROM OTHER ERAS.
WHAT KIND OF STUFF?
THAT ANSWER YOUR QUESTION?
AVENGERS...

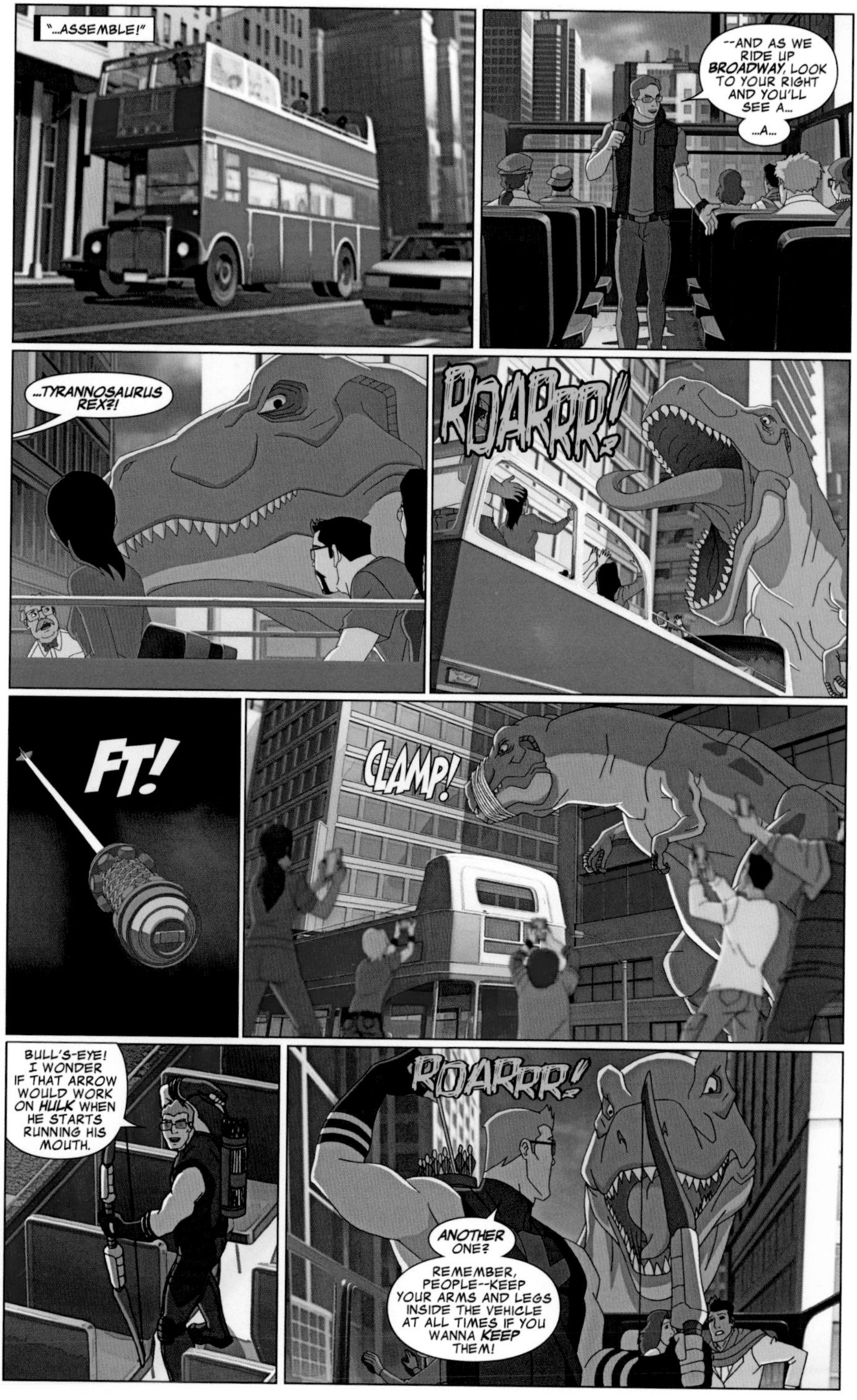
"...ASSEMBLE!"
--AND AS WE RIDE UP BROADWAY, LOOK TO YOUR RIGHT AND YOU'LL SEE A...
...A...
...TYRANNOSAURUS REX?!
ROARRR!
FT!
CLAMP!
BULL'S-EYE! I WONDER IF THAT ARROW WOULD WORK ON HULK WHEN HE STARTS RUNNING HIS MOUTH.
ROARRR!
ANOTHER ONE?
REMEMBER, PEOPLE--KEEP YOUR ARMS AND LEGS INSIDE THE VEHICLE AT ALL TIMES IF YOU WANNA KEEP THEM!

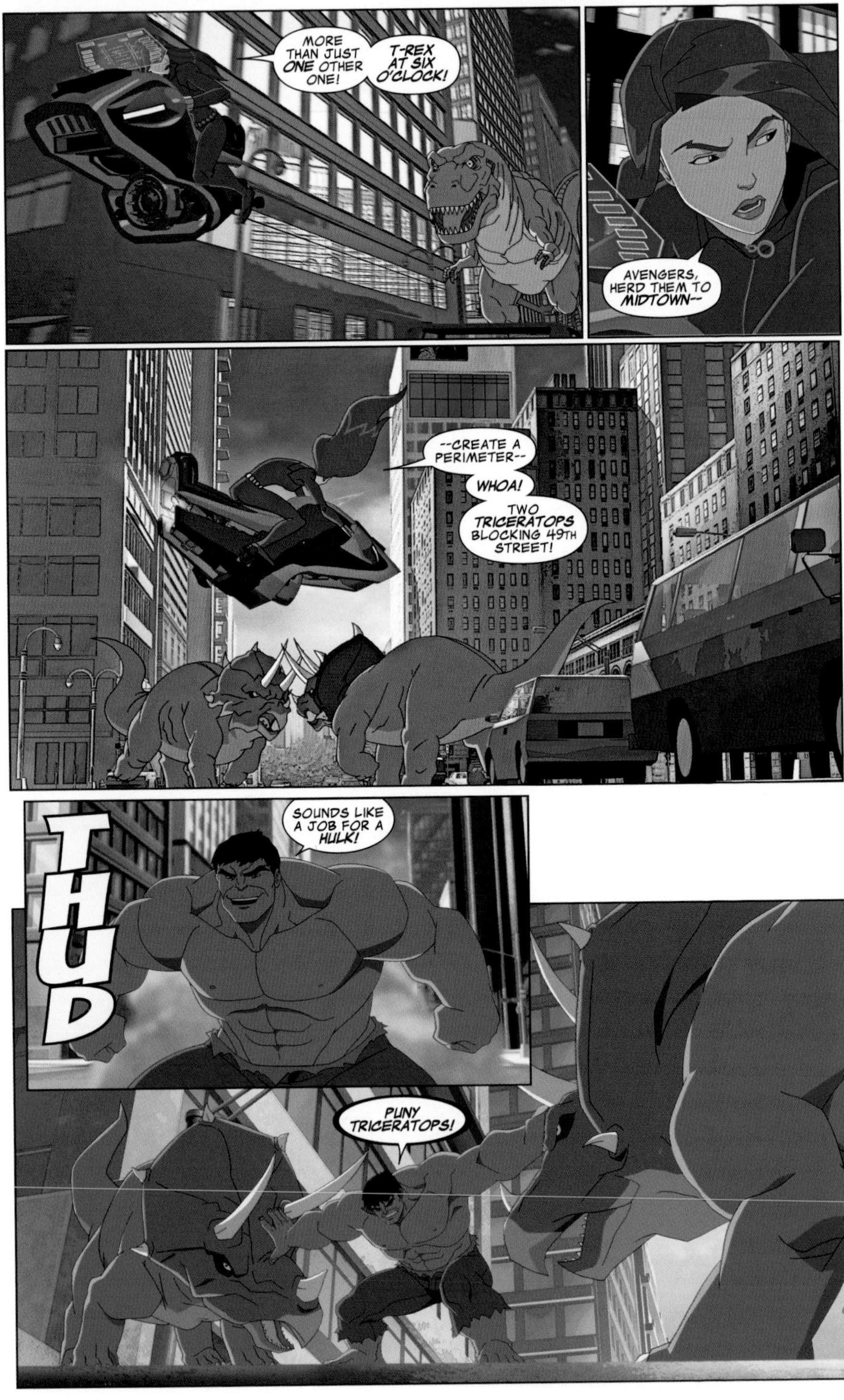
MORE THAN JUST ONE OTHER ONE!
T-REX AT SIX O'CLOCK!
AVENGERS, HERD THEM TO MIDTOWN--
--CREATE A PERIMETER--
WHOA!
TWO TRICERATOPS BLOCKING 49TH STREET!
THUD
SOUNDS LIKE A JOB FOR A HULK!
PUNY TRICERATOPS!

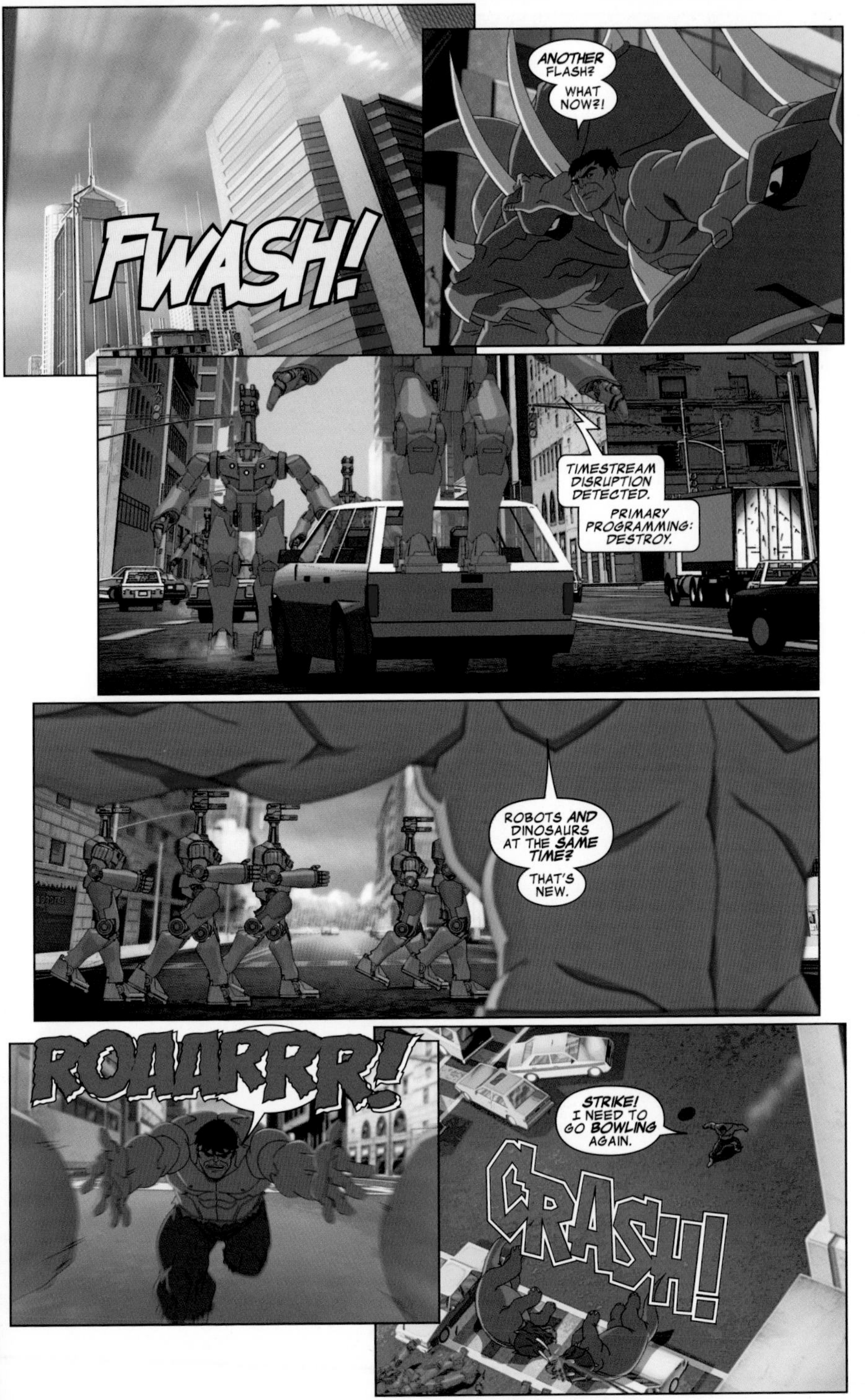
FWASH!
ANOTHER FLASH? WHAT NOW?!
TIMESTREAM DISRUPTION DETECTED.
PRIMARY PROGRAMMING: DESTROY.
ROBOTS AND DINOSAURS AT THE SAME TIME?
THAT'S NEW.
ROAARRR!
STRIKE! I NEED TO GO BOWLING AGAIN.
CRASH!

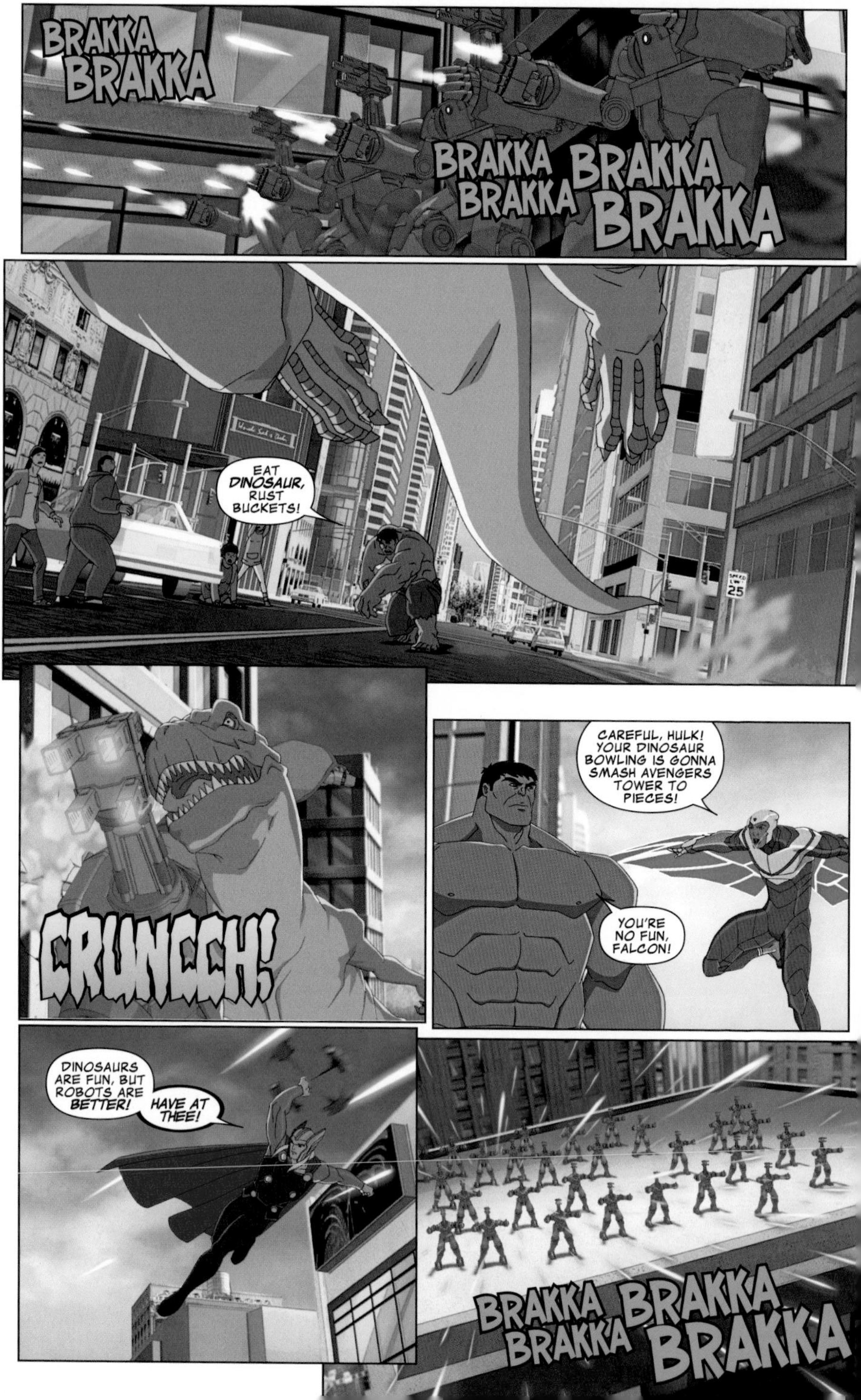
BRAKKA BRAKKA
BRAKKA BRAKKA BRAKKA BRAKKA
EAT DINOSAUR, RUST BUCKETS!
CRUNCCH!
CAREFUL, HULK! YOUR DINOSAUR BOWLING IS GONNA SMASH AVENGERS TOWER TO PIECES!
YOU'RE NO FUN, FALCON!
DINOSAURS ARE FUN, BUT ROBOTS ARE BETTER!
HAVE AT THEE!
BRAKKA BRAKKA BRAKKA BRAKKA

INSIDE.

WHAT'S HAPPENING DOWN THERE? THE TOWER'S TAKING DAMAGE!

THIS IS SO LAME!

I CAN'T GET THIS ARMOR TO WORK ON ME. AND I KEEP GETTING YOUNGER AND YOUNGER!

YOU HAVE TO BE *PATIENT*, TONY.

YOU MEAN MORE LIKE *YOU*?

GUESS WHAT? I'M *NOT* THE GREAT CAPTAIN AMERICA, *OKAY*?

BR-KOOM!

WHAT'S THAT?

YOUNG SIR, THERE'S BEEN A DISTURBANCE ON THE HOLDING CELL FLOOR.

CELL BREACH!

I KNEW THE FIGHTING WAS TOO CLOSE TO THE TOWER FOR COMFORT. YOU STAY AND TRY TO FIGURE OUT YOUR ARMOR--

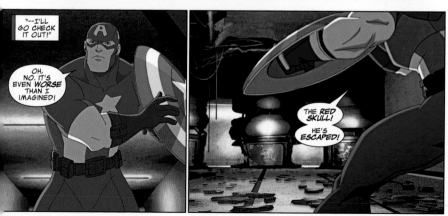

"--I'LL GO CHECK IT OUT!"

OH, NO. IT'S EVEN *WORSE* THAN I IMAGINED!

THE *RED SKULL*! HE'S ESCAPED!

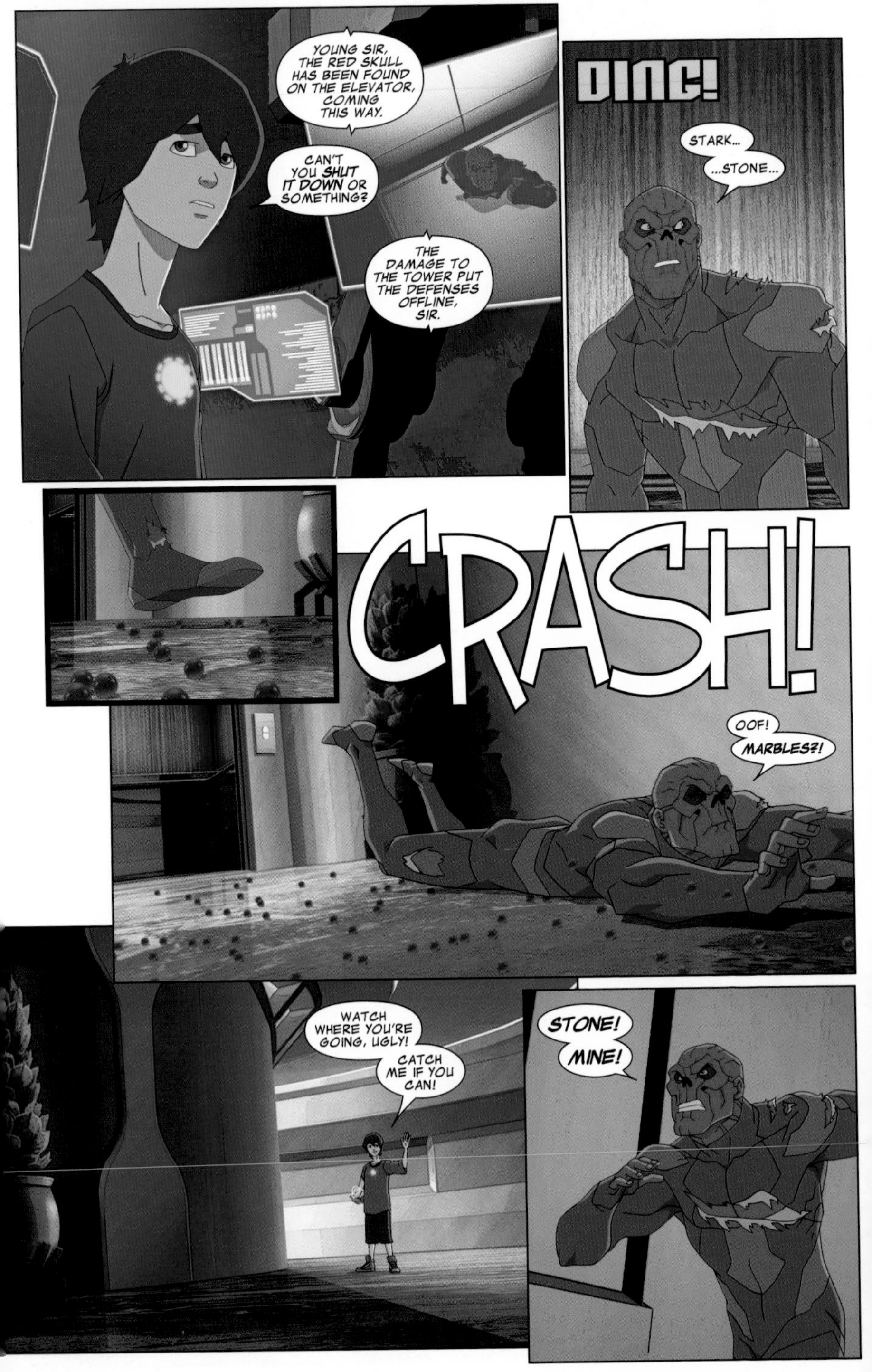
YOUNG SIR, THE RED SKULL HAS BEEN FOUND ON THE ELEVATOR, COMING THIS WAY.
CAN'T YOU **SHUT IT DOWN** OR SOMETHING?
THE DAMAGE TO THE TOWER PUT THE DEFENSES OFFLINE, SIR.
DING!
STARK...
...STONE...
CRASH!
OOF! **MARBLES?!**
WATCH WHERE YOU'RE GOING, UGLY!
CATCH ME IF YOU CAN!
STONE!
MINE!

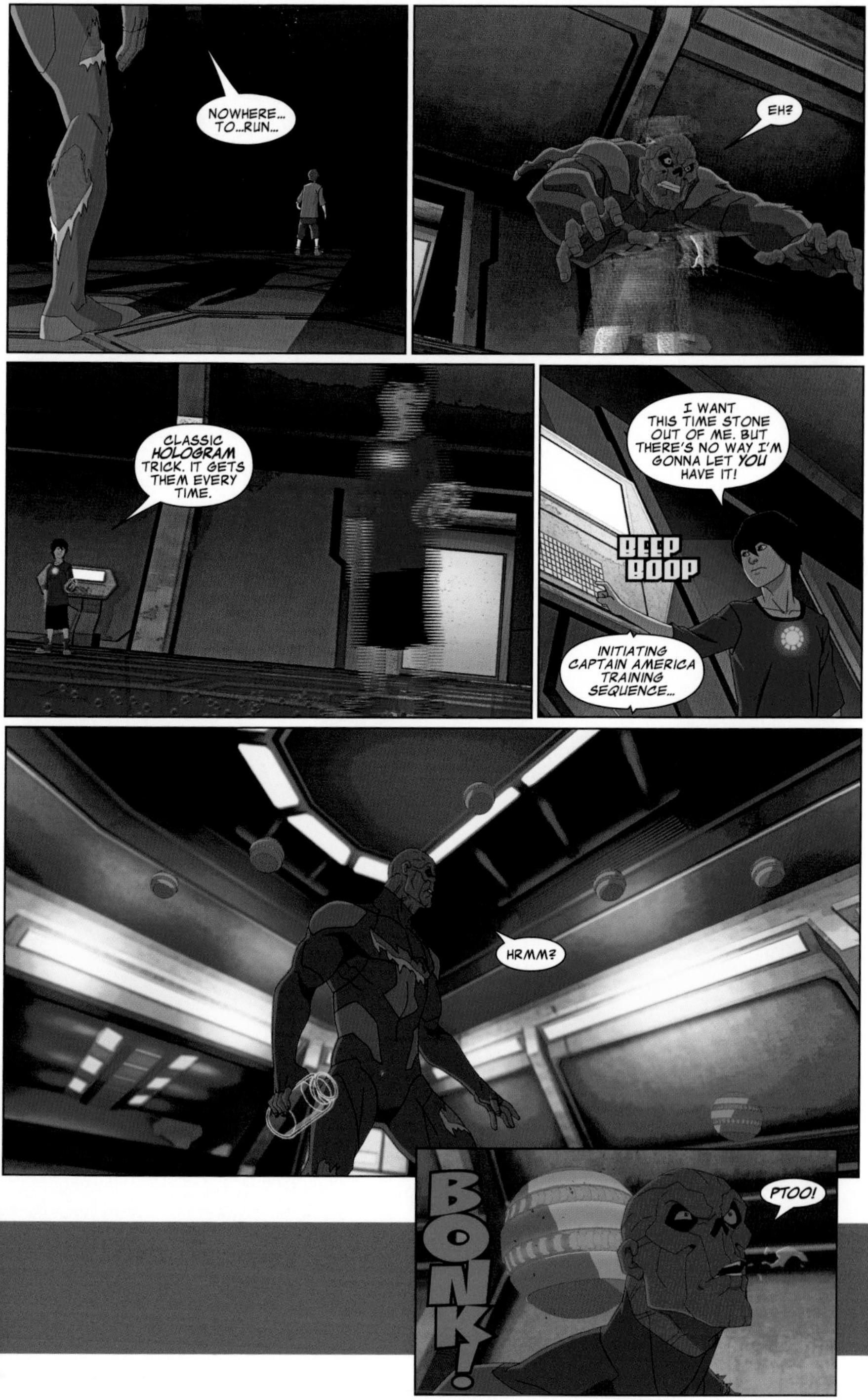
NOWHERE... TO...RUN...
EH?
CLASSIC HOLOGRAM TRICK. IT GETS THEM EVERY TIME.
I WANT THIS TIME STONE OUT OF ME. BUT THERE'S NO WAY I'M GONNA LET YOU HAVE IT!
BEEP BOOP
INITIATING CAPTAIN AMERICA TRAINING SEQUENCE...
HRMM?
BONK!
PTOO!

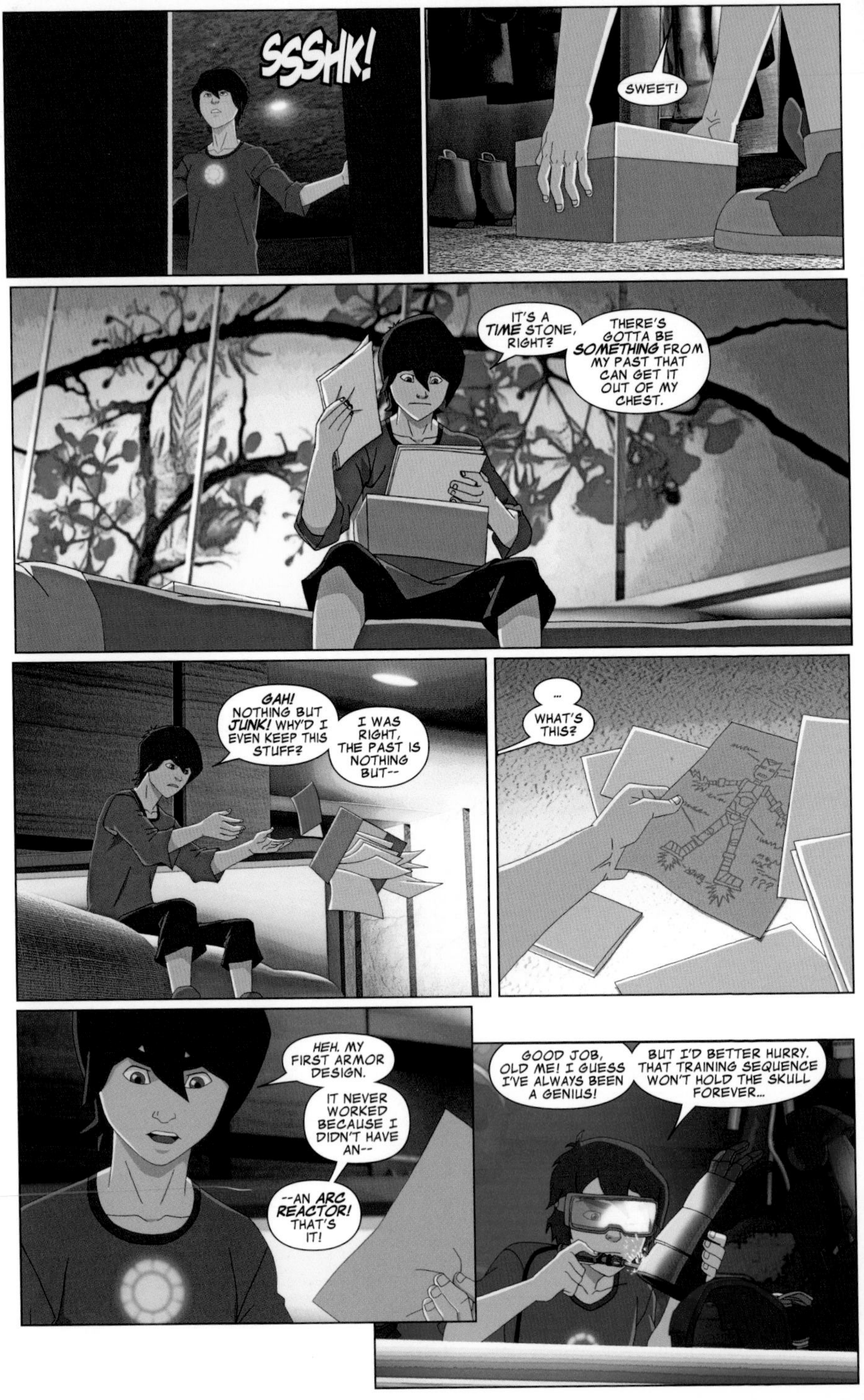
SSSHK!
SWEET!
IT'S A TIME STONE, RIGHT?
THERE'S GOTTA BE SOMETHING FROM MY PAST THAT CAN GET IT OUT OF MY CHEST.
GAH! NOTHING BUT JUNK! WHY'D I EVEN KEEP THIS STUFF?
I WAS RIGHT, THE PAST IS NOTHING BUT--
...
WHAT'S THIS?
HEH. MY FIRST ARMOR DESIGN.
IT NEVER WORKED BECAUSE I DIDN'T HAVE AN--
--AN ARC REACTOR! THAT'S IT!
GOOD JOB, OLD ME! I GUESS I'VE ALWAYS BEEN A GENIUS!
BUT I'D BETTER HURRY. THAT TRAINING SEQUENCE WON'T HOLD THE SKULL FOREVER...

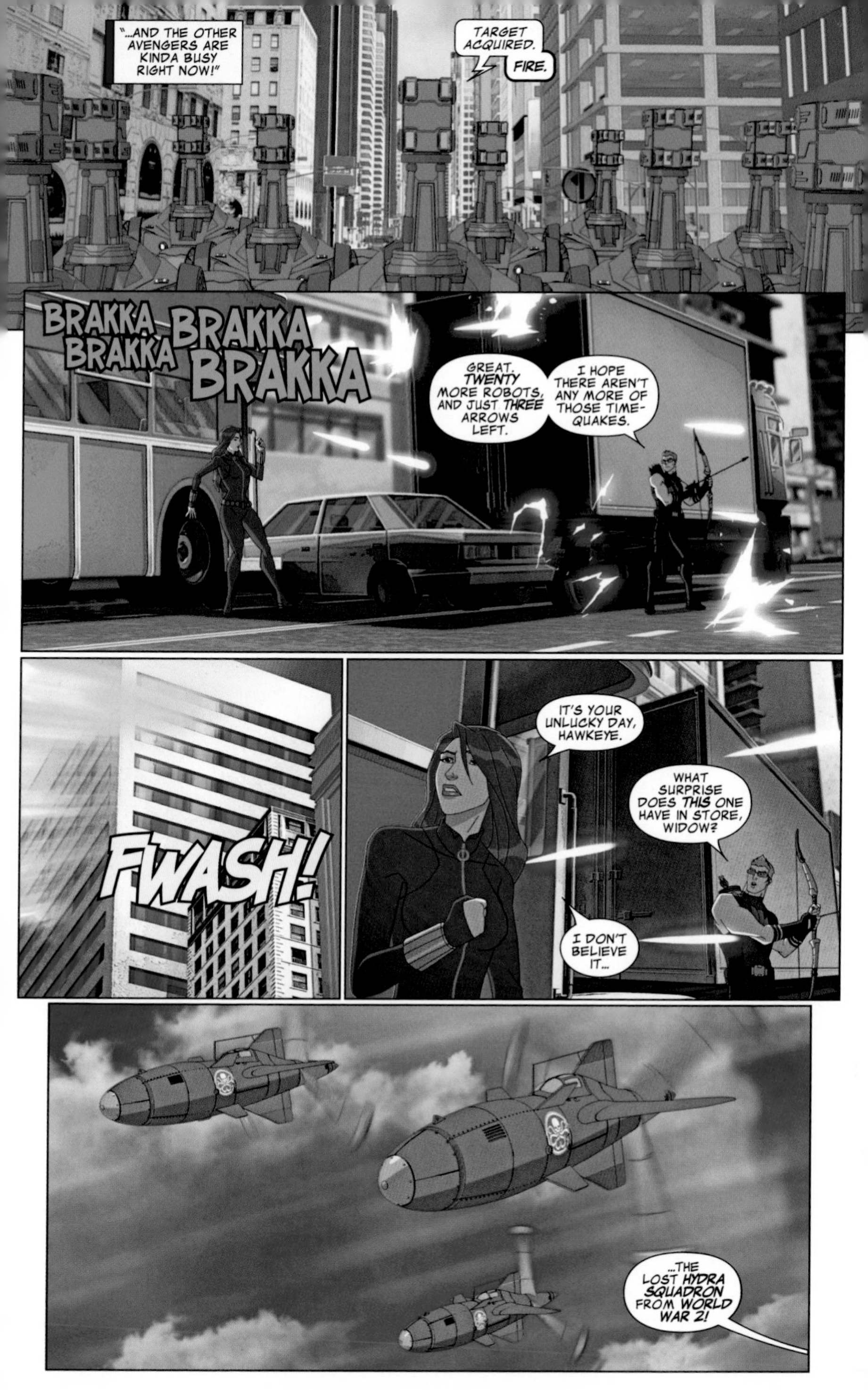
"...AND THE OTHER AVENGERS ARE KINDA BUSY RIGHT NOW!"
TARGET ACQUIRED.
FIRE.
BRAKKA BRAKKA BRAKKA BRAKKA
GREAT. TWENTY MORE ROBOTS, AND JUST THREE ARROWS LEFT.
I HOPE THERE AREN'T ANY MORE OF THOSE TIME-QUAKES.
FWASH!
IT'S YOUR UNLUCKY DAY, HAWKEYE.
WHAT SURPRISE DOES THIS ONE HAVE IN STORE, WIDOW?
I DON'T BELIEVE IT...
...THE LOST HYDRA SQUADRON FROM WORLD WAR 2!

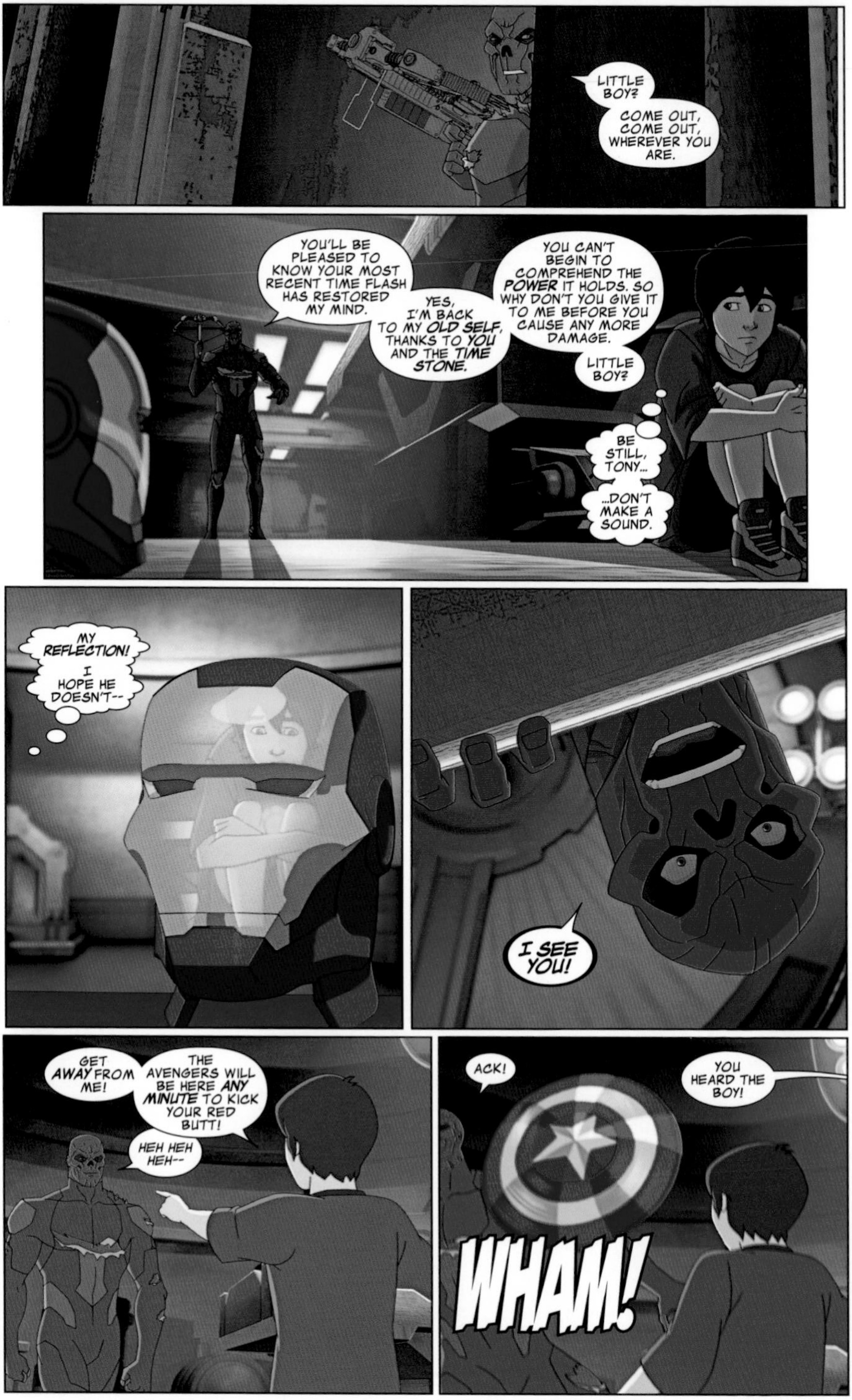

LITTLE BOY?
COME OUT, COME OUT, WHEREVER YOU ARE.
YOU'LL BE PLEASED TO KNOW YOUR MOST RECENT TIME FLASH HAS RESTORED MY MIND.
YES, I'M BACK TO MY OLD SELF, THANKS TO YOU AND THE TIME STONE.
YOU CAN'T BEGIN TO COMPREHEND THE POWER IT HOLDS. SO WHY DON'T YOU GIVE IT TO ME BEFORE YOU CAUSE ANY MORE DAMAGE.
LITTLE BOY?
BE STILL, TONY...
...DON'T MAKE A SOUND.
MY REFLECTION!
I HOPE HE DOESN'T--
I SEE YOU!
GET AWAY FROM ME!
THE AVENGERS WILL BE HERE ANY MINUTE TO KICK YOUR RED BUTT!
HEH HEH HEH--
ACK!
YOU HEARD THE BOY!
WHAM!

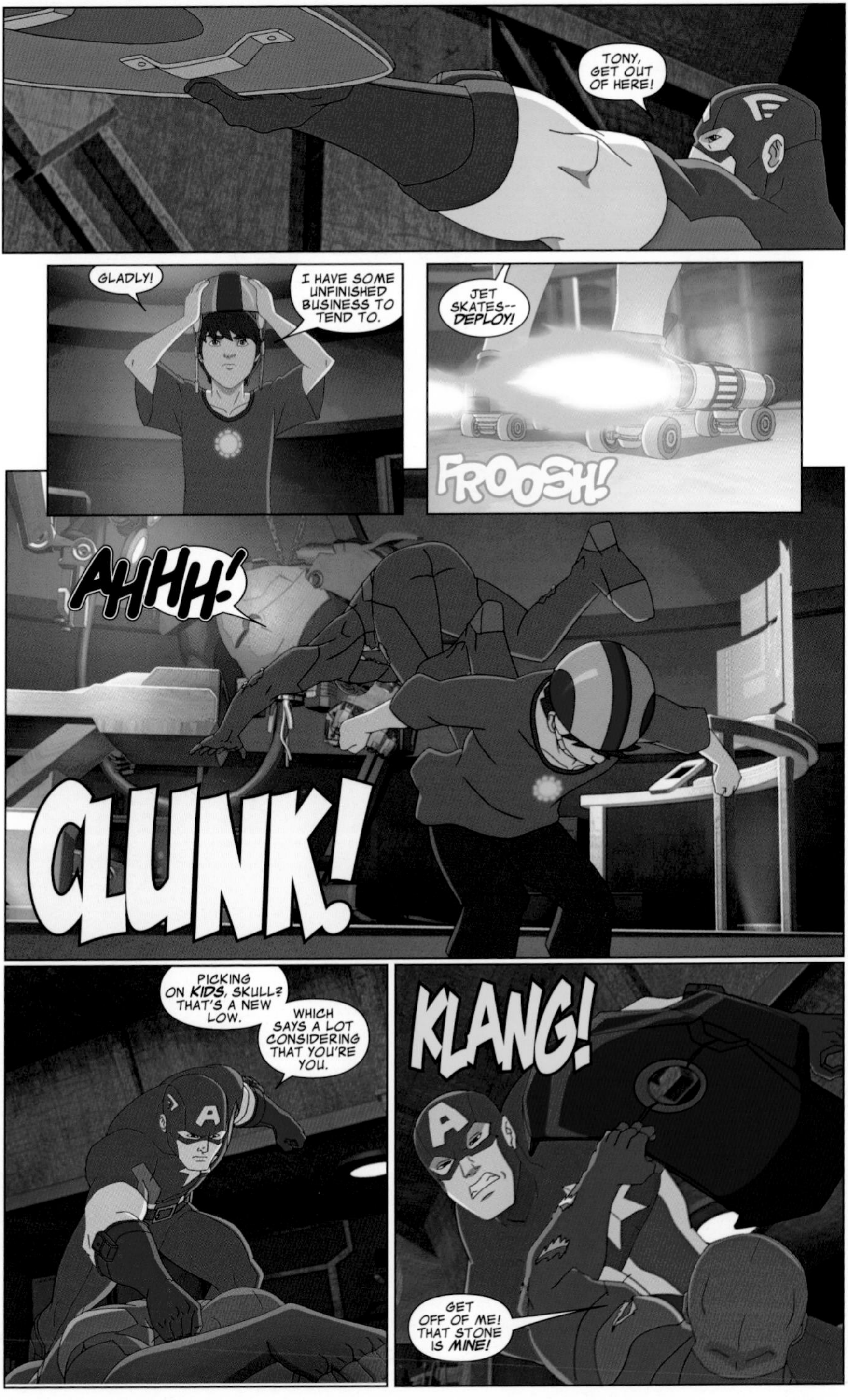
TONY, GET OUT OF HERE!
GLADLY!
I HAVE SOME UNFINISHED BUSINESS TO TEND TO.
JET SKATES-- DEPLOY!
FROOSH!
AHHH!
CLUNK!
PICKING ON KIDS, SKULL? THAT'S A NEW LOW.
WHICH SAYS A LOT CONSIDERING THAT YOU'RE YOU.
KLANG!
GET OFF OF ME! THAT STONE IS MINE!

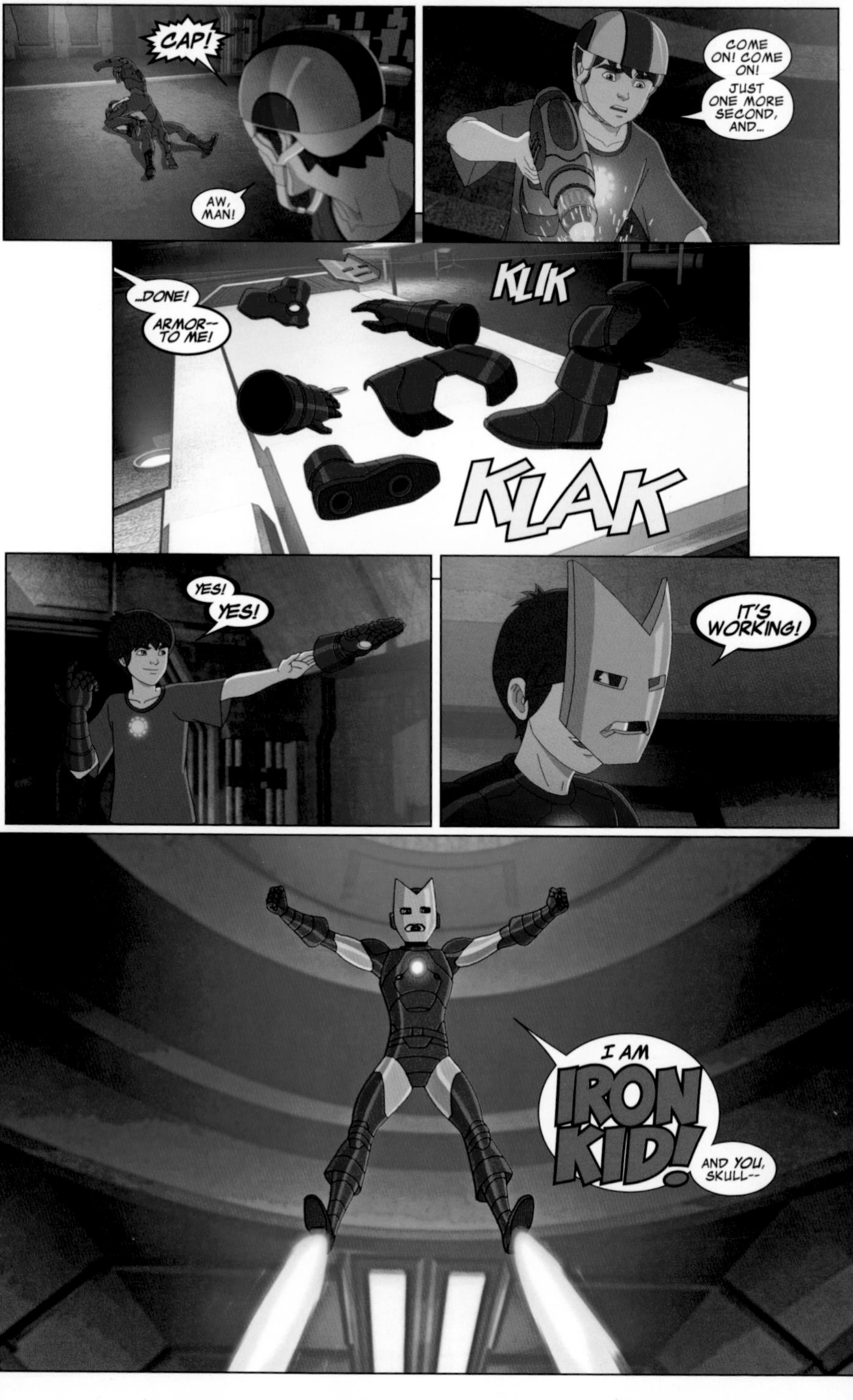
CAP!
AW, MAN!
COME ON! COME ON! JUST ONE MORE SECOND, AND...
...DONE! ARMOR--TO ME!
KLIK
KLAK
YES! YES!
IT'S WORKING!
I AM IRON KID!
AND YOU, SKULL--

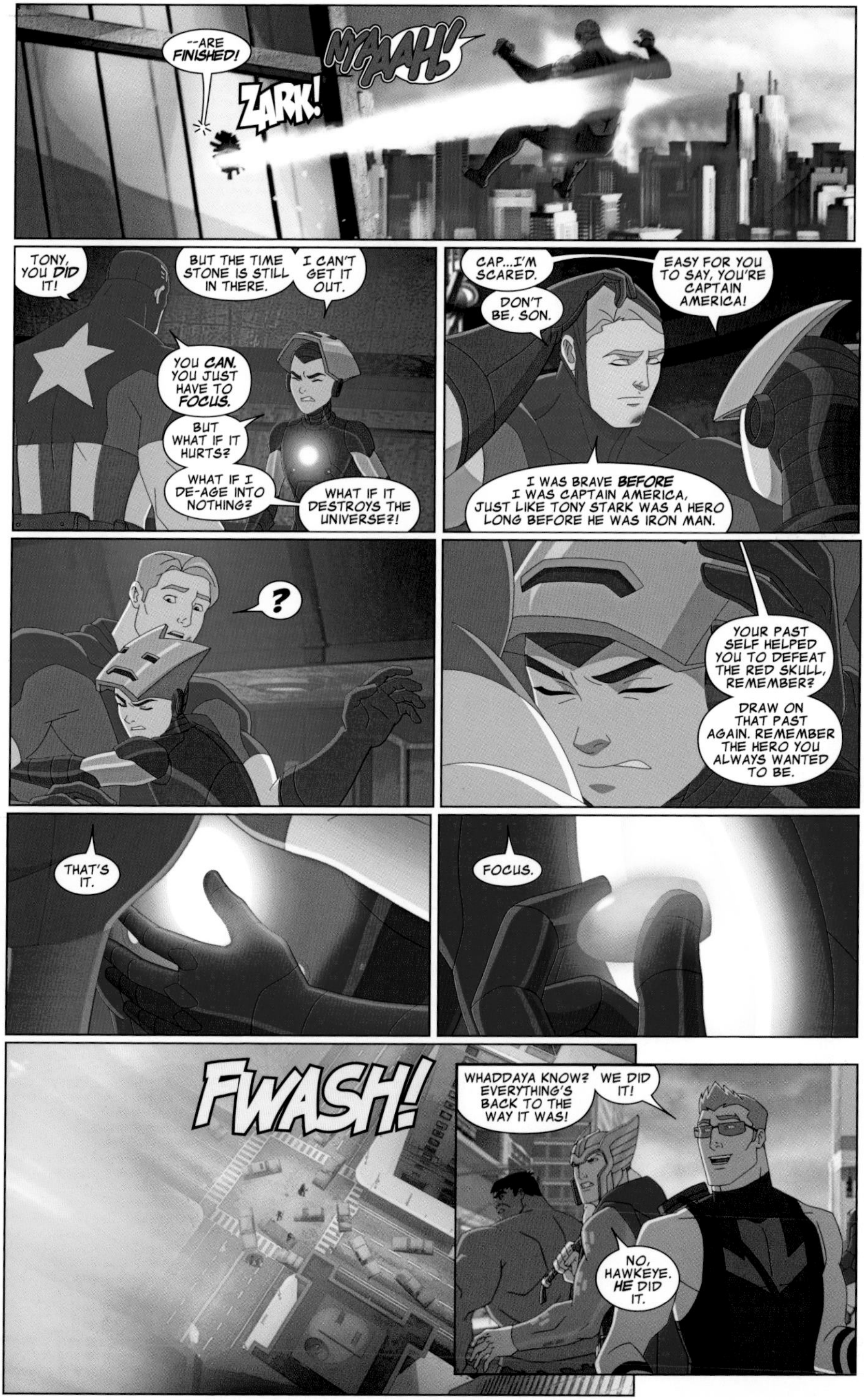
--ARE FINISHED!
ZARK!
NYAAAH!
TONY, YOU DID IT!
BUT THE TIME STONE IS STILL IN THERE.
I CAN'T GET IT OUT.
YOU CAN. YOU JUST HAVE TO FOCUS.
BUT WHAT IF IT HURTS?
WHAT IF I DE-AGE INTO NOTHING?
WHAT IF IT DESTROYS THE UNIVERSE?!
CAP...I'M SCARED.
DON'T BE, SON.
EASY FOR YOU TO SAY, YOU'RE CAPTAIN AMERICA!
I WAS BRAVE BEFORE I WAS CAPTAIN AMERICA, JUST LIKE TONY STARK WAS A HERO LONG BEFORE HE WAS IRON MAN.
?
YOUR PAST SELF HELPED YOU TO DEFEAT THE RED SKULL, REMEMBER?
DRAW ON THAT PAST AGAIN. REMEMBER THE HERO YOU ALWAYS WANTED TO BE.
THAT'S IT.
FOCUS.
FWASH!
WHADDAYA KNOW? EVERYTHING'S BACK TO THE WAY IT WAS!
WE DID IT!
NO, HAWKEYE. HE DID IT.

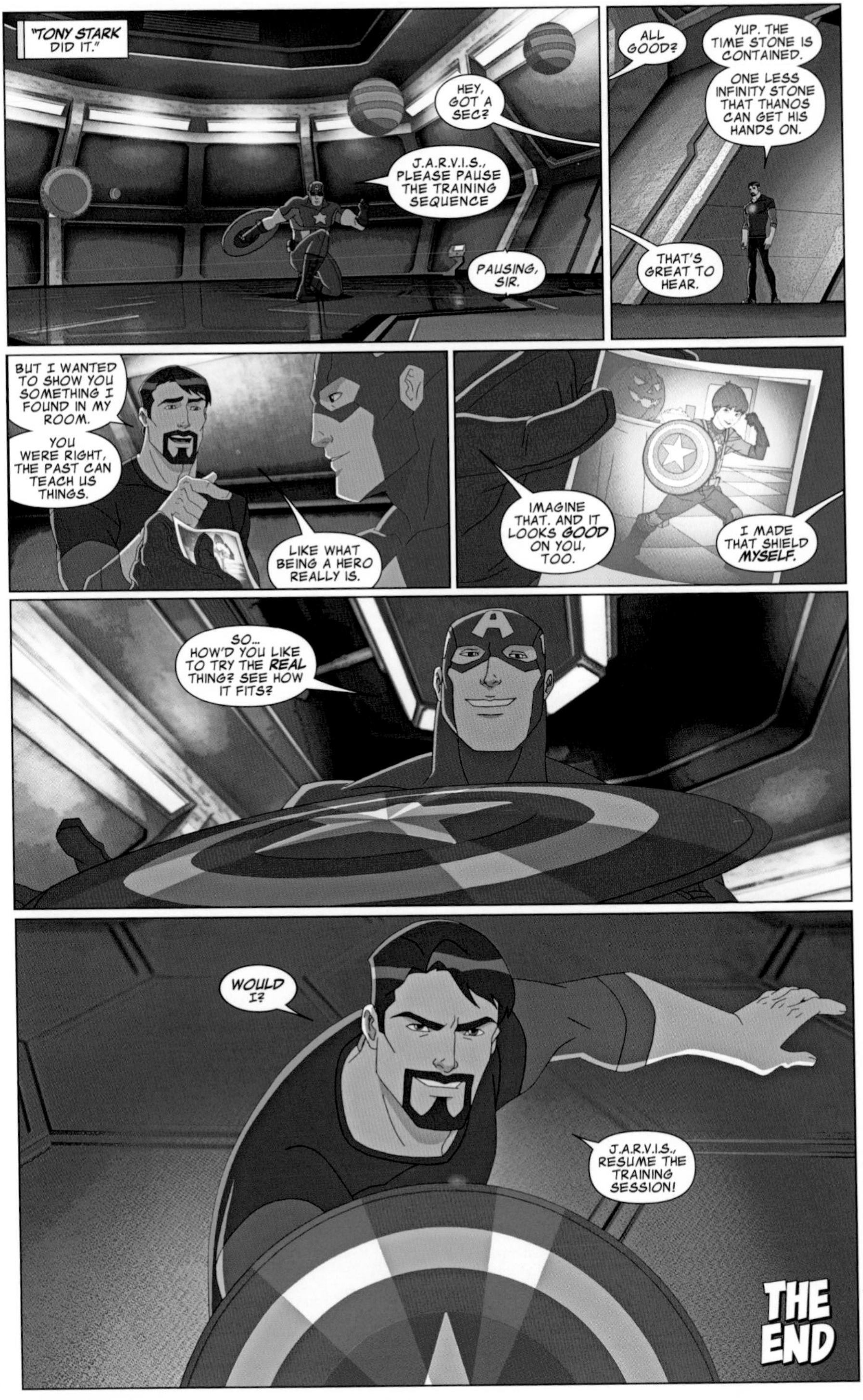
"TONY STARK DID IT."
HEY, GOT A SEC?
J.A.R.V.I.S., PLEASE PAUSE THE TRAINING SEQUENCE
PAUSING, SIR.
ALL GOOD?
YUP. THE TIME STONE IS CONTAINED.
ONE LESS INFINITY STONE THAT THANOS CAN GET HIS HANDS ON.
THAT'S GREAT TO HEAR.
BUT I WANTED TO SHOW YOU SOMETHING I FOUND IN MY ROOM.
YOU WERE RIGHT, THE PAST CAN TEACH US THINGS.
LIKE WHAT BEING A HERO REALLY IS.
IMAGINE THAT. AND IT LOOKS GOOD ON YOU, TOO.
I MADE THAT SHIELD MYSELF.
SO... HOW'D YOU LIKE TO TRY THE REAL THING? SEE HOW IT FITS?
WOULD I?
J.A.R.V.I.S., RESUME THE TRAINING SESSION!
THE END

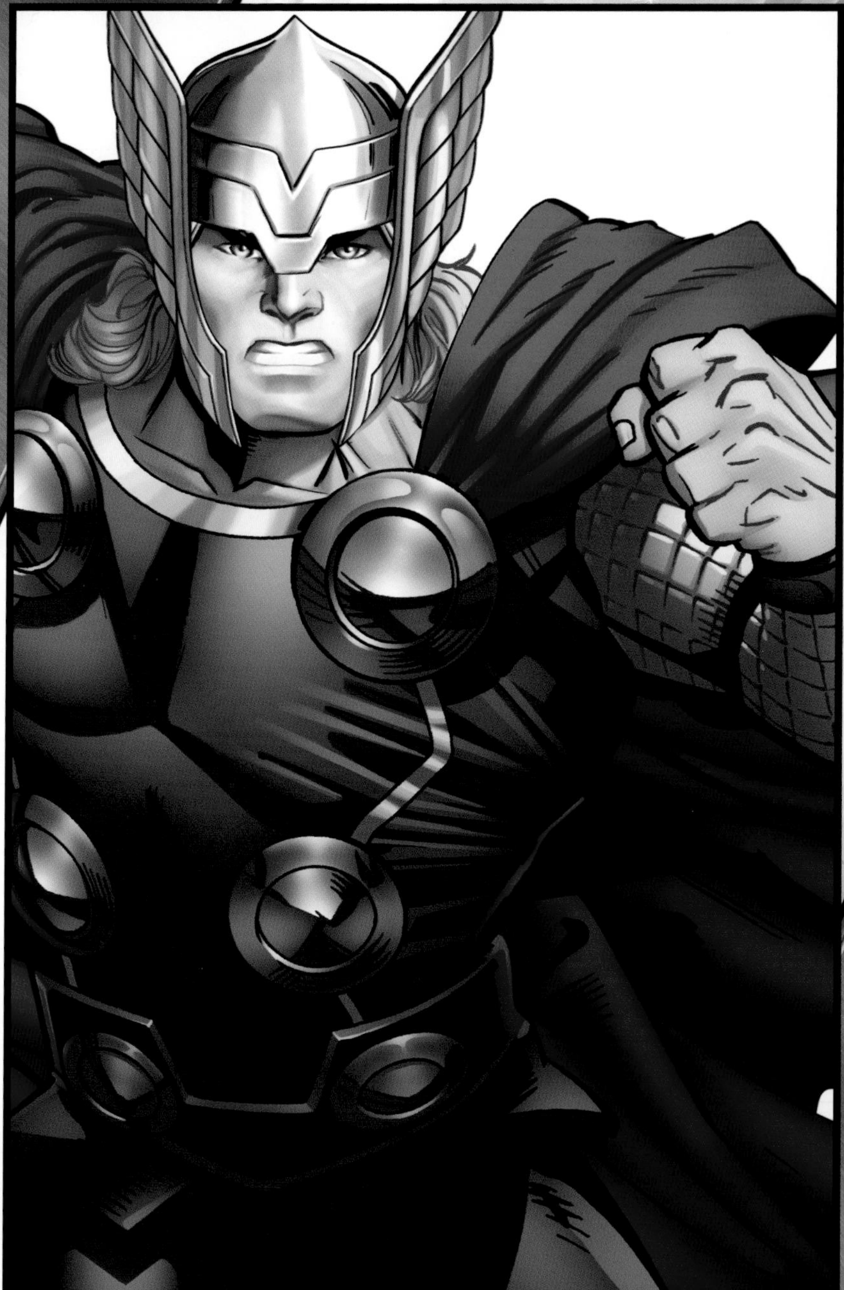

BASED ON "ALL-FATHER'S DAY" #7

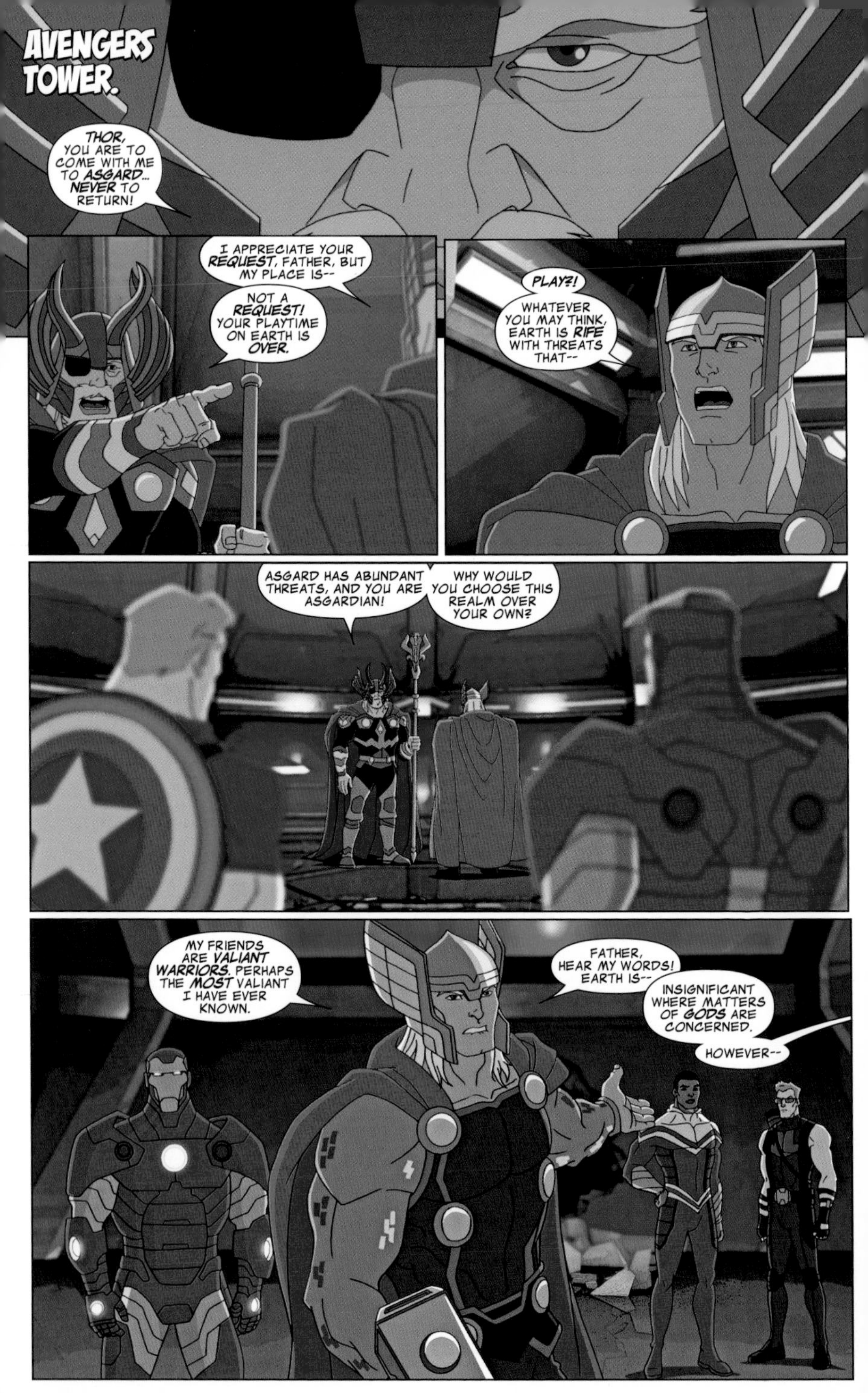
AVENGERS TOWER.
THOR, YOU ARE TO COME WITH ME TO ASGARD... NEVER TO RETURN!
I APPRECIATE YOUR REQUEST, FATHER, BUT MY PLACE IS--
NOT A REQUEST! YOUR PLAYTIME ON EARTH IS OVER.
PLAY?!
WHATEVER YOU MAY THINK, EARTH IS RIFE WITH THREATS THAT--
ASGARD HAS ABUNDANT THREATS, AND YOU ARE ASGARDIAN!
WHY WOULD YOU CHOOSE THIS REALM OVER YOUR OWN?
MY FRIENDS ARE VALIANT WARRIORS. PERHAPS THE MOST VALIANT I HAVE EVER KNOWN.
FATHER, HEAR MY WORDS! EARTH IS--
INSIGNIFICANT WHERE MATTERS OF GODS ARE CONCERNED.
HOWEVER--

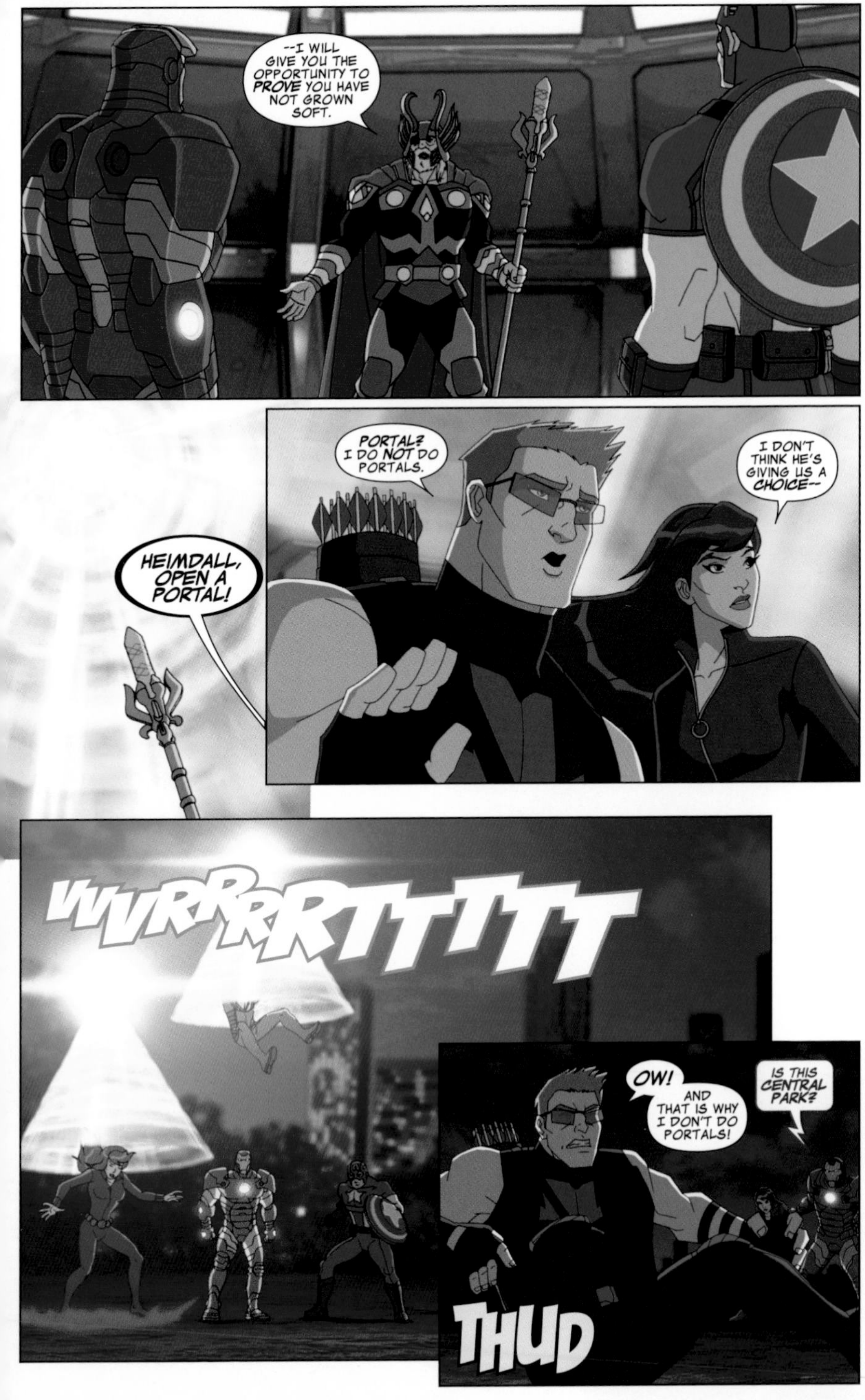
--I WILL GIVE YOU THE OPPORTUNITY TO PROVE YOU HAVE NOT GROWN SOFT.
HEIMDALL, OPEN A PORTAL!
PORTAL? I DO NOT DO PORTALS.
I DON'T THINK HE'S GIVING US A CHOICE--
WVRRRRTTTTT
OW!
AND THAT IS WHY I DON'T DO PORTALS!
IS THIS CENTRAL PARK?
THUD

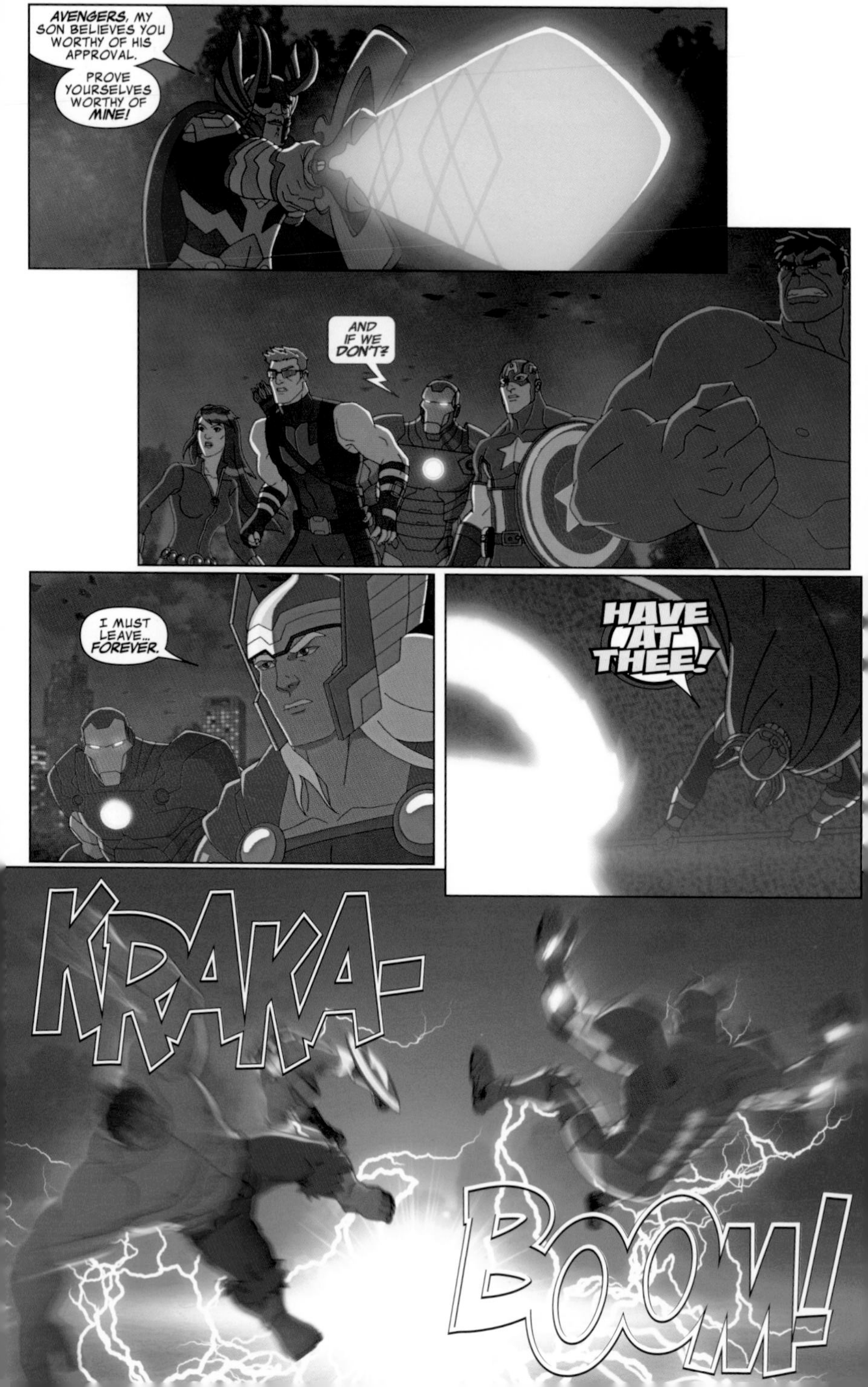
AVENGERS, MY SON BELIEVES YOU WORTHY OF HIS APPROVAL.
PROVE YOURSELVES WORTHY OF MINE!
AND IF WE DON'T?
I MUST LEAVE... FOREVER.
HAVE AT THEE!
KRAKA-
BOOM!

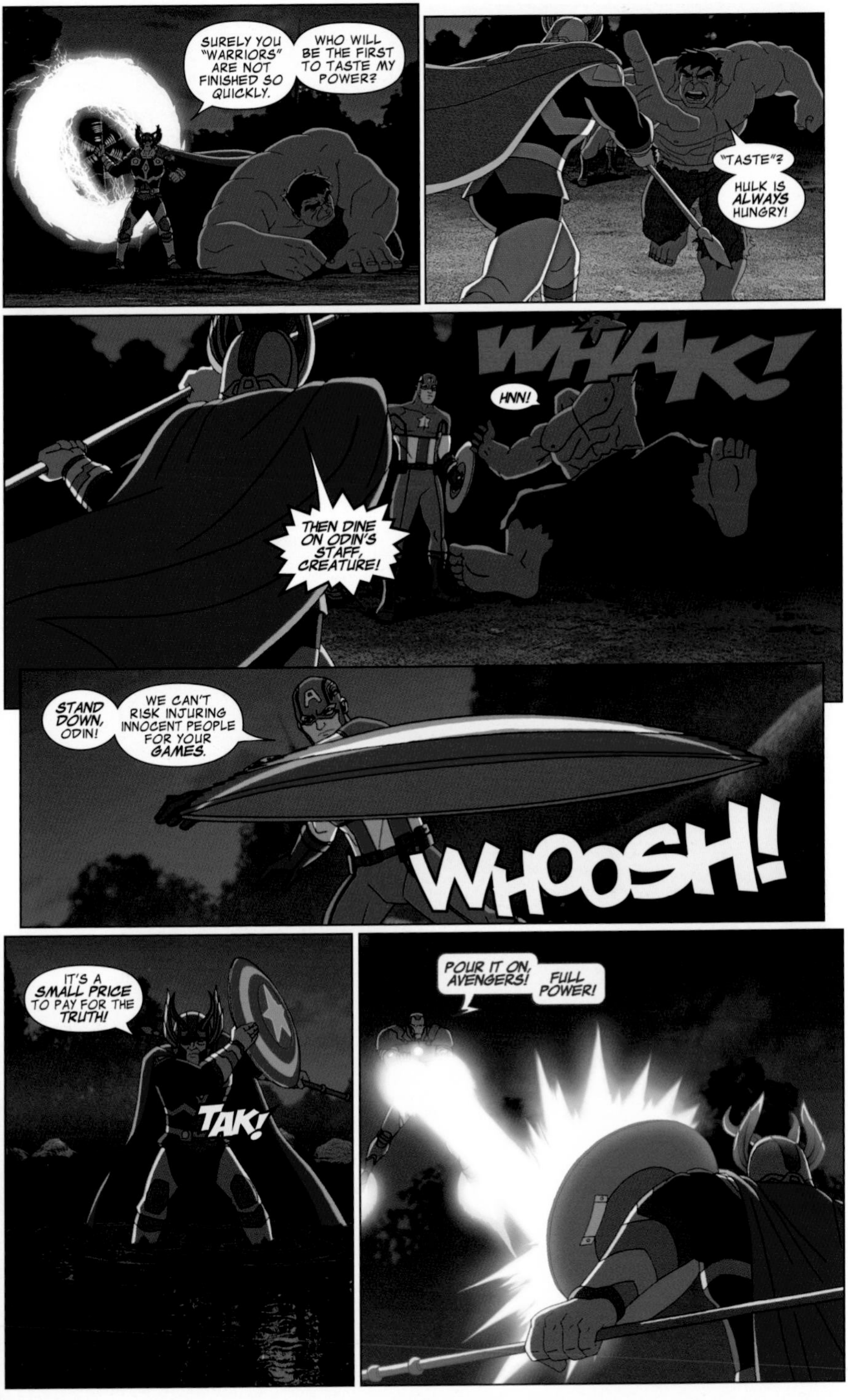
SURELY YOU "WARRIORS" ARE NOT FINISHED SO QUICKLY.
WHO WILL BE THE FIRST TO TASTE MY POWER?
"TASTE"?
HULK IS ALWAYS HUNGRY!
WHAK!
HNN!
THEN DINE ON ODIN'S STAFF, CREATURE!
STAND DOWN, ODIN!
WE CAN'T RISK INJURING INNOCENT PEOPLE FOR YOUR GAMES.
WHOOSH!
IT'S A SMALL PRICE TO PAY FOR THE TRUTH!
TAK!
POUR IT ON, AVENGERS!
FULL POWER!

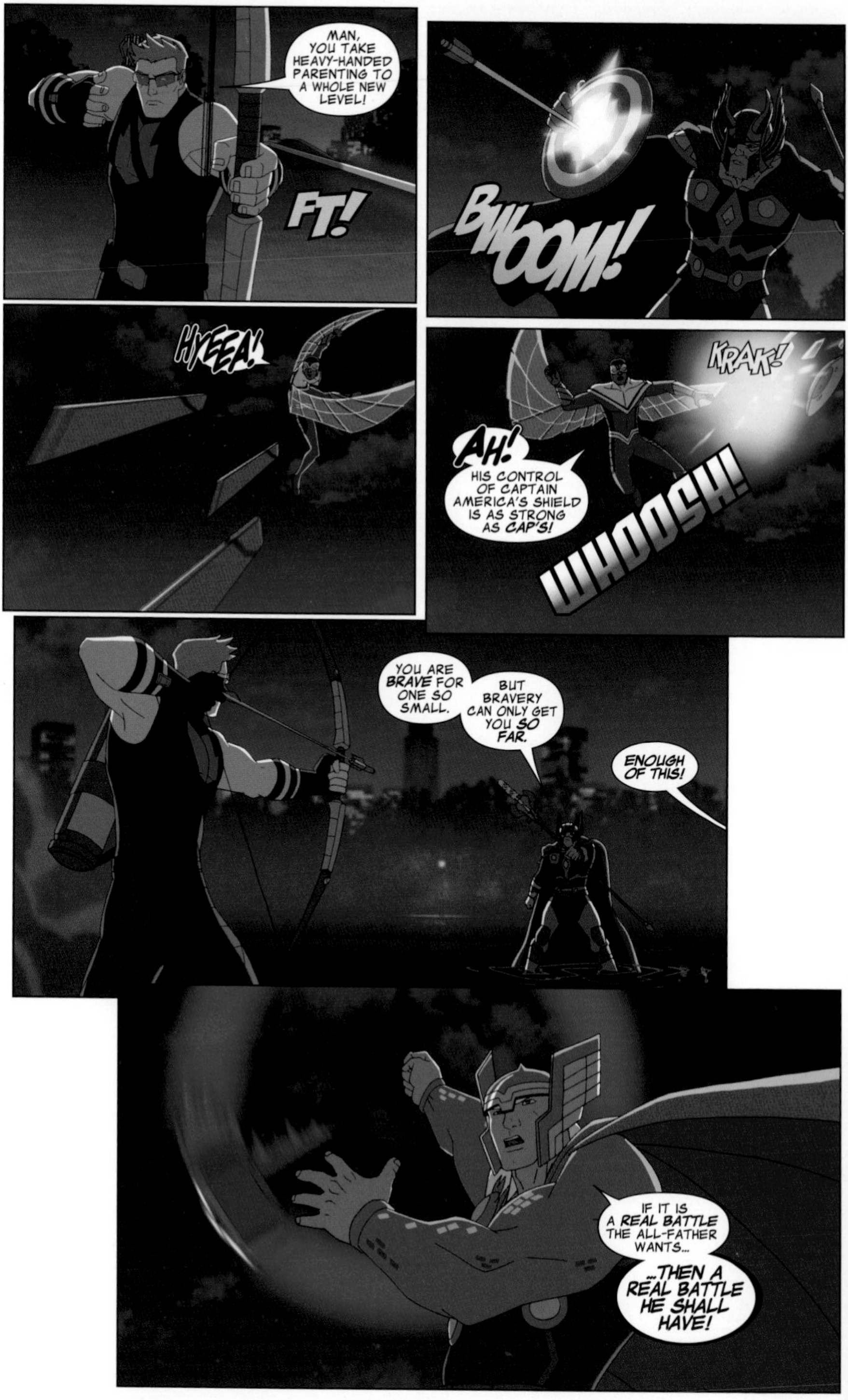

MAN, YOU TAKE HEAVY-HANDED PARENTING TO A WHOLE NEW LEVEL!
FT!
BWOOOM!
HYEEA!
KRAK!
AH!
HIS CONTROL OF CAPTAIN AMERICA'S SHIELD IS AS STRONG AS CAP'S!
WHOOSH!
YOU ARE BRAVE FOR ONE SO SMALL.
BUT BRAVERY CAN ONLY GET YOU SO FAR.
ENOUGH OF THIS!
IF IT IS A REAL BATTLE THE ALL-FATHER WANTS...
...THEN A REAL BATTLE HE SHALL HAVE!

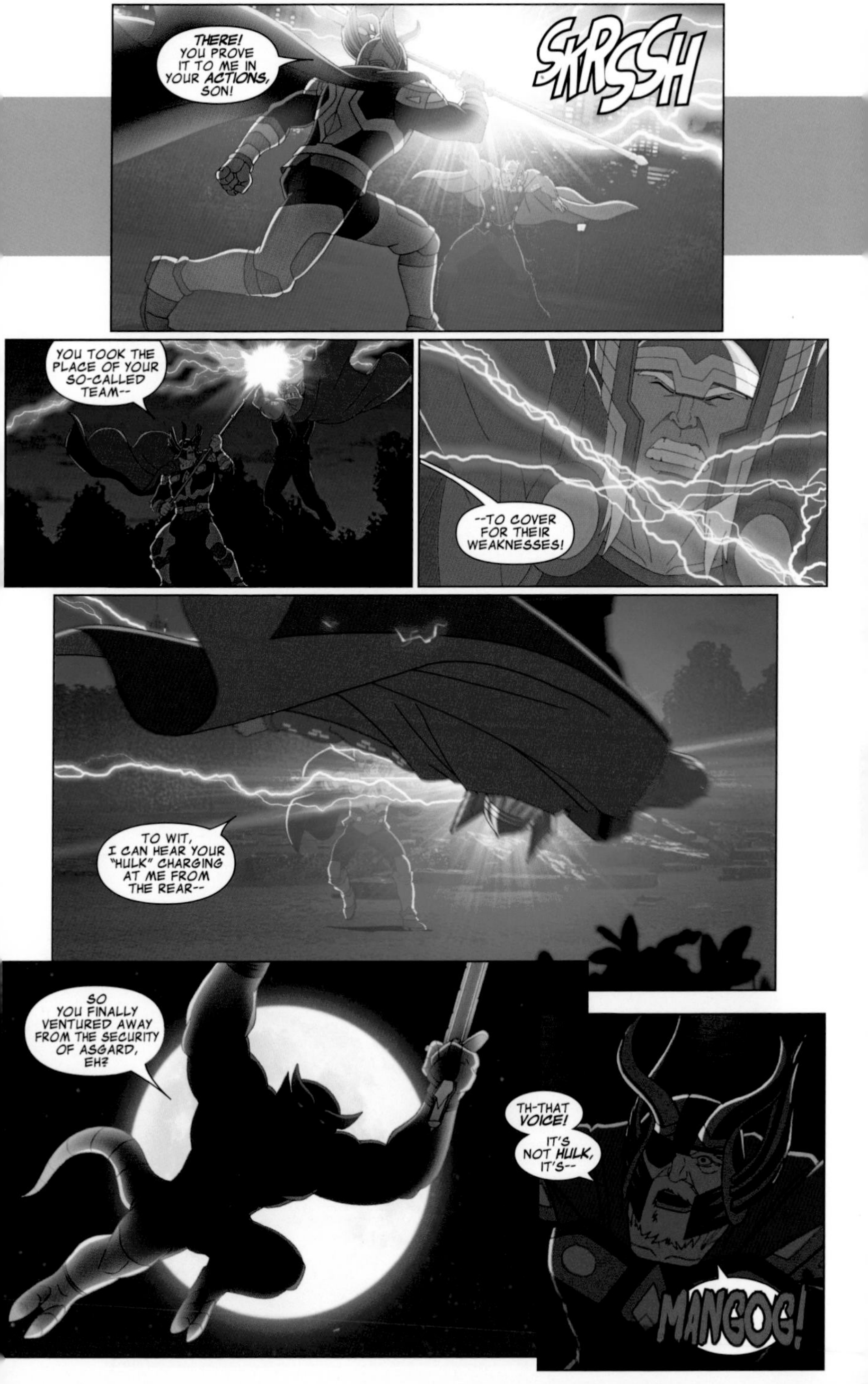
SKRSSH
THERE! YOU PROVE IT TO ME IN YOUR ACTIONS, SON!
YOU TOOK THE PLACE OF YOUR SO-CALLED TEAM--
--TO COVER FOR THEIR WEAKNESSES!
TO WIT, I CAN HEAR YOUR "HULK" CHARGING AT ME FROM THE REAR--
SO YOU FINALLY VENTURED AWAY FROM THE SECURITY OF ASGARD, EH?
TH-THAT VOICE! IT'S NOT HULK, IT'S--
MANGOG!

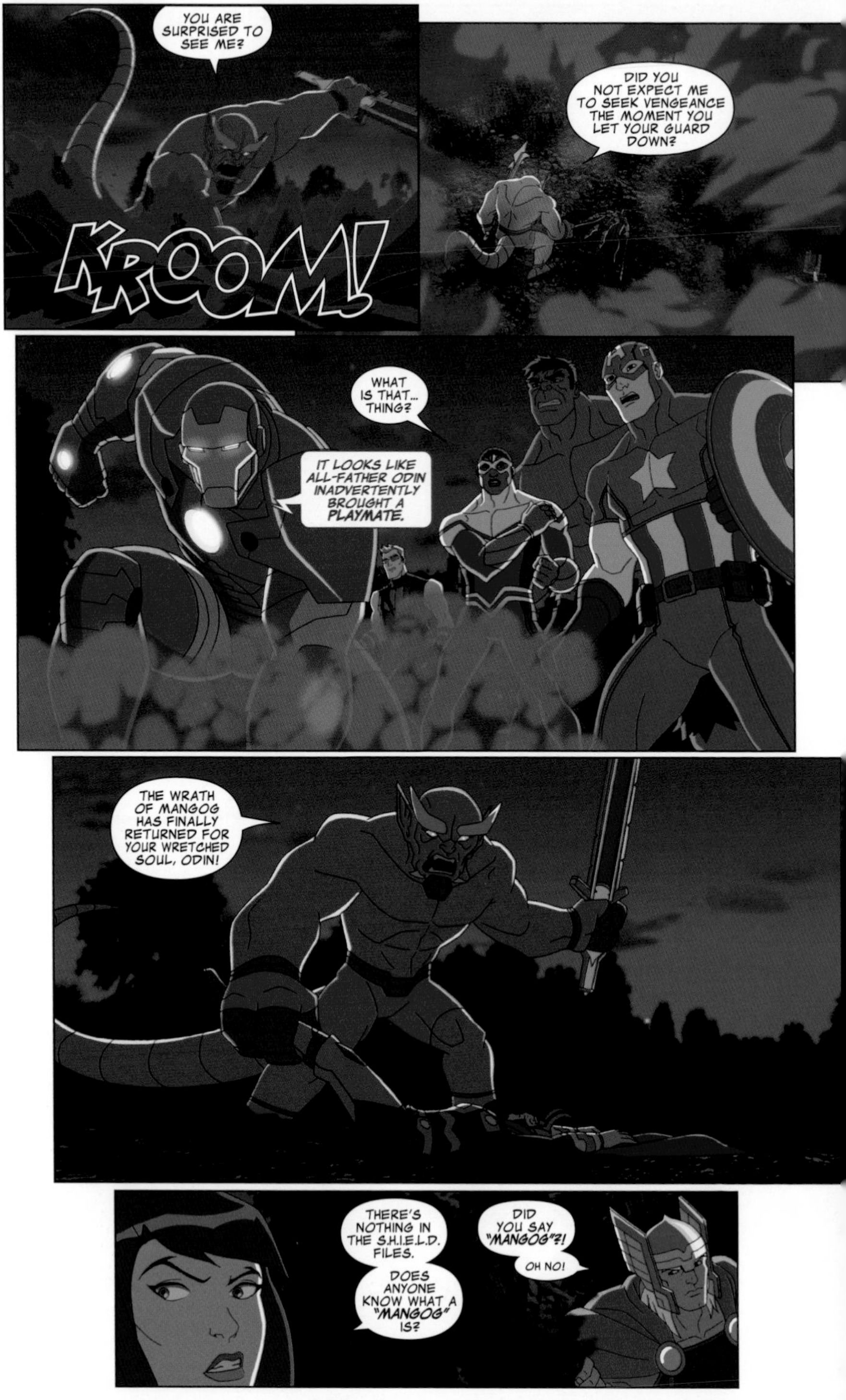
YOU ARE SURPRISED TO SEE ME?
KROOM!
DID YOU NOT EXPECT ME TO SEEK VENGEANCE THE MOMENT YOU LET YOUR GUARD DOWN?
WHAT IS THAT... THING?
IT LOOKS LIKE ALL-FATHER ODIN INADVERTENTLY BROUGHT A PLAYMATE.
THE WRATH OF MANGOG HAS FINALLY RETURNED FOR YOUR WRETCHED SOUL, ODIN!
THERE'S NOTHING IN THE S.H.I.E.L.D. FILES.
DOES ANYONE KNOW WHAT A "MANGOG" IS?
DID YOU SAY "MANGOG"?!
OH NO!

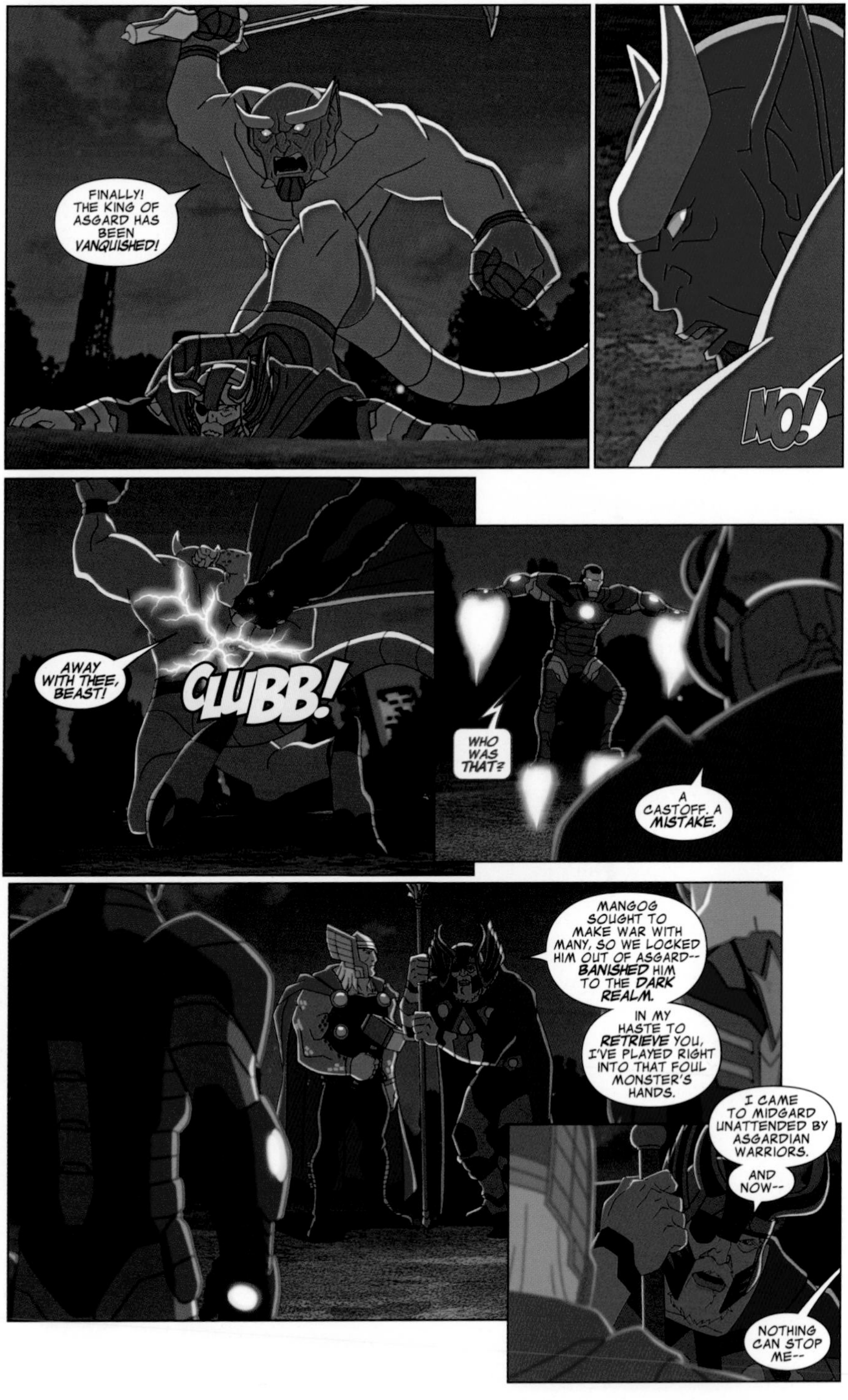
FINALLY! THE KING OF ASGARD HAS BEEN VANQUISHED!
NO!
AWAY WITH THEE, BEAST!
CLUBB!
WHO WAS THAT?
A CASTOFF. A MISTAKE.
MANGOG SOUGHT TO MAKE WAR WITH MANY, SO WE LOCKED HIM OUT OF ASGARD-- BANISHED HIM TO THE DARK REALM.
IN MY HASTE TO RETRIEVE YOU, I'VE PLAYED RIGHT INTO THAT FOUL MONSTER'S HANDS.
I CAME TO MIDGARD UNATTENDED BY ASGARDIAN WARRIORS.
AND NOW--
NOTHING CAN STOP ME--

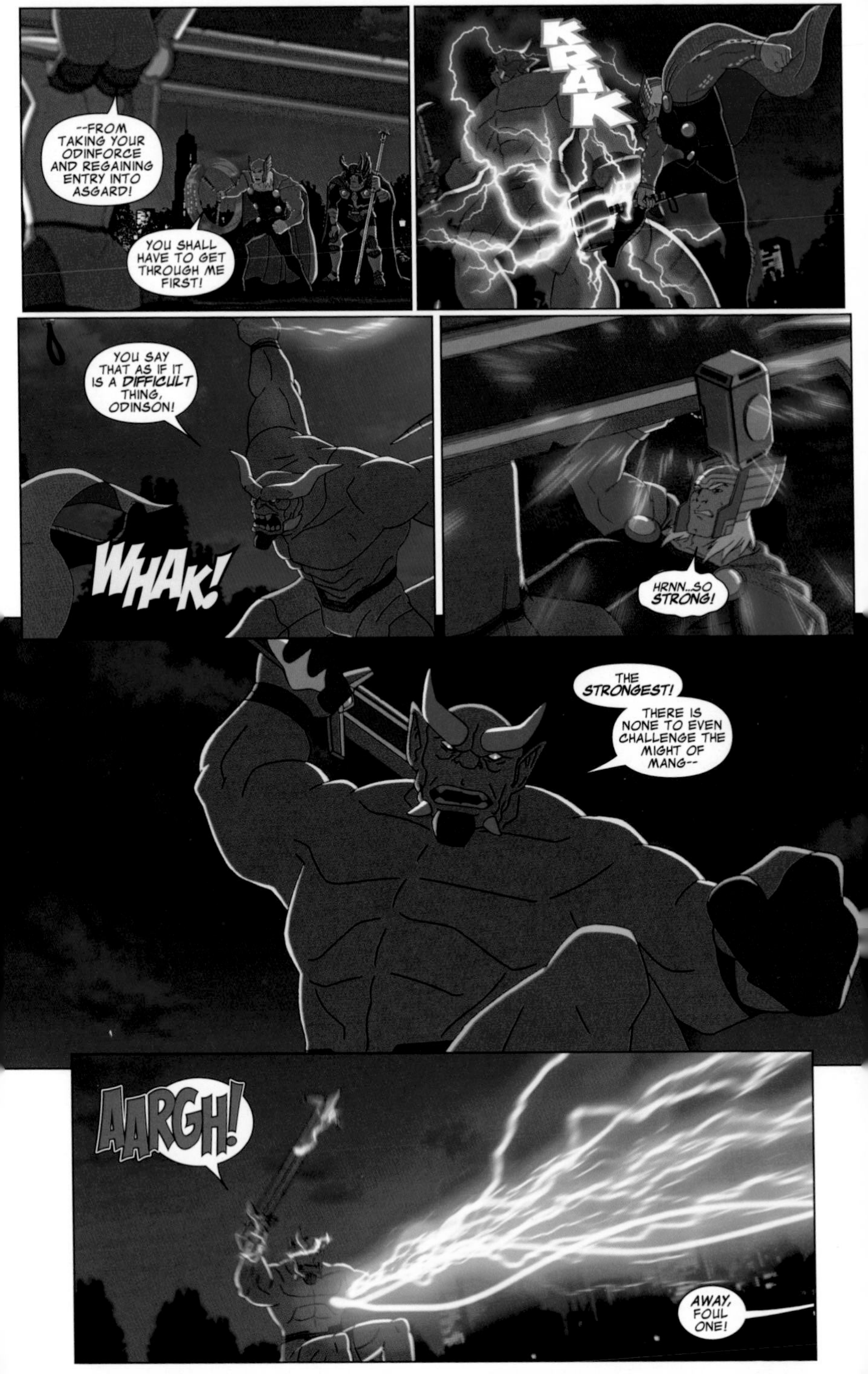
--FROM TAKING YOUR ODINFORCE AND REGAINING ENTRY INTO ASGARD!
YOU SHALL HAVE TO GET THROUGH ME FIRST!
KRAK
YOU SAY THAT AS IF IT IS A DIFFICULT THING, ODINSON!
WHAK!
HRNN...SO STRONG!
THE STRONGEST!
THERE IS NONE TO EVEN CHALLENGE THE MIGHT OF MANG--
AARGH!
AWAY, FOUL ONE!

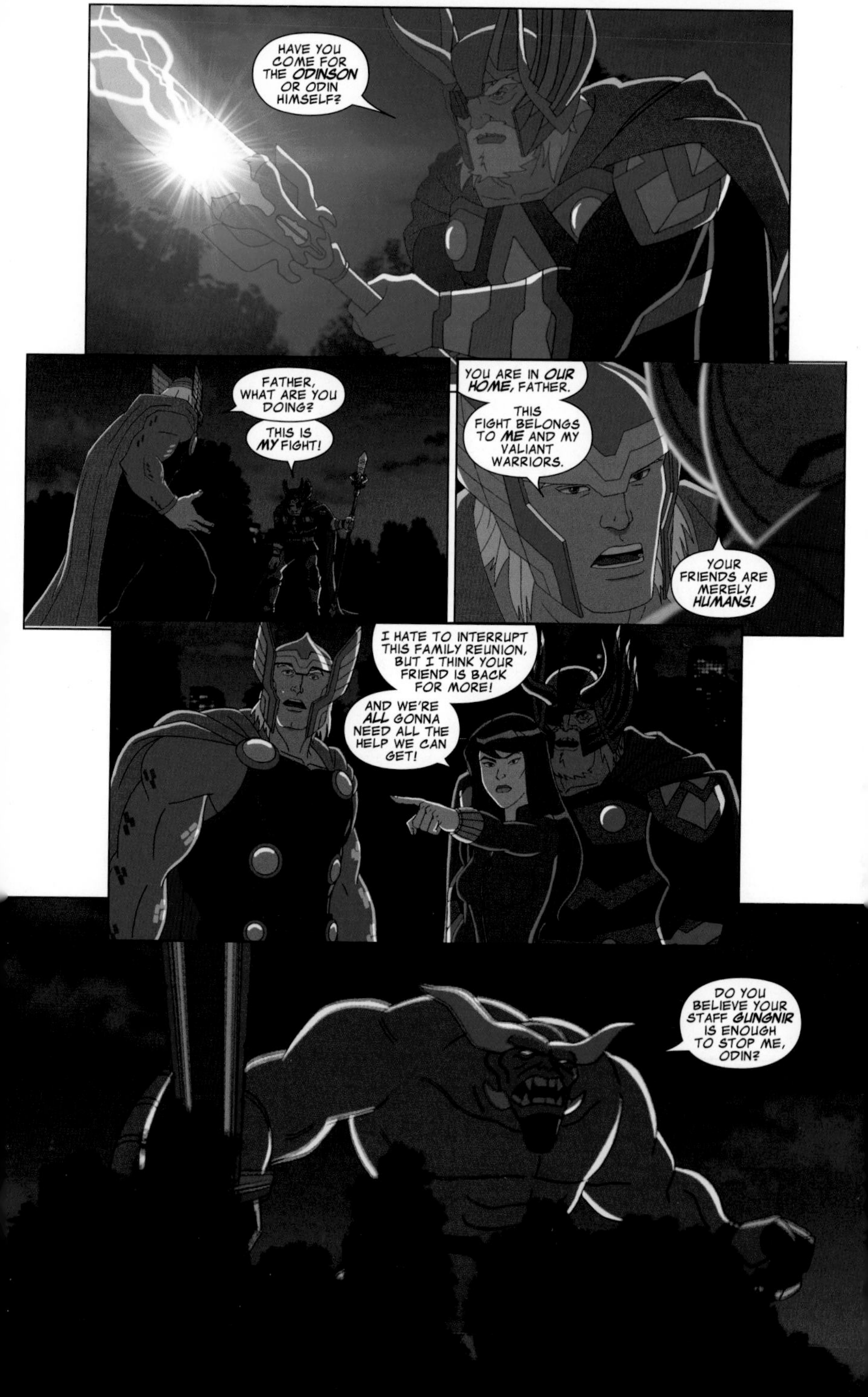
HAVE YOU COME FOR THE ODINSON OR ODIN HIMSELF?
FATHER, WHAT ARE YOU DOING?
THIS IS MY FIGHT!
YOU ARE IN OUR HOME, FATHER.
THIS FIGHT BELONGS TO ME AND MY VALIANT WARRIORS.
YOUR FRIENDS ARE MERELY HUMANS!
I HATE TO INTERRUPT THIS FAMILY REUNION, BUT I THINK YOUR FRIEND IS BACK FOR MORE!
AND WE'RE ALL GONNA NEED ALL THE HELP WE CAN GET!
DO YOU BELIEVE YOUR STAFF GUNGNIR IS ENOUGH TO STOP ME, ODIN?

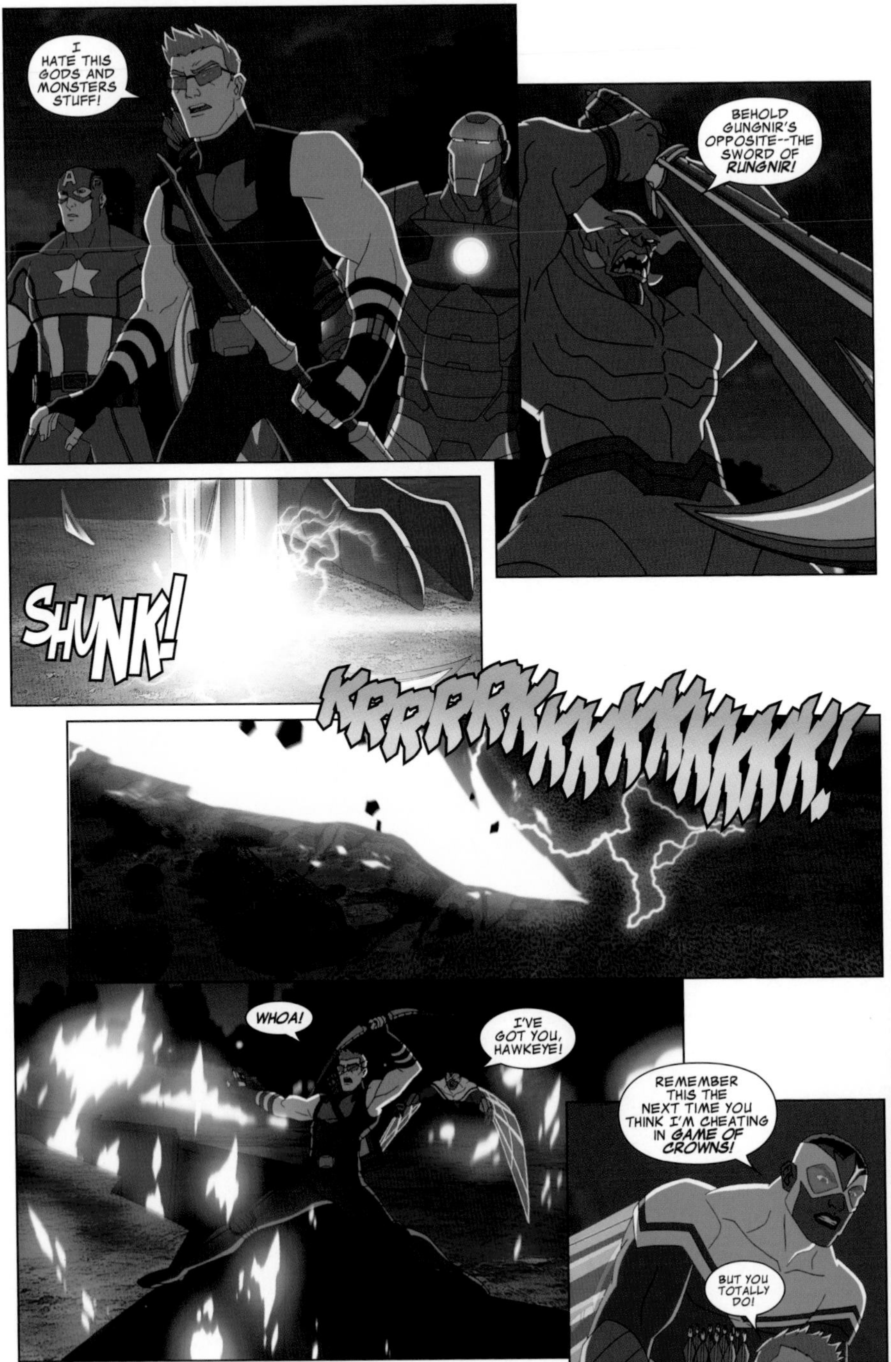
I HATE THIS GODS AND MONSTERS STUFF!
BEHOLD GUNGNIR'S OPPOSITE--THE SWORD OF RUNGNIR!
SHUNK!
KRRRRKKKKKKKKKK!
WHOA!
I'VE GOT YOU, HAWKEYE!
REMEMBER THIS THE NEXT TIME YOU THINK I'M CHEATING IN GAME OF CROWNS!
BUT YOU TOTALLY DO!

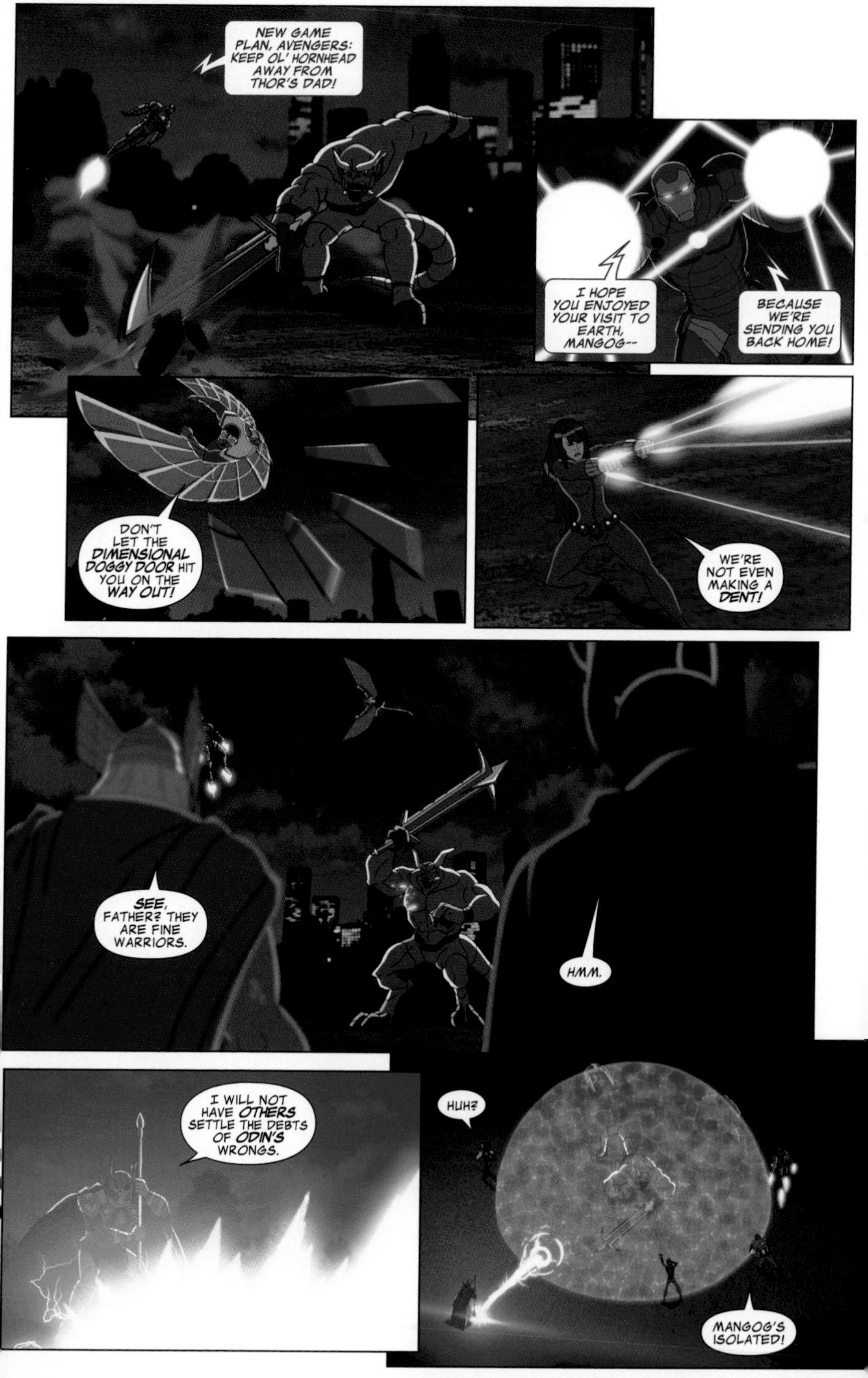
NEW GAME PLAN, AVENGERS: KEEP OL' HORNHEAD AWAY FROM THOR'S DAD!
I HOPE YOU ENJOYED YOUR VISIT TO EARTH, MANGOG--
BECAUSE WE'RE SENDING YOU BACK HOME!
DON'T LET THE DIMENSIONAL DOGGY DOOR HIT YOU ON THE WAY OUT!
WE'RE NOT EVEN MAKING A DENT!
SEE, FATHER? THEY ARE FINE WARRIORS.
HMM.
I WILL NOT HAVE OTHERS SETTLE THE DEBTS OF ODIN'S WRONGS.
HUH?
MANGOG'S ISOLATED!

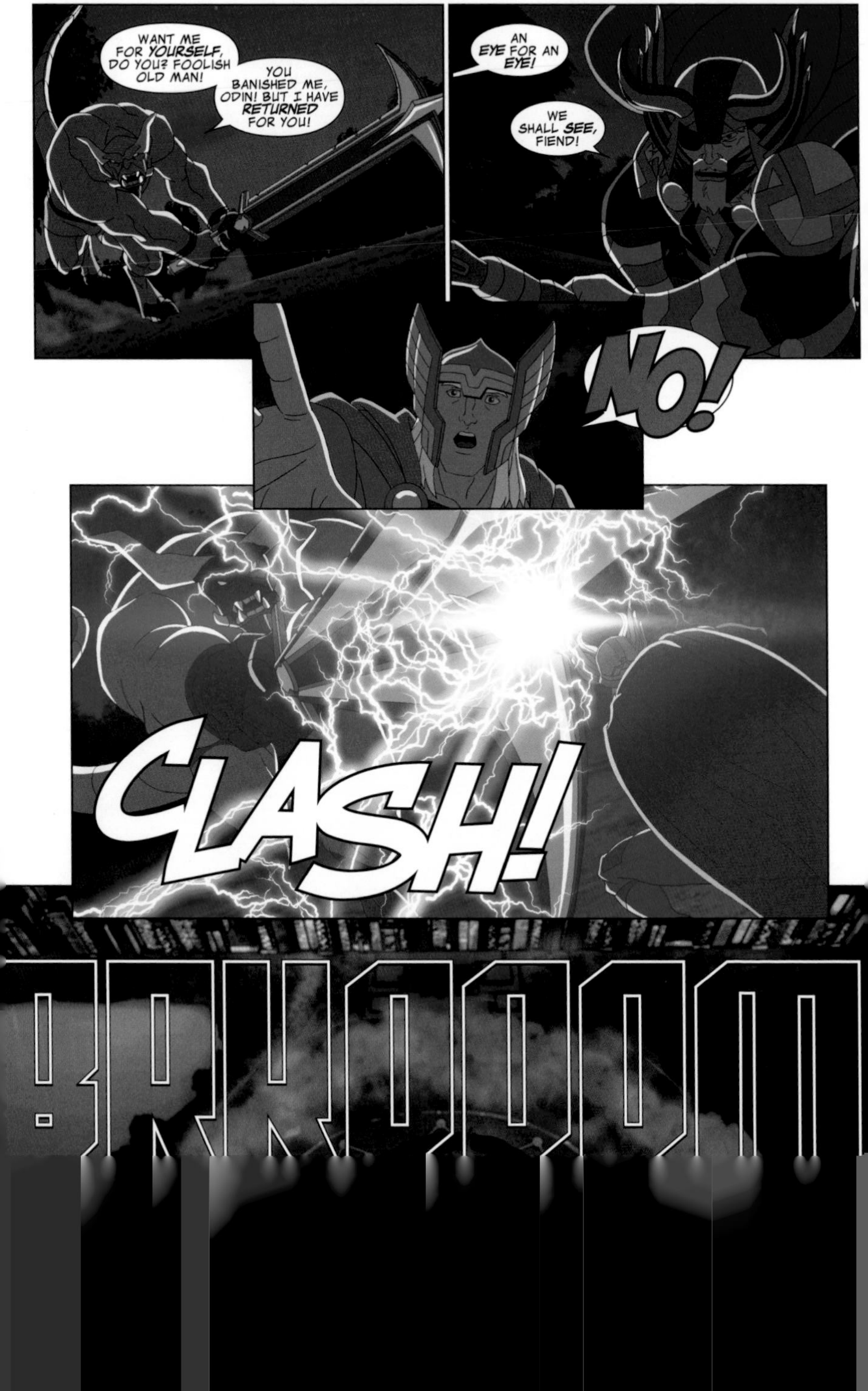
WANT ME FOR YOURSELF, DO YOU? FOOLISH OLD MAN!
YOU BANISHED ME, ODIN! BUT I HAVE RETURNED FOR YOU!
AN EYE FOR AN EYE!
WE SHALL SEE, FIEND!
NO!
CLASH!
BRKOOOM

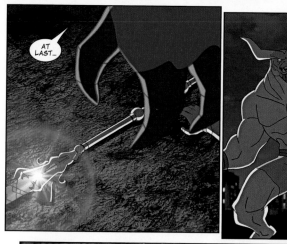

AT LAST...

...THE ODINFORCE IS MINE!

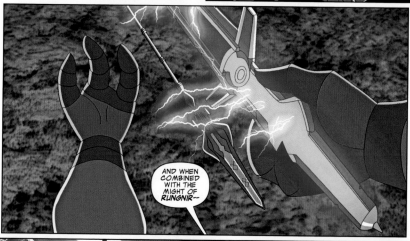

AND WHEN COMBINED WITH THE MIGHT OF RUNGNIR--

--MANGOG WILL RULE OVER ALL REALMS!

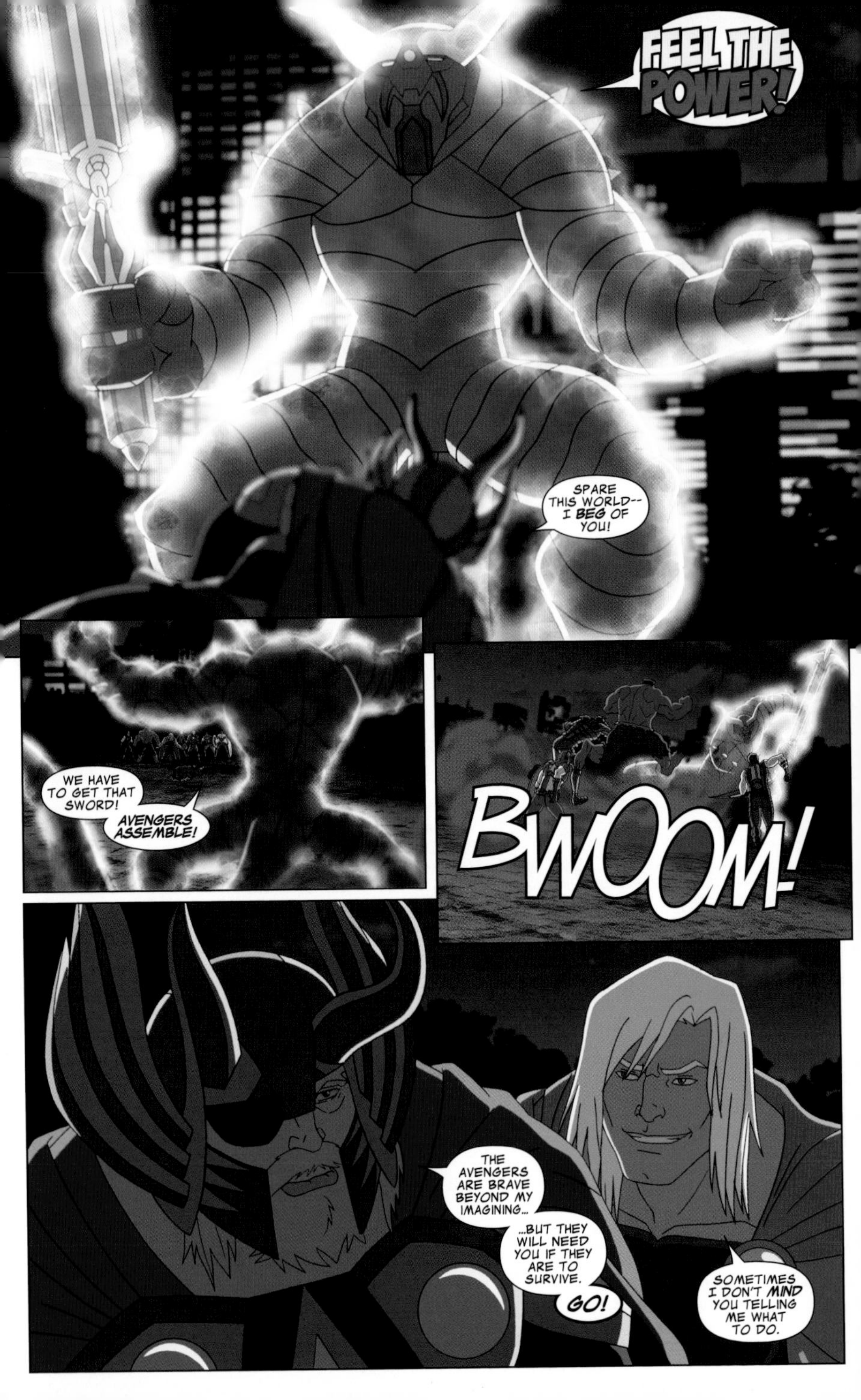
FEEL THE POWER!
SPARE THIS WORLD-- I BEG OF YOU!
WE HAVE TO GET THAT SWORD!
AVENGERS ASSEMBLE!
BWOOM!
THE AVENGERS ARE BRAVE BEYOND MY IMAGINING...
...BUT THEY WILL NEED YOU IF THEY ARE TO SURVIVE.
GO!
SOMETIMES I DON'T MIND YOU TELLING ME WHAT TO DO.

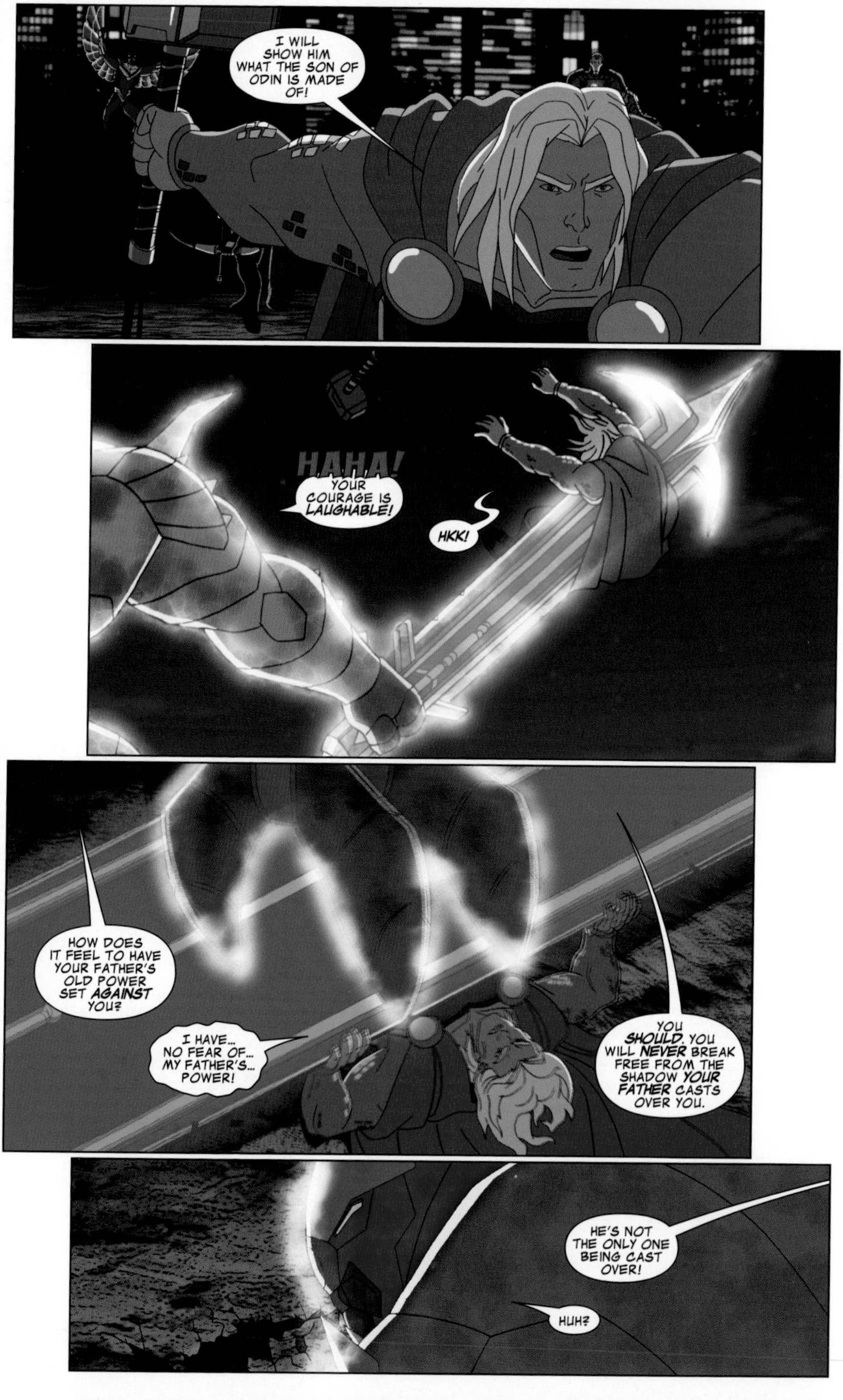
I WILL SHOW HIM WHAT THE SON OF ODIN IS MADE OF!
HAHA!
YOUR COURAGE IS LAUGHABLE!
HKK!
HOW DOES IT FEEL TO HAVE YOUR FATHER'S OLD POWER SET AGAINST YOU?
I HAVE... NO FEAR OF... MY FATHER'S... POWER!
YOU SHOULD. YOU WILL NEVER BREAK FREE FROM THE SHADOW YOUR FATHER CASTS OVER YOU.
HE'S NOT THE ONLY ONE BEING CAST OVER!
HUH?

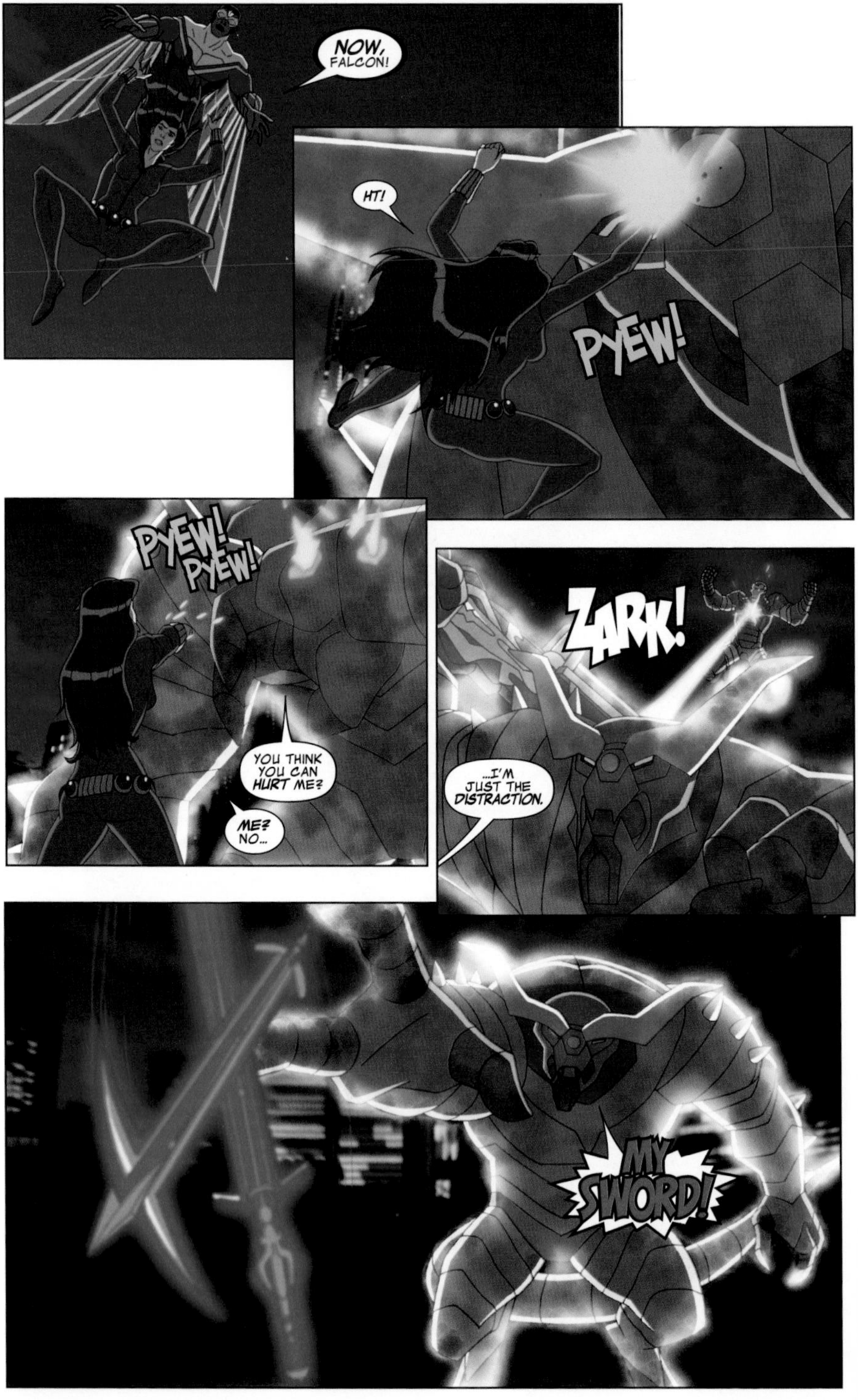
NOW, FALCON!
HT!
PYEW!
PYEW! PYEW!
YOU THINK YOU CAN HURT ME?
ME? NO...
ZARK!
...I'M JUST THE DISTRACTION.
MY SWORD!

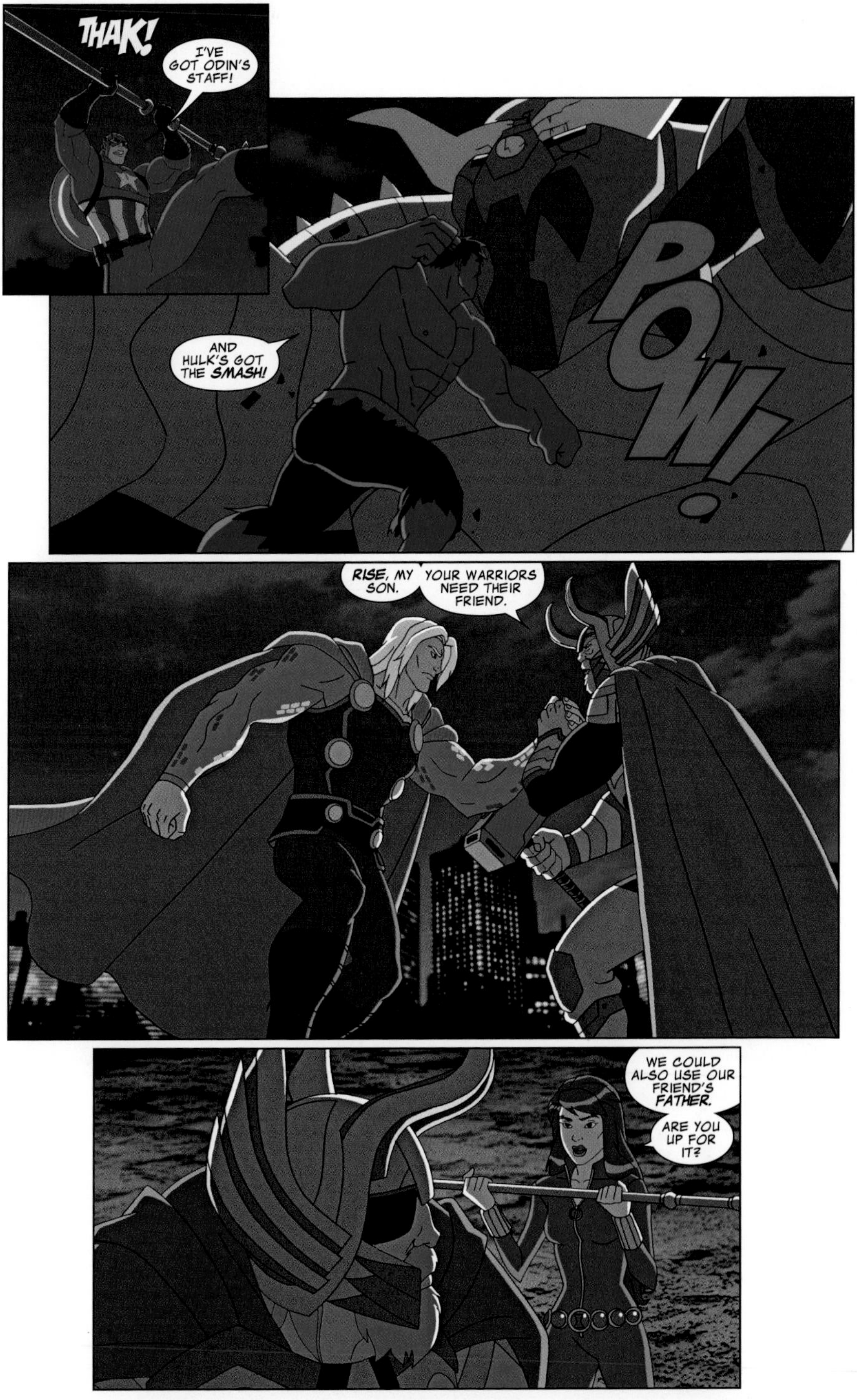
THAK!
I'VE GOT ODIN'S STAFF!
AND HULK'S GOT THE SMASH!
POW!
RISE, MY SON.
YOUR WARRIORS NEED THEIR FRIEND.
WE COULD ALSO USE OUR FRIEND'S FATHER.
ARE YOU UP FOR IT?

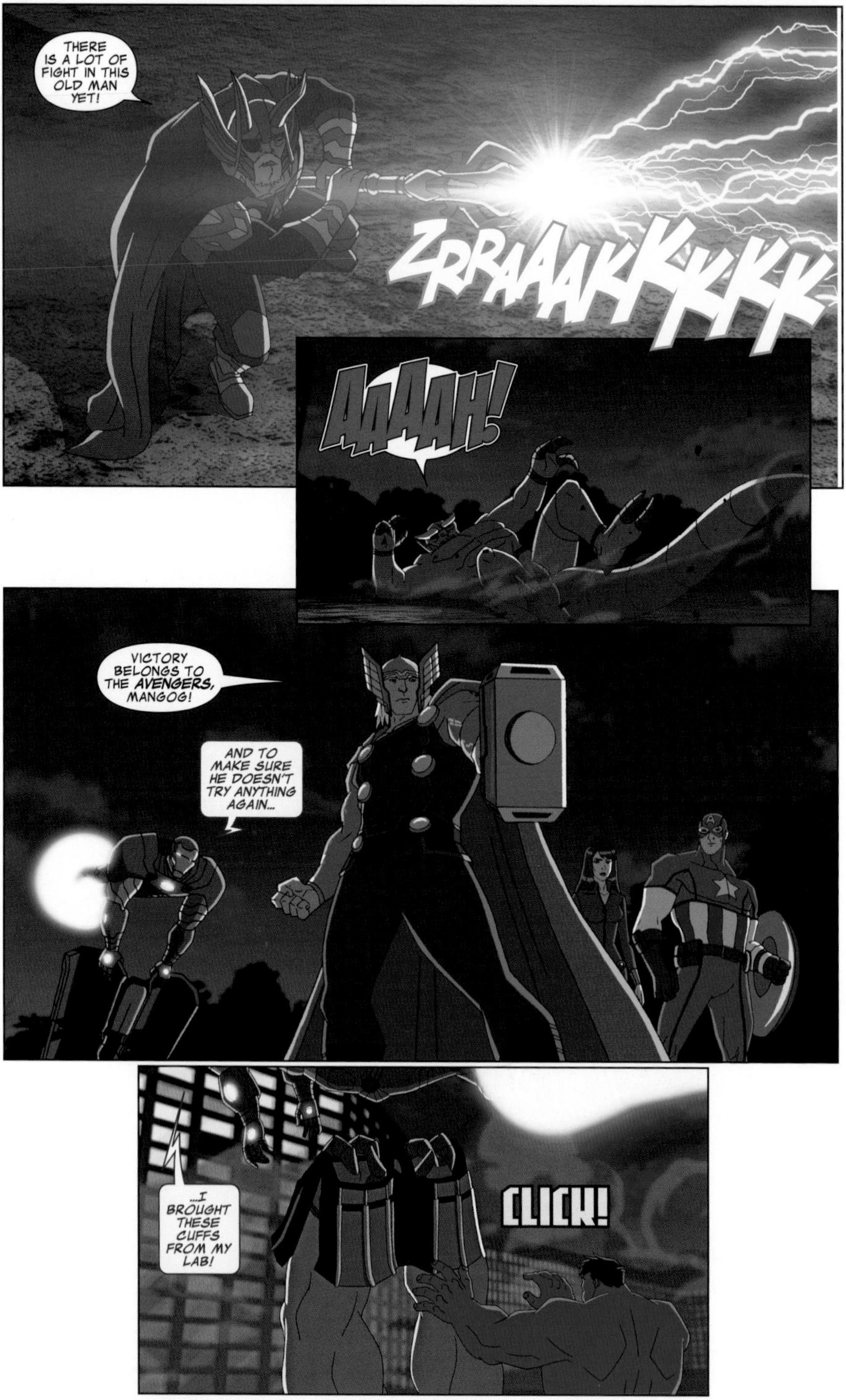
THERE IS A LOT OF FIGHT IN THIS OLD MAN YET!
ZRRAAAKKKKK
AAAAH!
VICTORY BELONGS TO THE AVENGERS, MANGOG!
AND TO MAKE SURE HE DOESN'T TRY ANYTHING AGAIN...
...I BROUGHT THESE CUFFS FROM MY LAB!
CLICK!

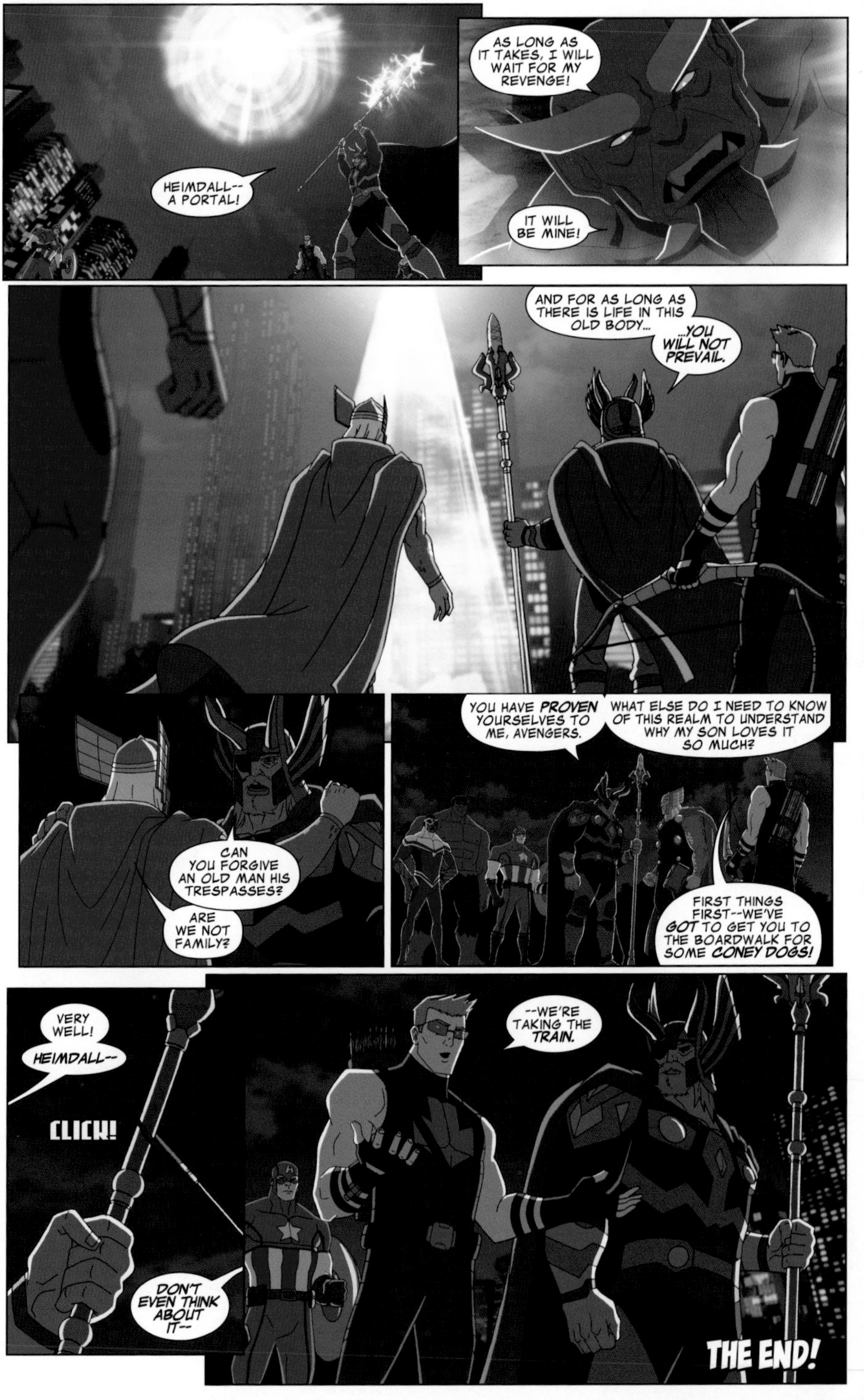
HEIMDALL-- A PORTAL!
AS LONG AS IT TAKES, I WILL WAIT FOR MY REVENGE!
IT WILL BE MINE!
AND FOR AS LONG AS THERE IS LIFE IN THIS OLD BODY...
...YOU WILL NOT PREVAIL.
CAN YOU FORGIVE AN OLD MAN HIS TRESPASSES?
ARE WE NOT FAMILY?
YOU HAVE PROVEN YOURSELVES TO ME, AVENGERS.
WHAT ELSE DO I NEED TO KNOW OF THIS REALM TO UNDERSTAND WHY MY SON LOVES IT SO MUCH?
FIRST THINGS FIRST--WE'VE GOT TO GET YOU TO THE BOARDWALK FOR SOME CONEY DOGS!
VERY WELL!
HEIMDALL--
CLICK!
DON'T EVEN THINK ABOUT IT--
--WE'RE TAKING THE TRAIN.
THE END!

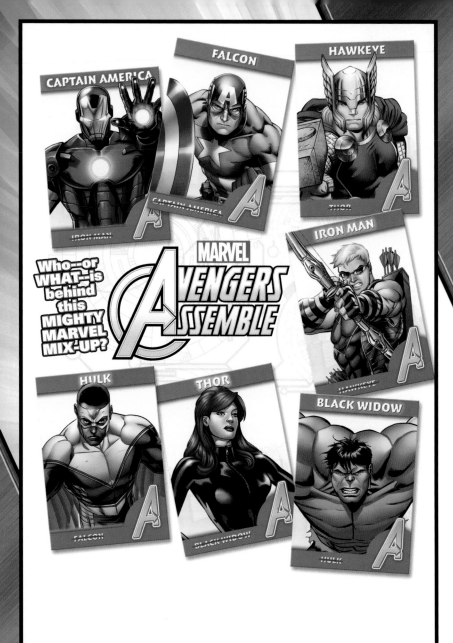

CAPTAIN AMERICA
IRON MAN

FALCON
CAPTAIN AMERICA

HAWKEYE
THOR

IRON MAN
HAWKEYE

HULK
FALCON

THOR
BLACK WIDOW

BLACK WIDOW
HULK

Who--or WHAT--is behind this MIGHTY MARVEL MIX-UP?

MARVEL
AVENGERS ASSEMBLE

#8 BASED ON "HEAD TO HEAD"

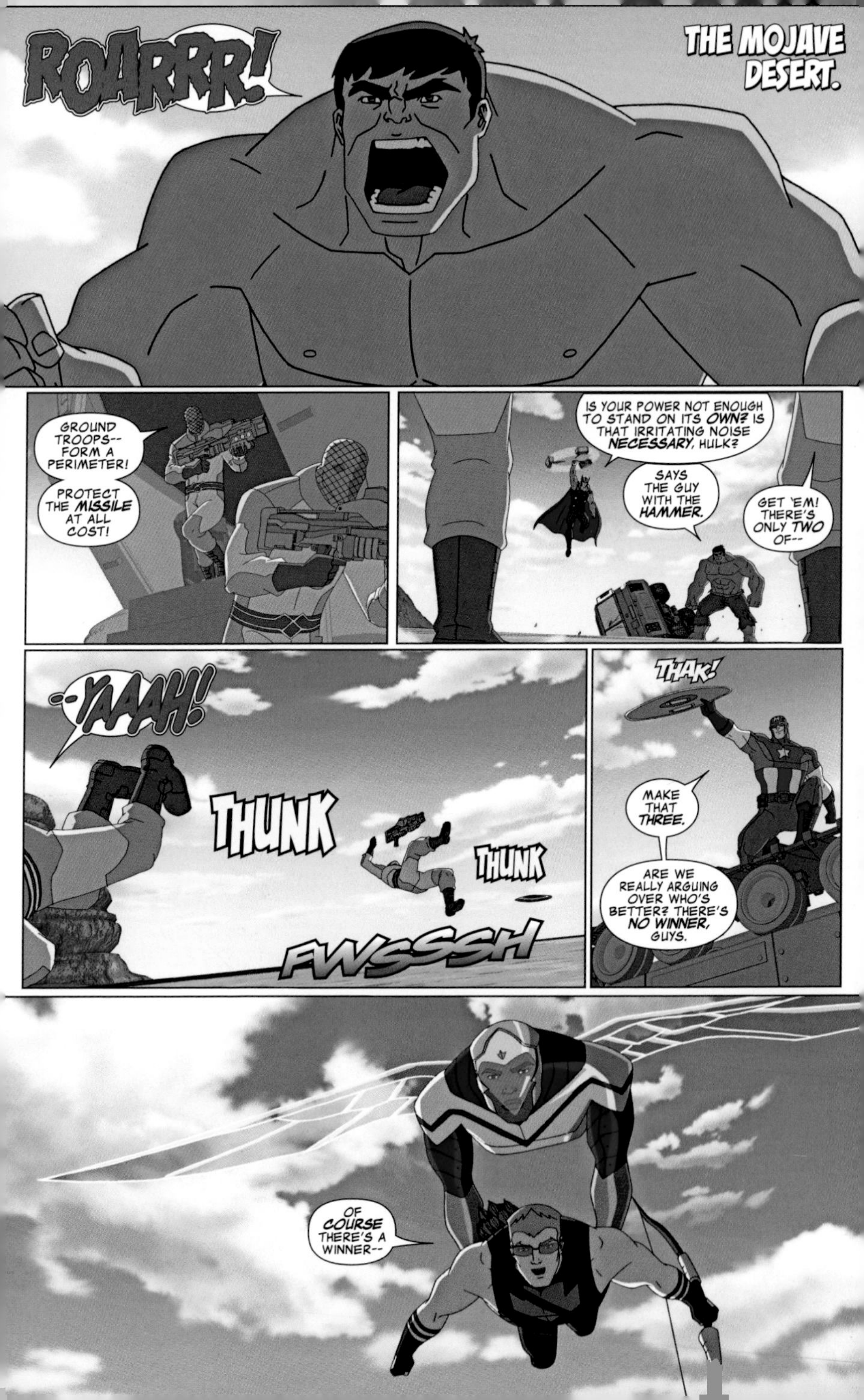
ROARRR!
THE MOJAVE DESERT.
GROUND TROOPS-- FORM A PERIMETER!
PROTECT THE MISSILE AT ALL COST!
IS YOUR POWER NOT ENOUGH TO STAND ON ITS OWN? IS THAT IRRITATING NOISE NECESSARY, HULK?
SAYS THE GUY WITH THE HAMMER.
GET 'EM! THERE'S ONLY TWO OF--
--YAAAH!
THUNK
THUNK
FWSSSH
THAK!
MAKE THAT THREE.
ARE WE REALLY ARGUING OVER WHO'S BETTER? THERE'S NO WINNER, GUYS.
OF COURSE THERE'S A WINNER--

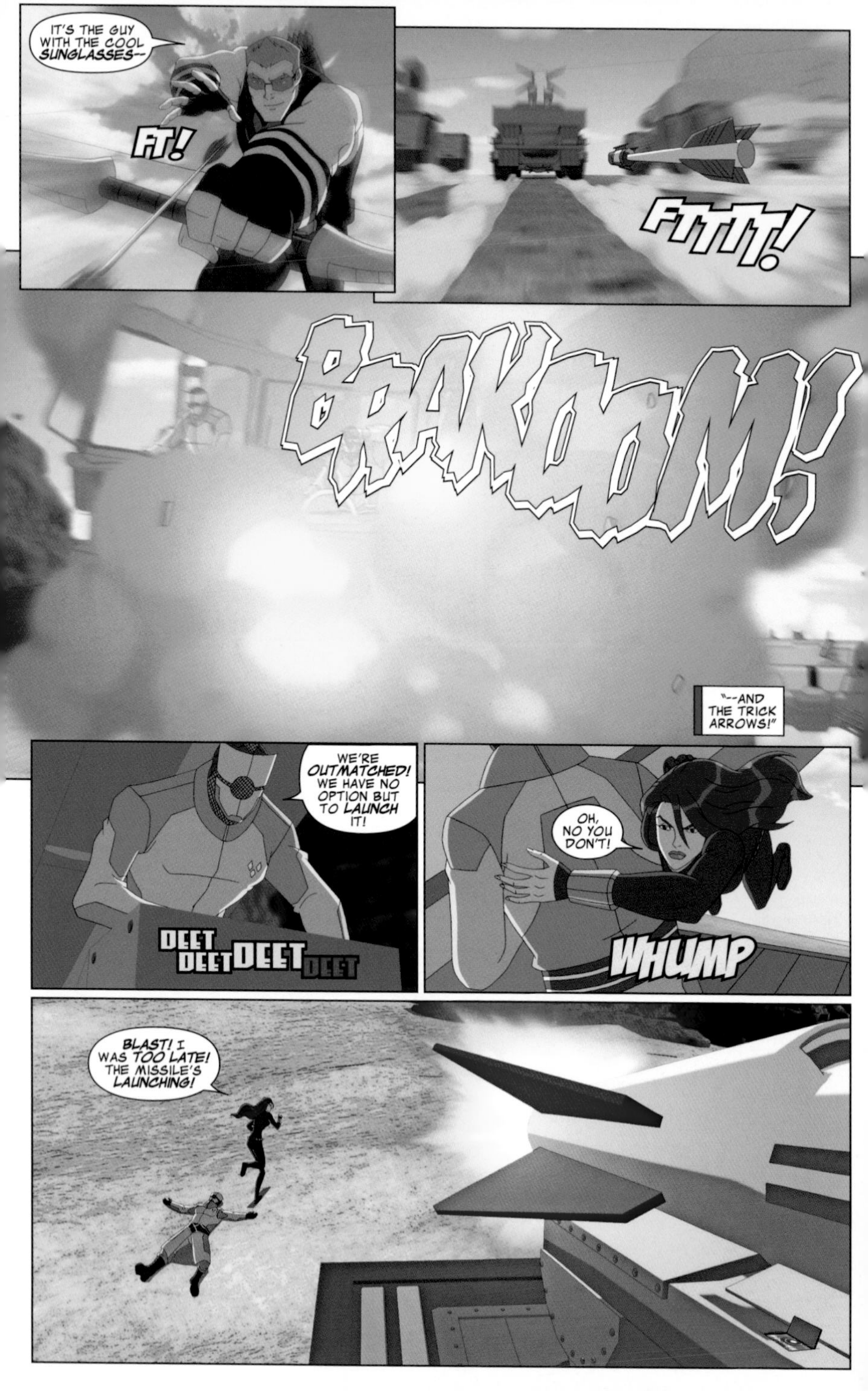
IT'S THE GUY WITH THE COOL SUNGLASSES--
FT!
FTTTT!
BRAKOOM!
"--AND THE TRICK ARROWS!"
WE'RE OUTMATCHED! WE HAVE NO OPTION BUT TO LAUNCH IT!
DEET DEET DEET DEET
OH, NO YOU DON'T!
WHUMP
BLAST! I WAS TOO LATE! THE MISSILE'S LAUNCHING!

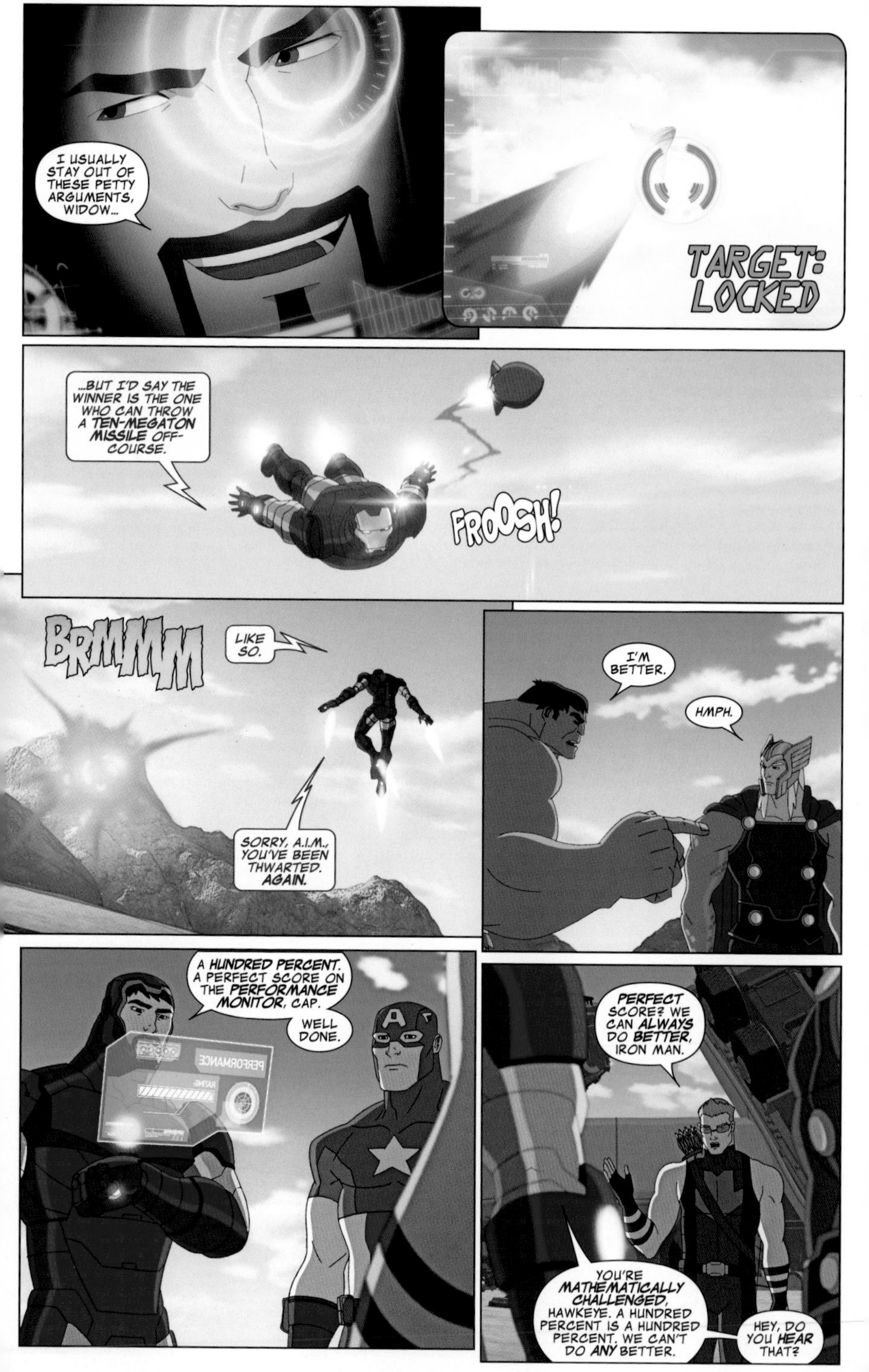
I USUALLY STAY OUT OF THESE PETTY ARGUMENTS, WIDOW...
TARGET: LOCKED
...BUT I'D SAY THE WINNER IS THE ONE WHO CAN THROW A TEN-MEGATON MISSILE OFF-COURSE.
FROOSH!
BRMMM
LIKE SO.
SORRY, A.I.M., YOU'VE BEEN THWARTED. AGAIN.
I'M BETTER.
HMPH.
A HUNDRED PERCENT. A PERFECT SCORE ON THE PERFORMANCE MONITOR, CAP.
WELL DONE.
PERFECT SCORE? WE CAN ALWAYS DO BETTER, IRON MAN.
YOU'RE MATHEMATICALLY CHALLENGED, HAWKEYE. A HUNDRED PERCENT IS A HUNDRED PERCENT. WE CAN'T DO ANY BETTER.
HEY, DO YOU HEAR THAT?

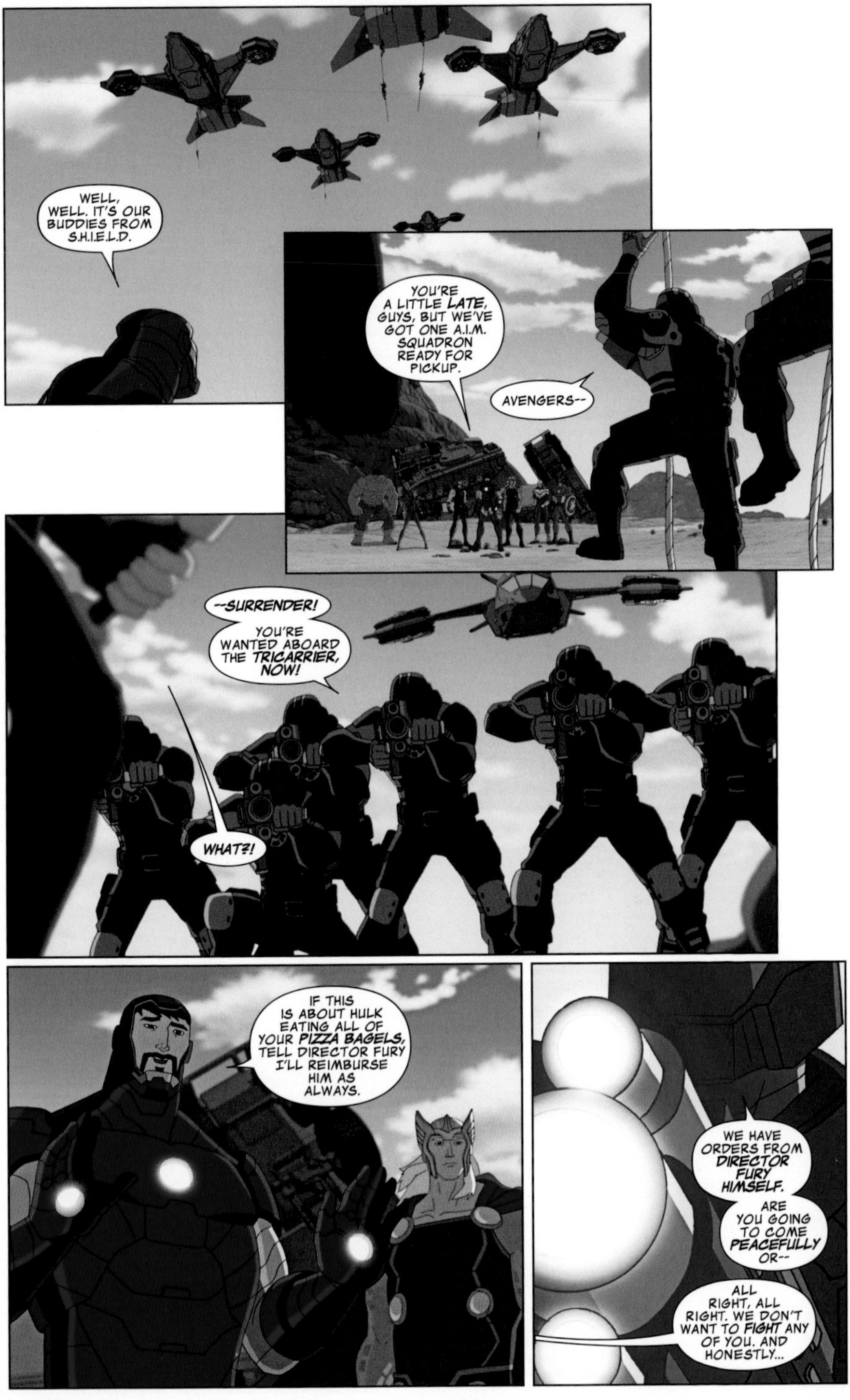
WELL, WELL. IT'S OUR BUDDIES FROM S.H.I.E.L.D.
YOU'RE A LITTLE LATE, GUYS, BUT WE'VE GOT ONE A.I.M. SQUADRON READY FOR PICKUP.
AVENGERS--
--SURRENDER!
YOU'RE WANTED ABOARD THE TRICARRIER, NOW!
WHAT?!
IF THIS IS ABOUT HULK EATING ALL OF YOUR PIZZA BAGELS, TELL DIRECTOR FURY I'LL REIMBURSE HIM AS ALWAYS.
WE HAVE ORDERS FROM DIRECTOR FURY HIMSELF.
ARE YOU GOING TO COME PEACEFULLY OR--
ALL RIGHT, ALL RIGHT. WE DON'T WANT TO FIGHT ANY OF YOU. AND HONESTLY...

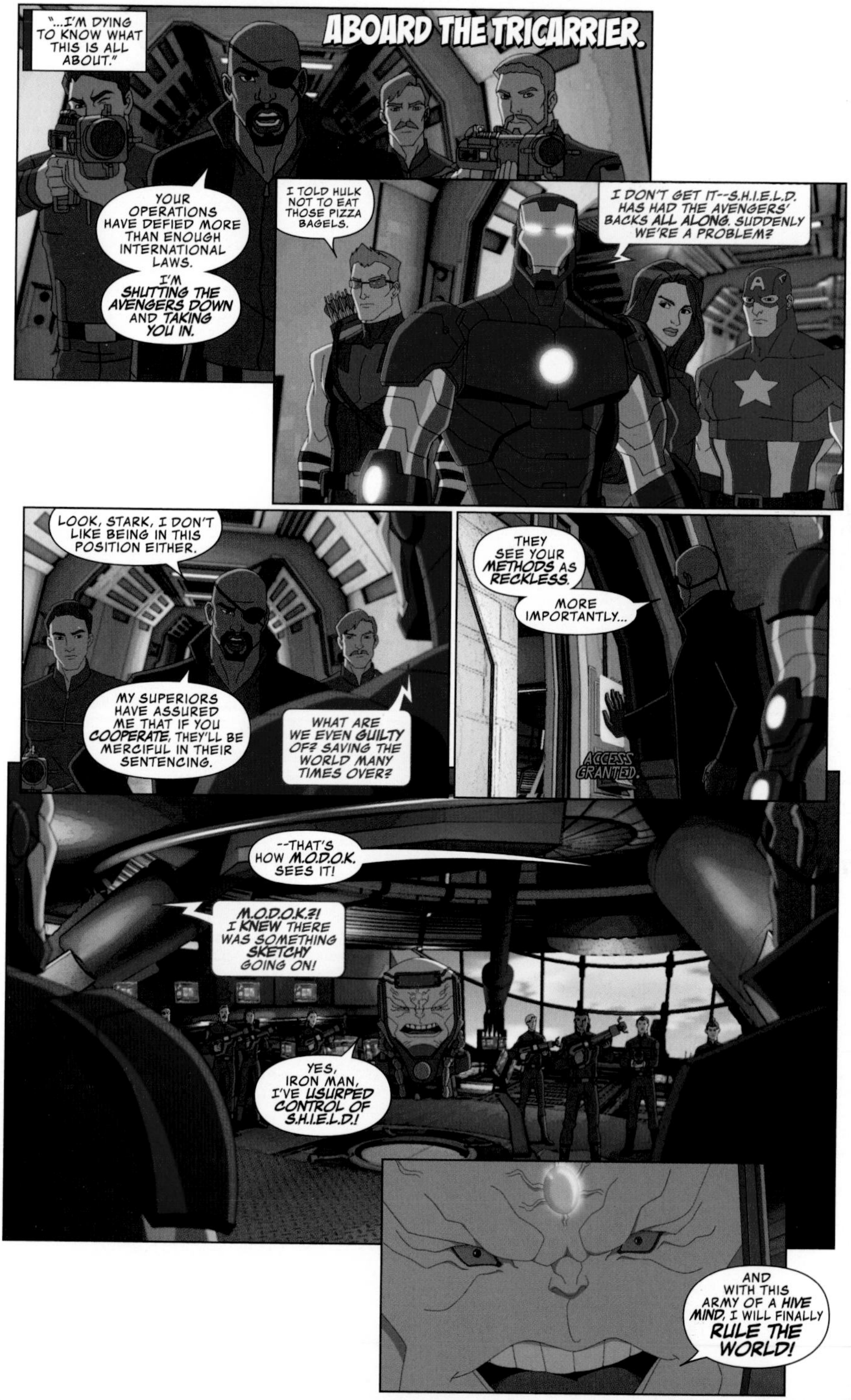
"...I'M DYING TO KNOW WHAT THIS IS ALL ABOUT."
ABOARD THE TRICARRIER.
YOUR OPERATIONS HAVE DEFIED MORE THAN ENOUGH INTERNATIONAL LAWS.
I'M SHUTTING THE AVENGERS DOWN AND TAKING YOU IN.
I TOLD HULK NOT TO EAT THOSE PIZZA BAGELS.
I DON'T GET IT--S.H.I.E.L.D. HAS HAD THE AVENGERS' BACKS ALL ALONG. SUDDENLY WE'RE A PROBLEM?
LOOK, STARK, I DON'T LIKE BEING IN THIS POSITION EITHER.
MY SUPERIORS HAVE ASSURED ME THAT IF YOU COOPERATE, THEY'LL BE MERCIFUL IN THEIR SENTENCING.
WHAT ARE WE EVEN GUILTY OF? SAVING THE WORLD MANY TIMES OVER?
THEY SEE YOUR METHODS AS RECKLESS.
MORE IMPORTANTLY...
ACCESS GRANTED.
--THAT'S HOW M.O.D.O.K. SEES IT!
M.O.D.O.K.?! I KNEW THERE WAS SOMETHING SKETCHY GOING ON!
YES, IRON MAN, I'VE USURPED CONTROL OF S.H.I.E.L.D.!
AND WITH THIS ARMY OF A HIVE MIND, I WILL FINALLY RULE THE WORLD!

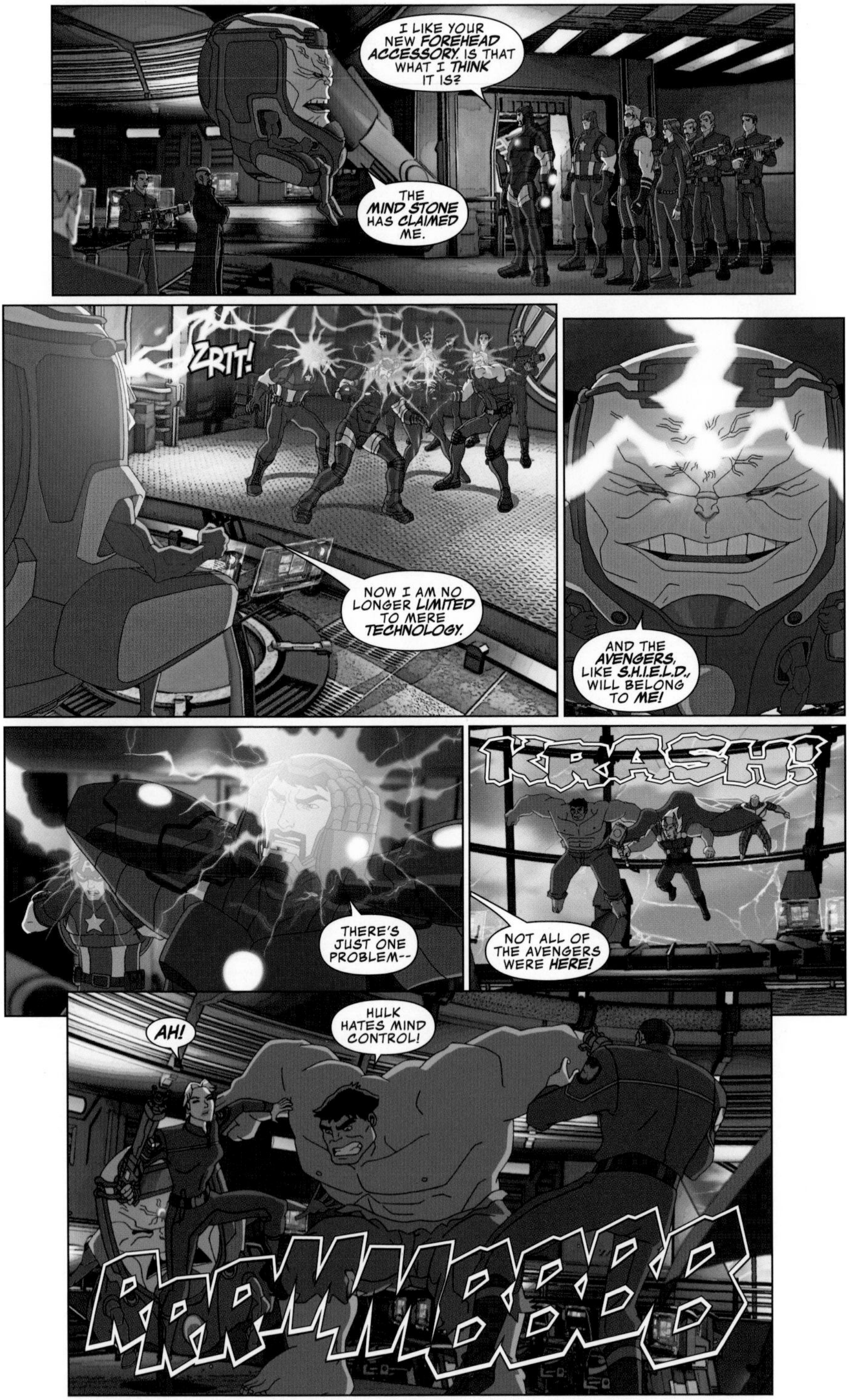

I LIKE YOUR NEW FOREHEAD ACCESSORY. IS THAT WHAT I THINK IT IS?
THE MIND STONE HAS CLAIMED ME.
ZRTT!
NOW I AM NO LONGER LIMITED TO MERE TECHNOLOGY.
AND THE AVENGERS, LIKE S.H.I.E.L.D., WILL BELONG TO ME!
THERE'S JUST ONE PROBLEM--
KRASH!
NOT ALL OF THE AVENGERS WERE HERE!
AH!
HULK HATES MIND CONTROL!

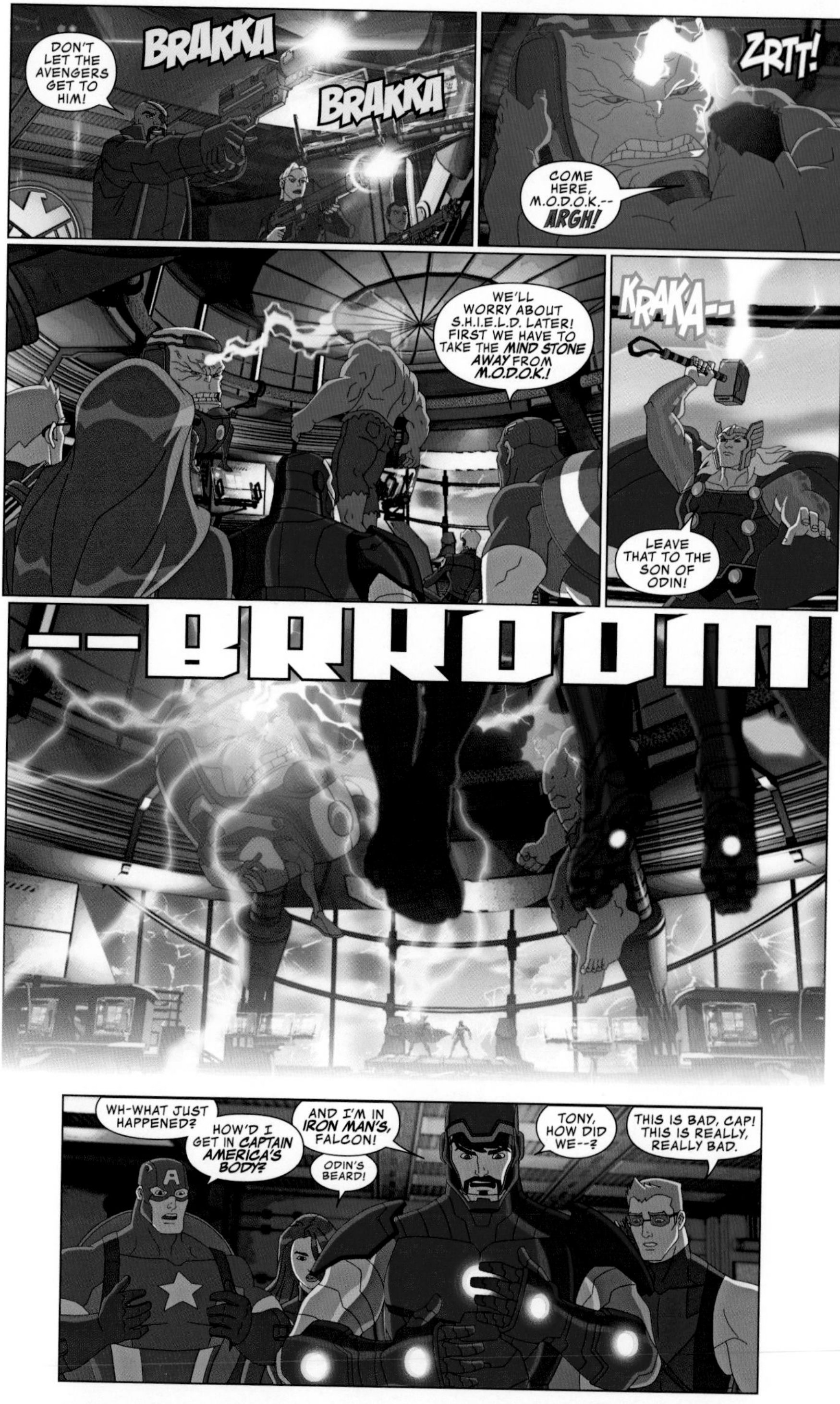
DON'T LET THE AVENGERS GET TO HIM!
BRAKKA
BRAKKA
ZRTT!
COME HERE, M.O.D.O.K.-- ARGH!
WE'LL WORRY ABOUT S.H.I.E.L.D. LATER! FIRST WE HAVE TO TAKE THE MIND STONE AWAY FROM M.O.D.O.K.!
KRAKA--
LEAVE THAT TO THE SON OF ODIN!
--BRROOM
WH-WHAT JUST HAPPENED?
HOW'D I GET IN CAPTAIN AMERICA'S BODY?
AND I'M IN IRON MAN'S, FALCON!
ODIN'S BEARD!
TONY, HOW DID WE--?
THIS IS BAD, CAP! THIS IS REALLY, REALLY BAD.

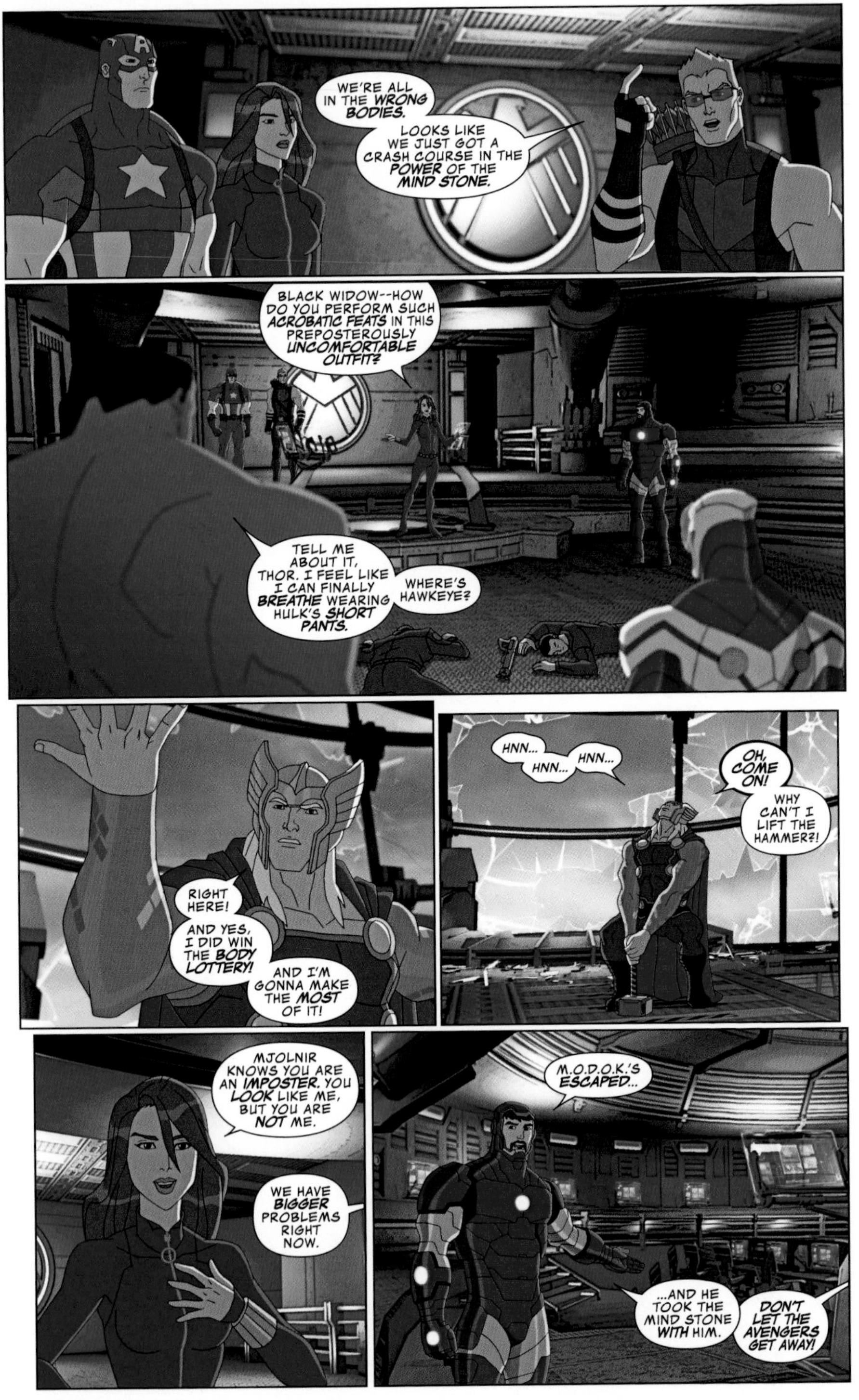

WE'RE ALL IN THE WRONG BODIES.
LOOKS LIKE WE JUST GOT A CRASH COURSE IN THE POWER OF THE MIND STONE.
BLACK WIDOW--HOW DO YOU PERFORM SUCH ACROBATIC FEATS IN THIS PREPOSTEROUSLY UNCOMFORTABLE OUTFIT?
TELL ME ABOUT IT, THOR. I FEEL LIKE I CAN FINALLY BREATHE WEARING HULK'S SHORT PANTS.
WHERE'S HAWKEYE?
RIGHT HERE!
AND YES, I DID WIN THE BODY LOTTERY!
AND I'M GONNA MAKE THE MOST OF IT!
HNN...
HNN...
HNN...
OH, COME ON!
WHY CAN'T I LIFT THE HAMMER?!
MJOLNIR KNOWS YOU ARE AN IMPOSTER. YOU LOOK LIKE ME, BUT YOU ARE NOT ME.
WE HAVE BIGGER PROBLEMS RIGHT NOW.
M.O.D.O.K.'S ESCAPED...
...AND HE TOOK THE MIND STONE WITH HIM.
DON'T LET THE AVENGERS GET AWAY!

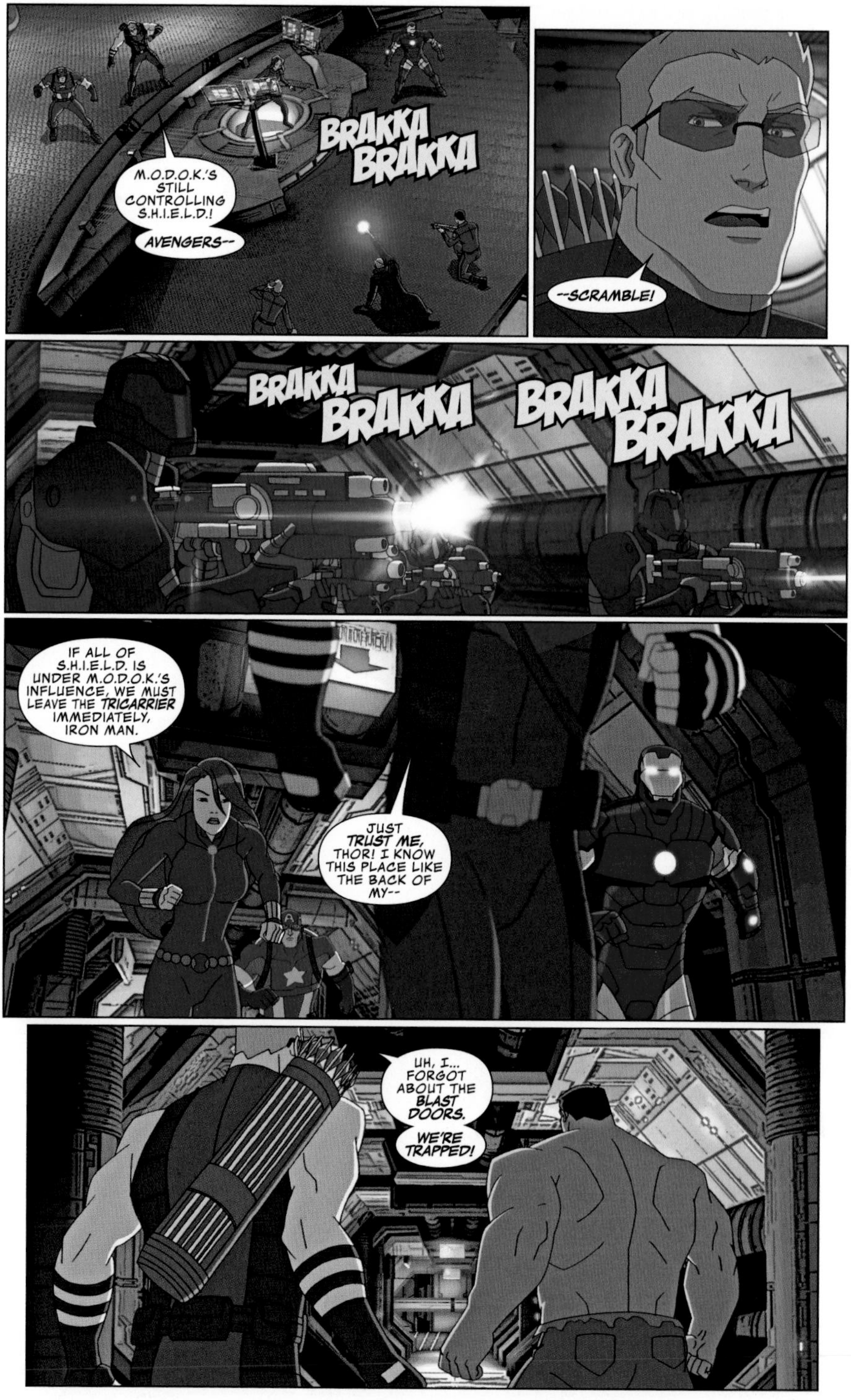

M.O.D.O.K.'S STILL CONTROLLING S.H.I.E.L.D.!
AVENGERS--
BRAKKA BRAKKA
--SCRAMBLE!
BRAKKA BRAKKA
BRAKKA BRAKKA
IF ALL OF S.H.I.E.L.D. IS UNDER M.O.D.O.K.'S INFLUENCE, WE MUST LEAVE THE TRICARRIER IMMEDIATELY, IRON MAN.
JUST TRUST ME, THOR! I KNOW THIS PLACE LIKE THE BACK OF MY--
UH, I... FORGOT ABOUT THE BLAST DOORS.
WE'RE TRAPPED!

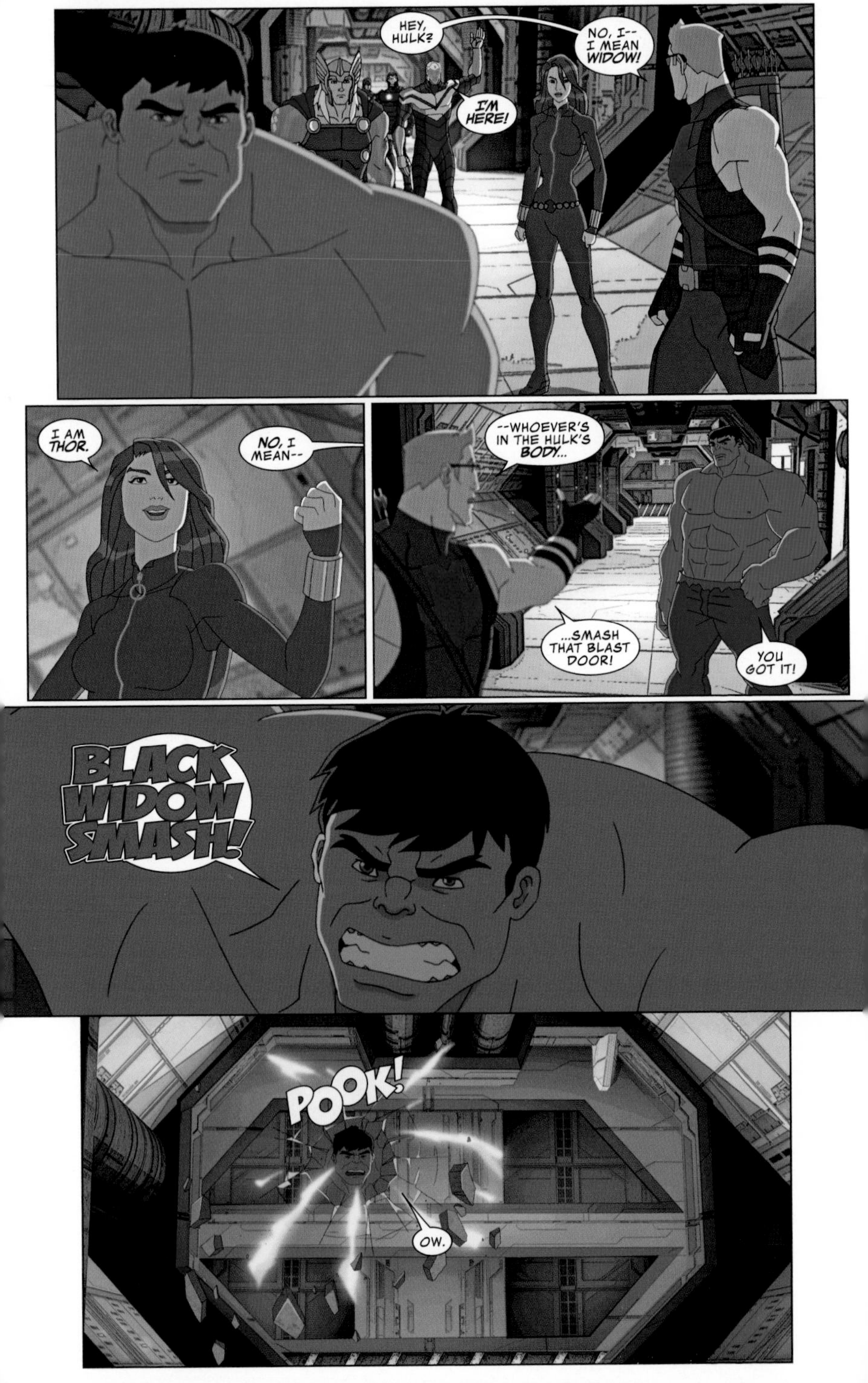
HEY, HULK?
NO, I-- I MEAN WIDOW!
I'M HERE!
I AM THOR.
NO, I MEAN--
--WHOEVER'S IN THE HULK'S BODY...
...SMASH THAT BLAST DOOR!
YOU GOT IT!
BLACK WIDOW SMASH!
POOK!
OW.

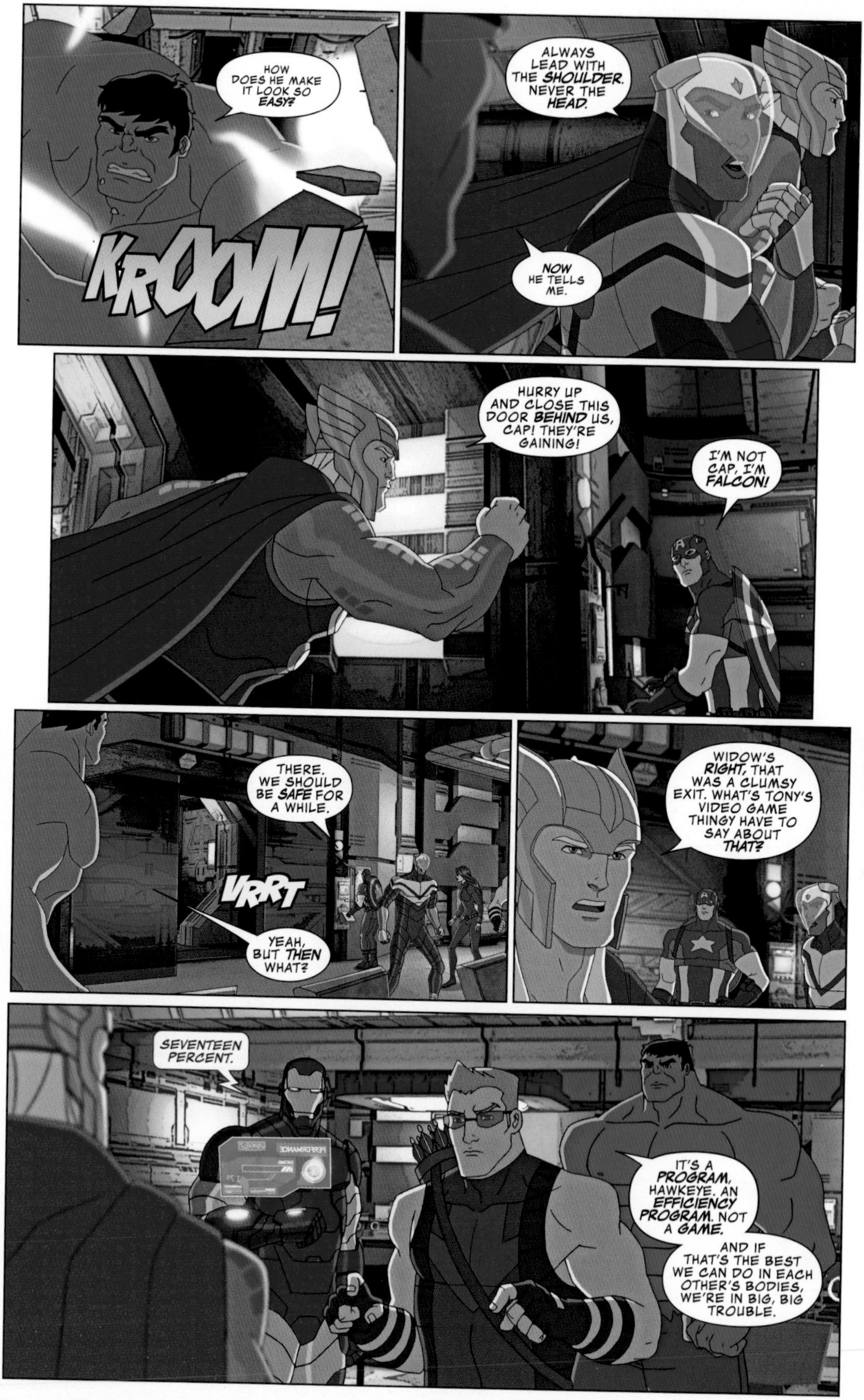
HOW DOES HE MAKE IT LOOK SO EASY?
KROOOM!
ALWAYS LEAD WITH THE SHOULDER. NEVER THE HEAD.
NOW HE TELLS ME.
HURRY UP AND CLOSE THIS DOOR BEHIND US, CAP! THEY'RE GAINING!
I'M NOT CAP, I'M FALCON!
THERE. WE SHOULD BE SAFE FOR A WHILE.
VRRT
YEAH, BUT THEN WHAT?
WIDOW'S RIGHT, THAT WAS A CLUMSY EXIT. WHAT'S TONY'S VIDEO GAME THINGY HAVE TO SAY ABOUT THAT?
SEVENTEEN PERCENT.
PERFORMANCE
IT'S A PROGRAM, HAWKEYE, AN EFFICIENCY PROGRAM. NOT A GAME.
AND IF THAT'S THE BEST WE CAN DO IN EACH OTHER'S BODIES, WE'RE IN BIG, BIG TROUBLE.

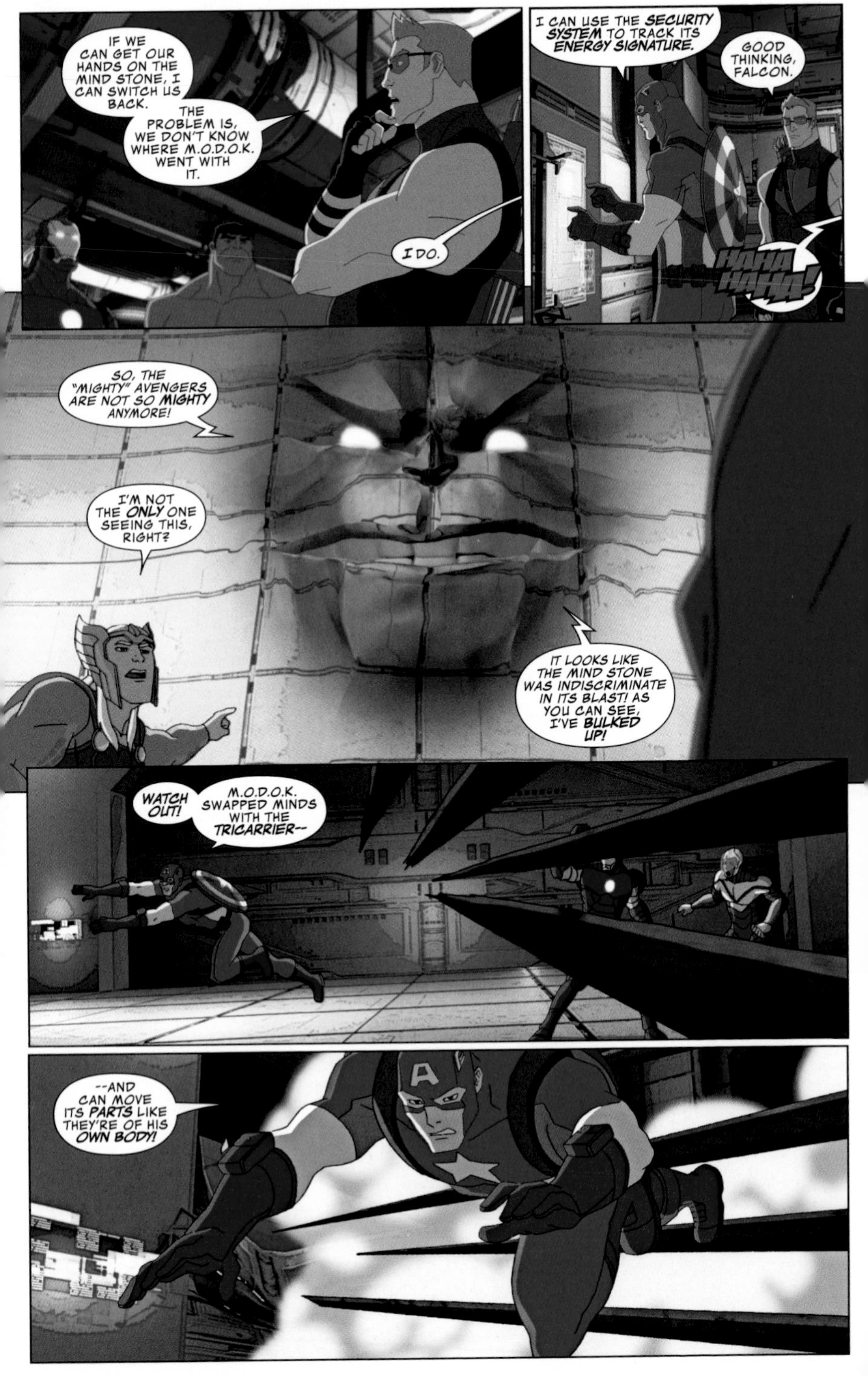
IF WE CAN GET OUR HANDS ON THE MIND STONE, I CAN SWITCH US BACK.
THE PROBLEM IS, WE DON'T KNOW WHERE M.O.D.O.K. WENT WITH IT.
I DO.
I CAN USE THE SECURITY SYSTEM TO TRACK ITS ENERGY SIGNATURE.
GOOD THINKING, FALCON.
HAHA HAHA!
SO, THE "MIGHTY" AVENGERS ARE NOT SO MIGHTY ANYMORE!
I'M NOT THE ONLY ONE SEEING THIS, RIGHT?
IT LOOKS LIKE THE MIND STONE WAS INDISCRIMINATE IN ITS BLAST! AS YOU CAN SEE, I'VE BULKED UP!
WATCH OUT!
M.O.D.O.K. SWAPPED MINDS WITH THE TRICARRIER--
--AND CAN MOVE ITS PARTS LIKE THEY'RE OF HIS OWN BODY!

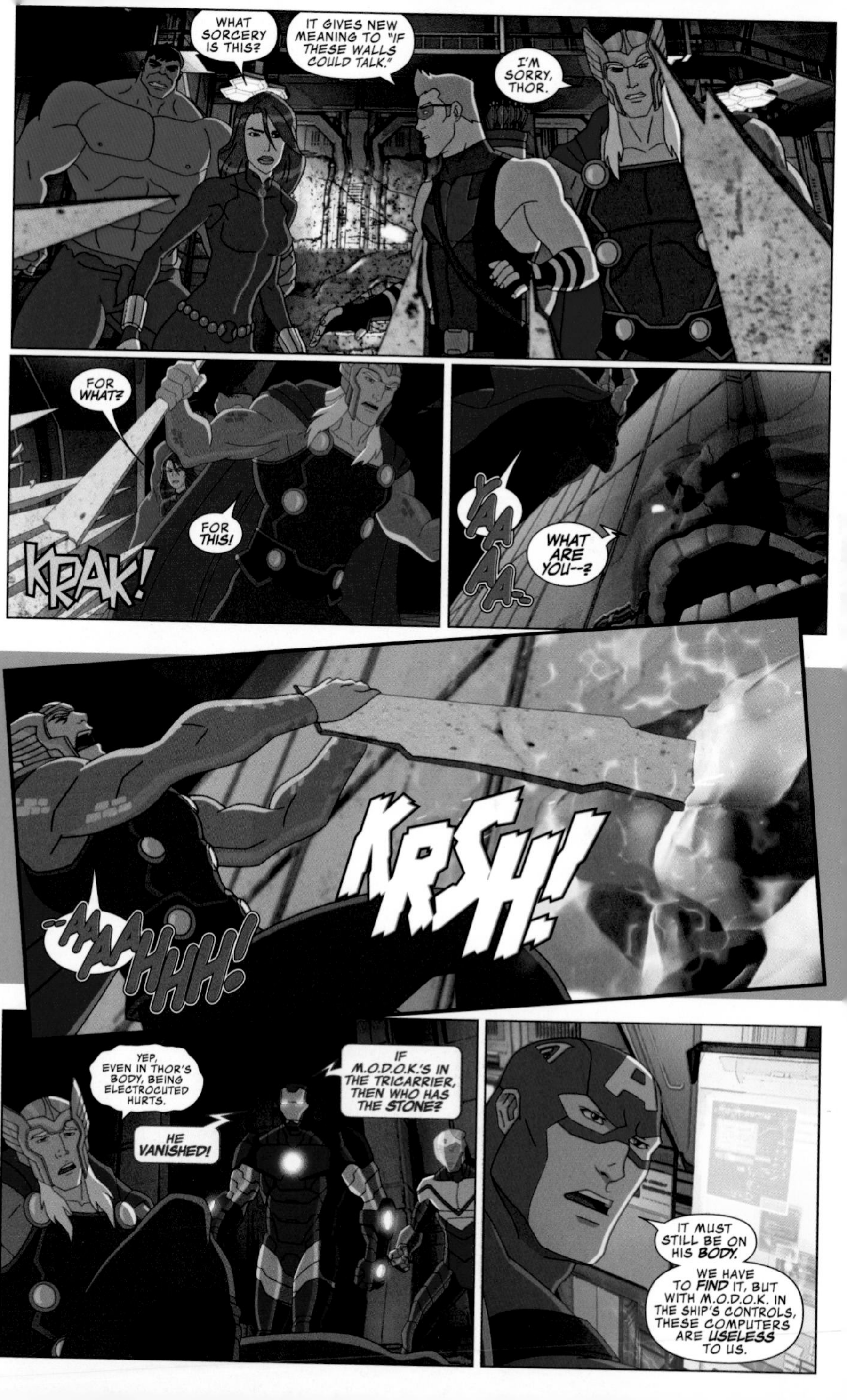
WHAT SORCERY IS THIS?
IT GIVES NEW MEANING TO "IF THESE WALLS COULD TALK."
I'M SORRY, THOR.
FOR WHAT?
FOR THIS!
KRAK!
YAAAAAA-
WHAT ARE YOU--?
KRSH!
-AAAAHHHH!
YEP, EVEN IN THOR'S BODY, BEING ELECTROCUTED HURTS.
HE VANISHED!
IF M.O.D.O.K.'S IN THE TRICARRIER, THEN WHO HAS THE STONE?
IT MUST STILL BE ON HIS BODY.
WE HAVE TO FIND IT, BUT WITH M.O.D.O.K. IN THE SHIP'S CONTROLS, THESE COMPUTERS ARE USELESS TO US.

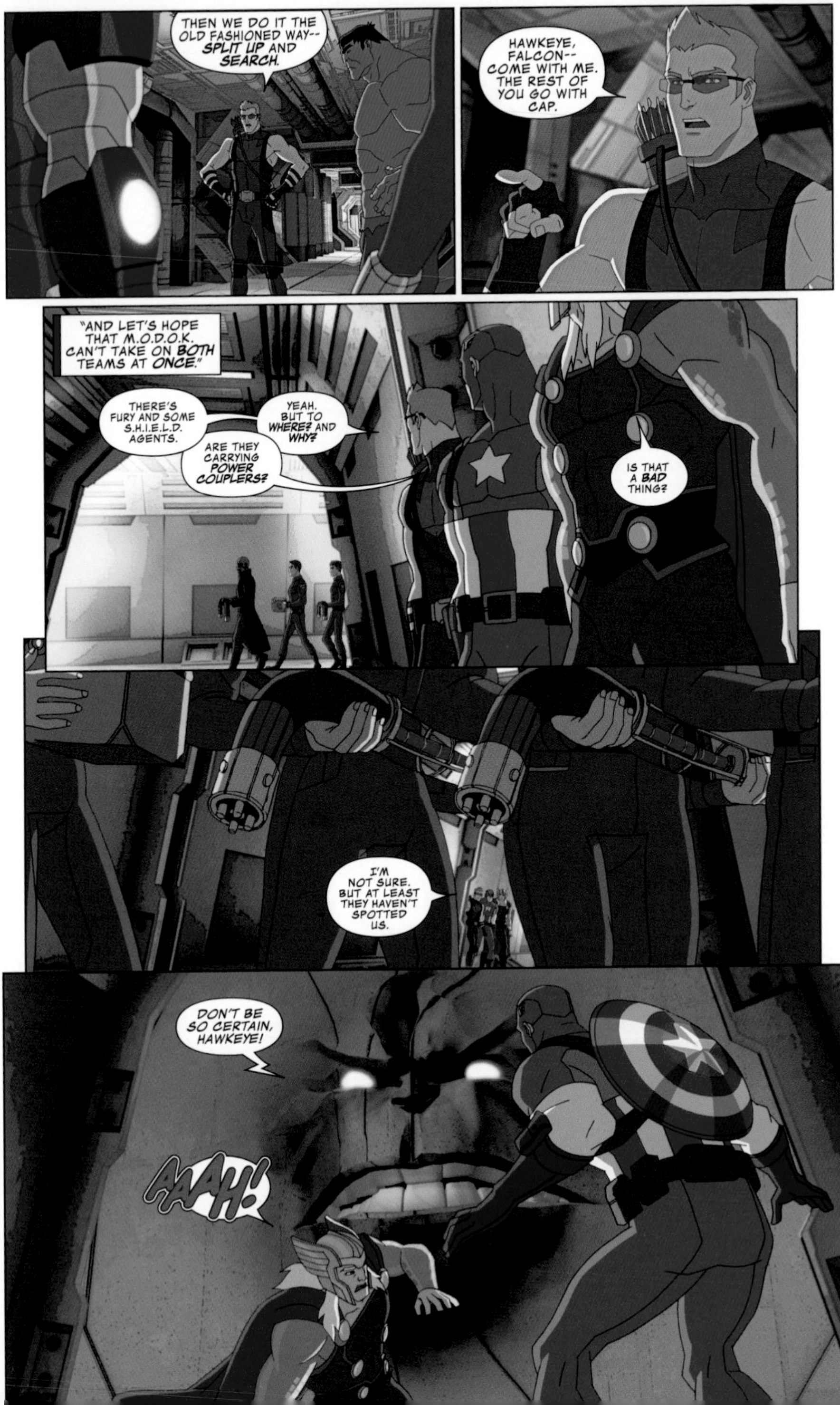
THEN WE DO IT THE OLD FASHIONED WAY-- SPLIT UP AND SEARCH.
HAWKEYE, FALCON-- COME WITH ME. THE REST OF YOU GO WITH CAP.
"AND LET'S HOPE THAT M.O.D.O.K. CAN'T TAKE ON BOTH TEAMS AT ONCE."
THERE'S FURY AND SOME S.H.I.E.L.D. AGENTS.
YEAH. BUT TO WHERE? AND WHY?
ARE THEY CARRYING POWER COUPLERS?
IS THAT A BAD THING?
I'M NOT SURE. BUT AT LEAST THEY HAVEN'T SPOTTED US.
DON'T BE SO CERTAIN, HAWKEYE!
AAAH!

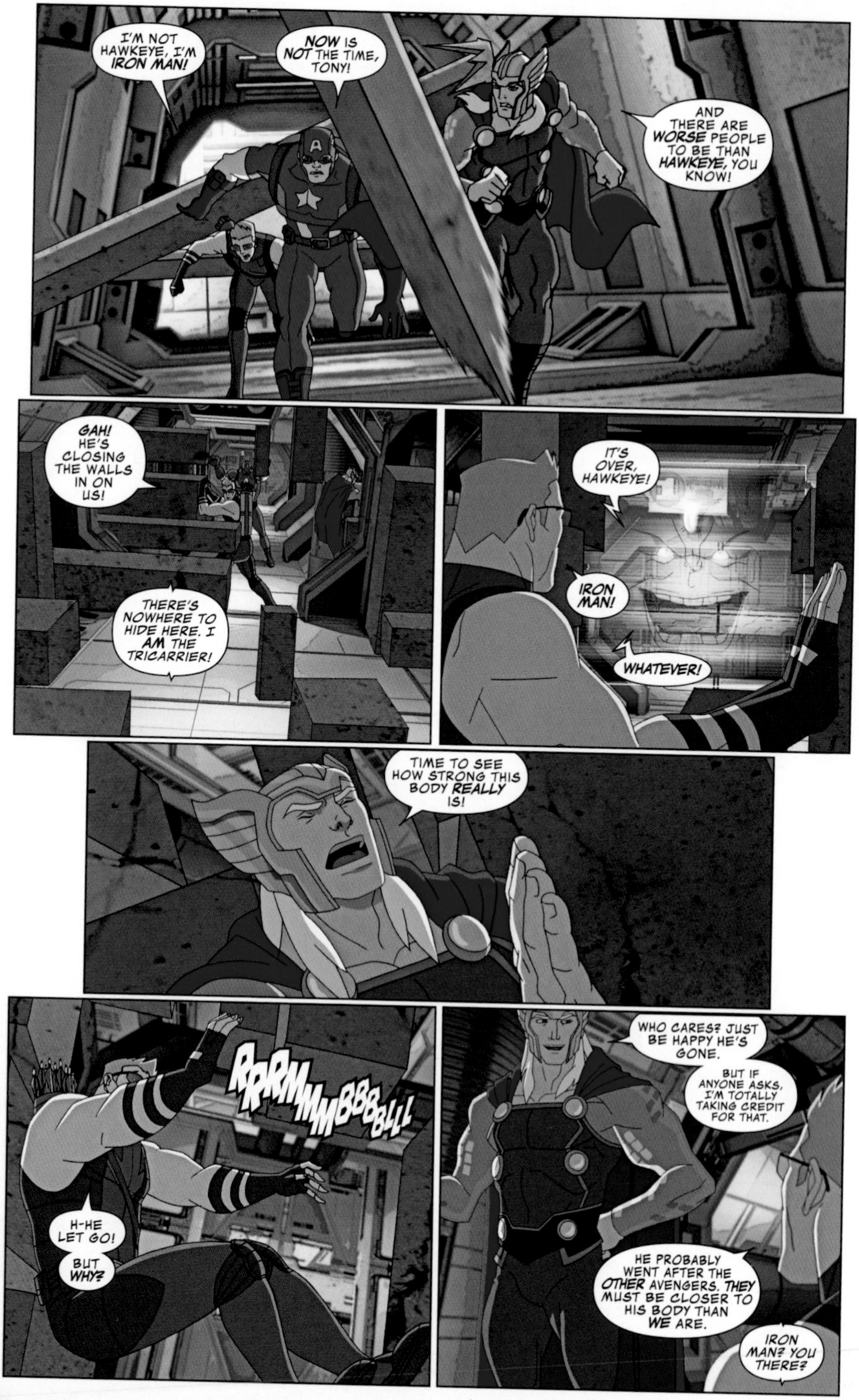
I'M NOT HAWKEYE, I'M IRON MAN!
NOW IS NOT THE TIME, TONY!
AND THERE ARE WORSE PEOPLE TO BE THAN HAWKEYE, YOU KNOW!
GAH! HE'S CLOSING THE WALLS IN ON US!
THERE'S NOWHERE TO HIDE HERE. I AM THE TRICARRIER!
IT'S OVER, HAWKEYE!
IRON MAN!
WHATEVER!
TIME TO SEE HOW STRONG THIS BODY REALLY IS!
RRRMMMBBBLLL
H-HE LET GO!
BUT WHY?
WHO CARES? JUST BE HAPPY HE'S GONE.
BUT IF ANYONE ASKS, I'M TOTALLY TAKING CREDIT FOR THAT.
HE PROBABLY WENT AFTER THE OTHER AVENGERS. THEY MUST BE CLOSER TO HIS BODY THAN WE ARE.
IRON MAN? YOU THERE?

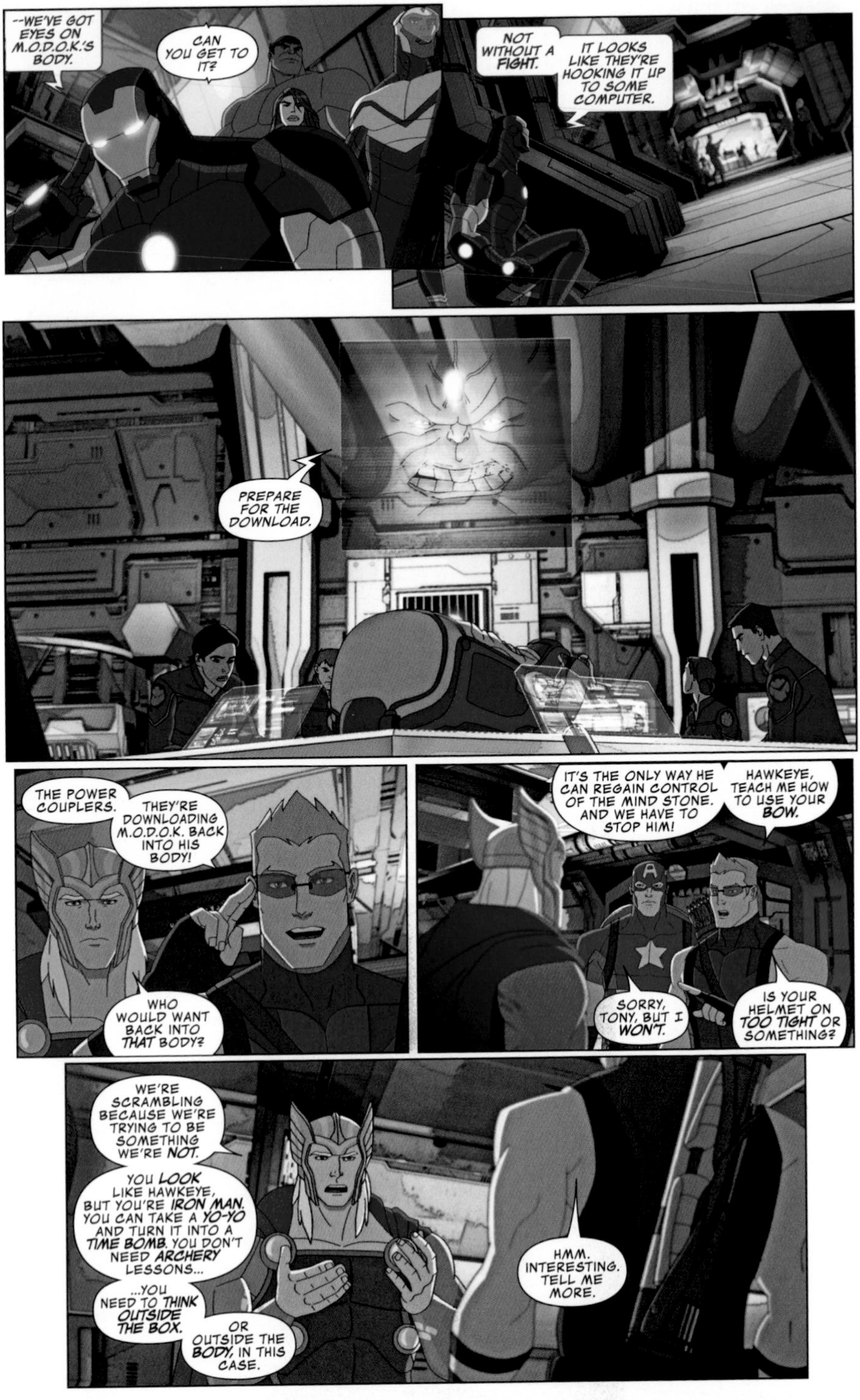
--WE'VE GOT EYES ON M.O.D.O.K.'S BODY.
CAN YOU GET TO IT?
NOT WITHOUT A FIGHT.
IT LOOKS LIKE THEY'RE HOOKING IT UP TO SOME COMPUTER.
PREPARE FOR THE DOWNLOAD.
THE POWER COUPLERS.
THEY'RE DOWNLOADING M.O.D.O.K. BACK INTO HIS BODY!
WHO WOULD WANT BACK INTO THAT BODY?
IT'S THE ONLY WAY HE CAN REGAIN CONTROL OF THE MIND STONE. AND WE HAVE TO STOP HIM!
HAWKEYE, TEACH ME HOW TO USE YOUR BOW.
SORRY, TONY, BUT I WON'T.
IS YOUR HELMET ON TOO TIGHT OR SOMETHING?
WE'RE SCRAMBLING BECAUSE WE'RE TRYING TO BE SOMETHING WE'RE NOT.
YOU LOOK LIKE HAWKEYE, BUT YOU'RE IRON MAN. YOU CAN TAKE A YO-YO AND TURN IT INTO A TIME BOMB. YOU DON'T NEED ARCHERY LESSONS...
...YOU NEED TO THINK OUTSIDE THE BOX.
OR OUTSIDE THE BODY, IN THIS CASE.
HMM. INTERESTING. TELL ME MORE.

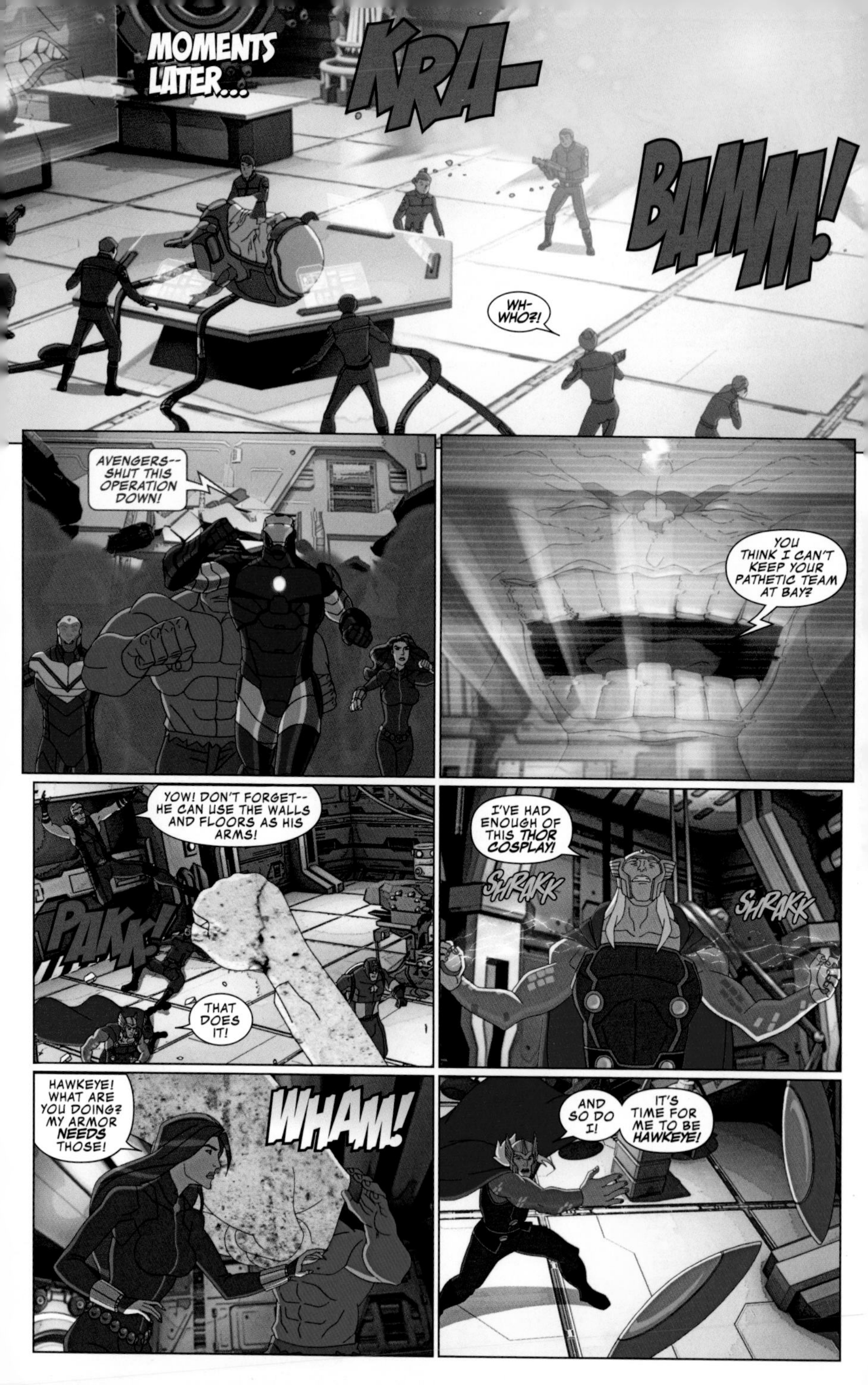
MOMENTS LATER...
KRA-
BAMM!
WH- WHO?!
AVENGERS-- SHUT THIS OPERATION DOWN!
YOU THINK I CAN'T KEEP YOUR PATHETIC TEAM AT BAY?
YOW! DON'T FORGET-- HE CAN USE THE WALLS AND FLOORS AS HIS ARMS!
PAKK!
THAT DOES IT!
I'VE HAD ENOUGH OF THIS THOR COSPLAY!
SHRAKK
SHRAKK
HAWKEYE! WHAT ARE YOU DOING? MY ARMOR NEEDS THOSE!
WHAM!
AND SO DO I!
IT'S TIME FOR ME TO BE HAWKEYE!

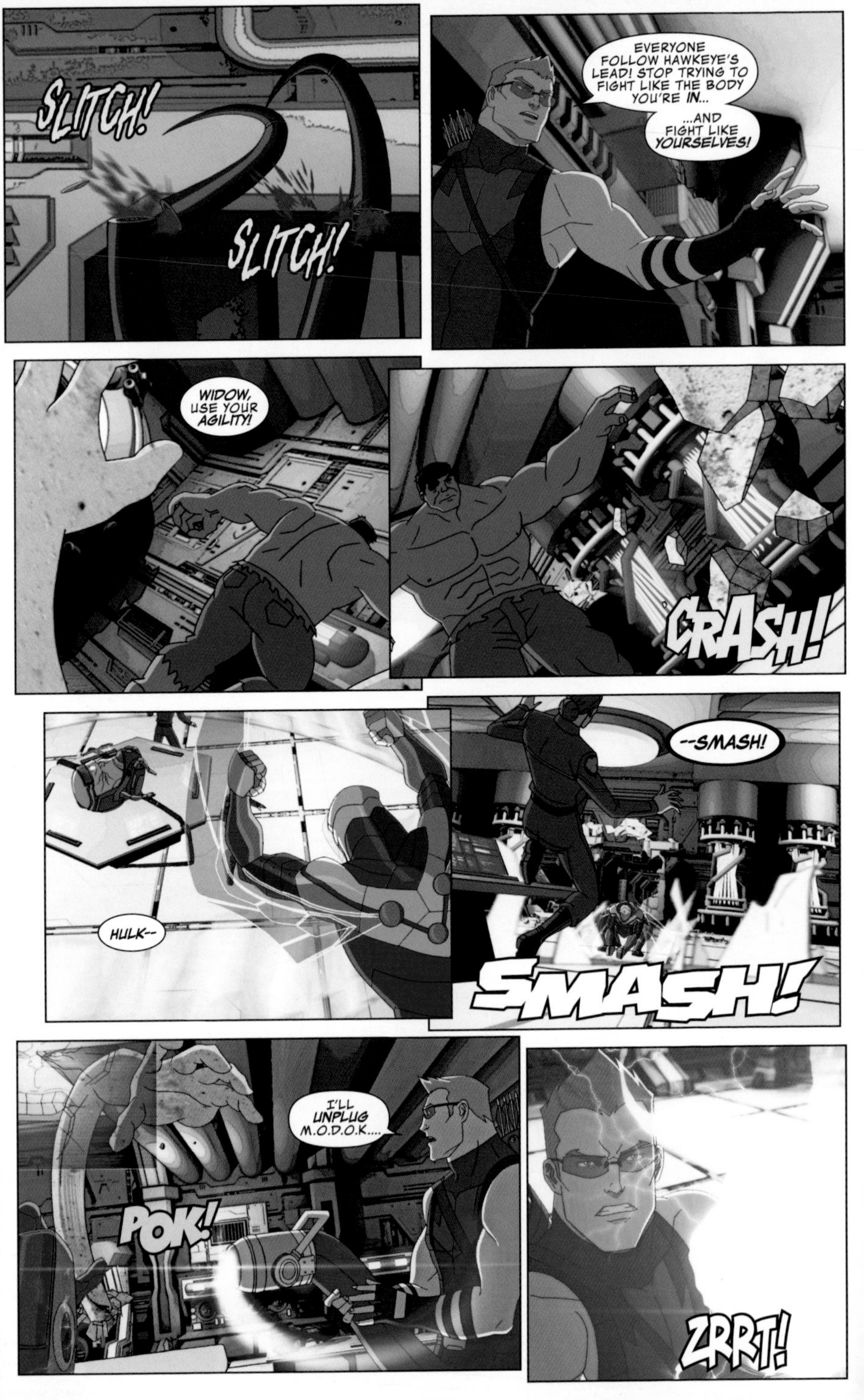
SLITCH!
SLITCH!
EVERYONE FOLLOW HAWKEYE'S LEAD! STOP TRYING TO FIGHT LIKE THE BODY YOU'RE IN...
...AND FIGHT LIKE YOURSELVES!
WIDOW, USE YOUR AGILITY!
CRASH!
HULK--
--SMASH!
SMASH!
I'LL UNPLUG M.O.D.O.K....
POK!
ZRRT!

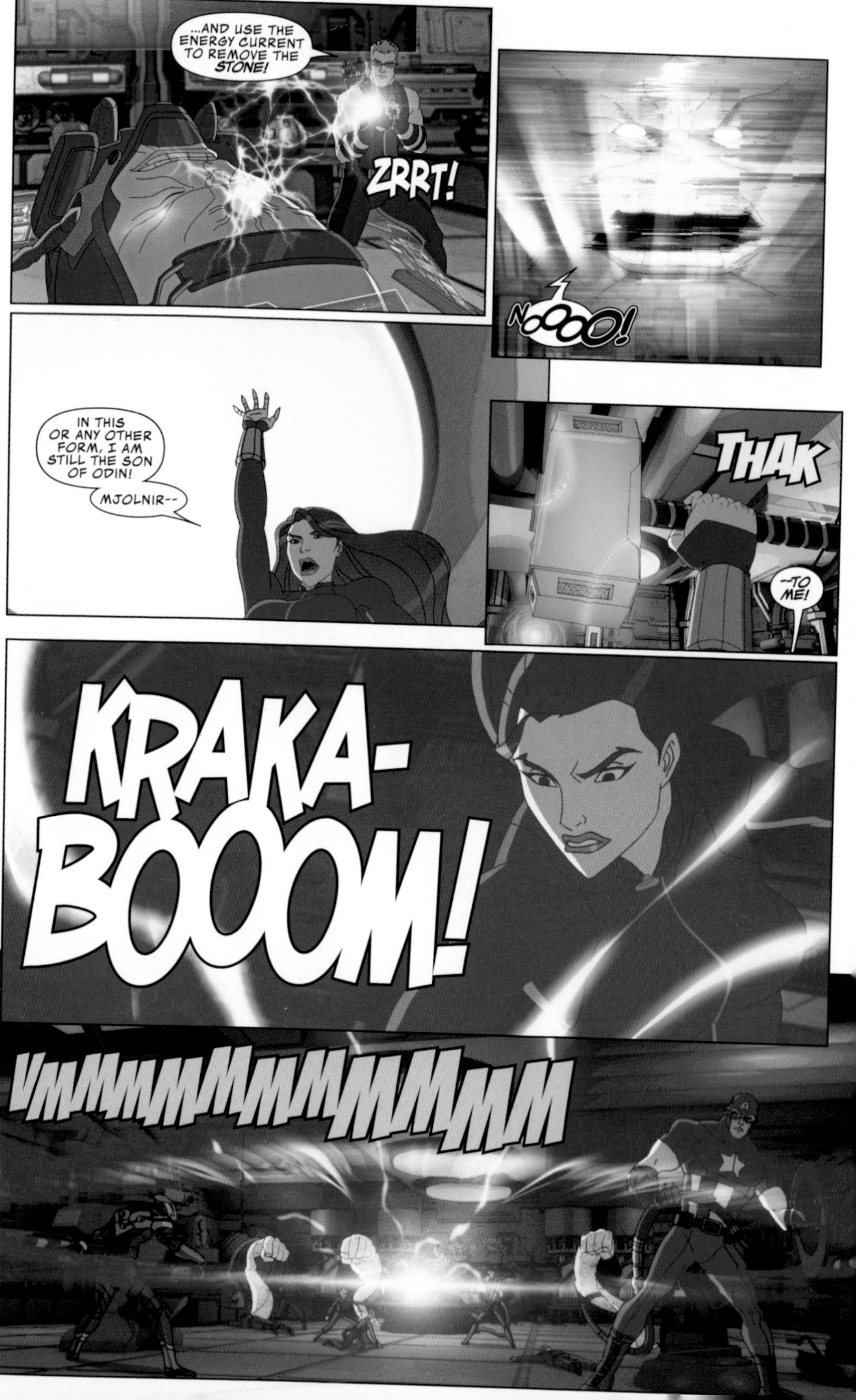
...AND USE THE ENERGY CURRENT TO REMOVE THE STONE!
ZRRT!
NOOOO!
IN THIS OR ANY OTHER FORM, I AM STILL THE SON OF ODIN!
MJOLNIR--
THAK
--TO ME!
KRAKA-BOOOM!
VMMMMMMMMMMMMMMM

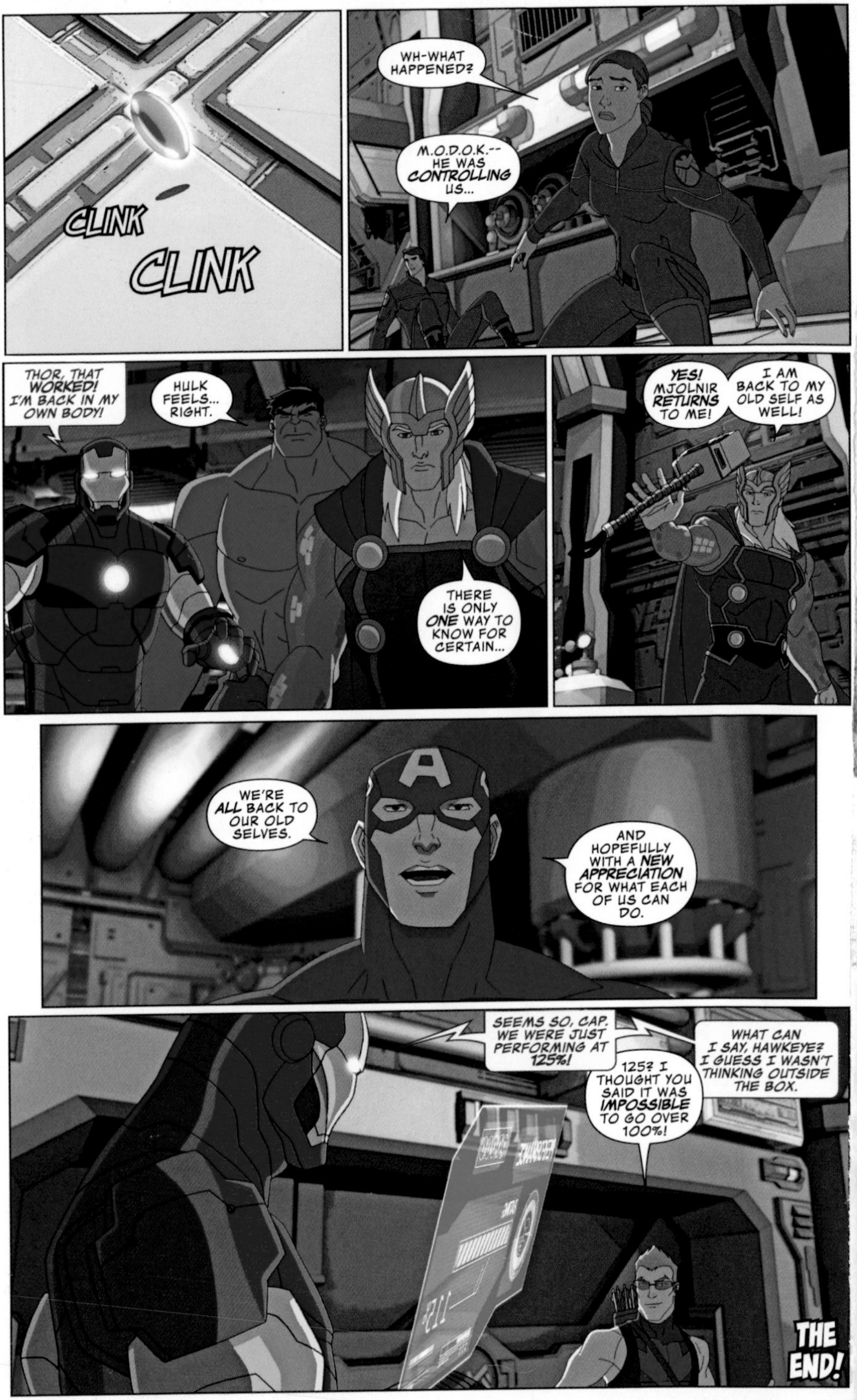
CLINK
CLINK
WH-WHAT HAPPENED?
M.O.D.O.K.-- HE WAS CONTROLLING US...
THOR, THAT WORKED! I'M BACK IN MY OWN BODY!
HULK FEELS... RIGHT.
THERE IS ONLY ONE WAY TO KNOW FOR CERTAIN...
YES! MJOLNIR RETURNS TO ME!
I AM BACK TO MY OLD SELF AS WELL!
WE'RE ALL BACK TO OUR OLD SELVES.
AND HOPEFULLY WITH A NEW APPRECIATION FOR WHAT EACH OF US CAN DO.
SEEMS SO, CAP. WE WERE JUST PERFORMING AT 125%!
125? I THOUGHT YOU SAID IT WAS IMPOSSIBLE TO GO OVER 100%!
WHAT CAN I SAY, HAWKEYE? I GUESS I WASN'T THINKING OUTSIDE THE BOX.
THE END!